The Blue Silence

MURDER NEW ORLEANS STYLE

Tim Chapman

Author of

A Trace of Gold

Kiddieland and other misfortunes

Thrilling Tales
Chicago, IL

Thrilling Tales
Chicago, IL

www.thrillingtales.com

Book and cover design by Tim Chapman

ISBN: 978-0-9862862-6-1

Library of Congress Control Number: 2017910031

This book is dedicated to the citizens of New Orleans, Venice, and (my sweet home) Chicago. Three beautiful cities in crisis.

The Drowned

We, who are alone, live far beneath
the murmuring waves—buoyant and
dangling, like marionettes.
Above us, the lucky ones chatter and
gossip, and their time hurries along
into their futures.

Our mouths move, but our voices, like
our bodies, remain suspended,
hovering in the too-viscous medium.
We, the unseen, are also the
unheard, and so we float,
adrift in the blue silence.

—Kim Katzman

The Blue Silence

ONE

Raymond Duchamp looked at himself in the little mirror in the forward stateroom and wondered why he felt so calm. His dark eyes showed no sign of fear, and when he looked down at his hand it was steady. *Steady and ready,* he thought. He flexed a bicep and smiled. They're just kids, barely out of their teens, but I suppose that doesn't make them any less dangerous. He had planned to get Sylvie out on the water alone. These friends of hers were an added inconvenience, nothing more. He felt the boat heel a bit. *What the hell are they doing up there?* He ran a comb through his wavy blond hair. *Too light. Guess I should try a darker shade.* Then, he bounded up the stairs and through the salon to the cockpit.

He looked out the cockpit window and saw the two girls up in the bow, smoking and staring out at the flat horizon. The boy was at the helm, stretched out in an easy chair he had brought up from the salon, and was drinking Duchamp's forty-year-old port from the bottle. Any qualms Duchamp had about killing the boy disappeared along with the six-hundred-dollars-a-bottle liquor. He tried to hide his anger as he called to the boy.

"Trevor, my fine fellow, what's happening? I thought you were going to try your hand at piloting the ship." He gestured toward the unmanned wheel.

Trevor slouched lower in the chair, his long legs stretched across half the cockpit. "Naw, that shit's lame. The sea never changes out here. It's all just flat. Besides, you can't get any speed out of this tub; it's too big."

Duchamp held out his hand for the bottle. "How about a swig for the captain?" The boy handed him the bottle, and

Duchamp took a sip and held the ruby liquid in his mouth. He closed his eyes and took a moment to appreciate the tawny's subtle notes of chocolate and oak. Then he swallowed the wine, reversed his grip on the bottle, and swung it against the side of Trevor's head. The bottle didn't break. Instead, it left a depression the size of an apricot in the boy's skull at his left temple, thrusting bits of bone into brain. Trevor twitched and shuddered for a minute or two, then lie still. Duchamp tossed the bottle onto his lap and walked out on deck to join the girls.

He couldn't remember the little, blond girl's name, Toni or Tami or something, so he directed his question to his niece. "So, what are we talking about girls?"

Sylvie flicked her cigarette over the side and turned to face him. "Please don't tell Dad I was smoking, Uncle Raymond. He gets a little hyper about stuff like that."

Duchamp shook his head. "Don't worry, ma chere. Your father and I haven't spoken since our last family gathering. Anyway, my lips are sealed."

"Thank you for letting me join the party, Mister Duchamp. It's nice and calm out here, very relaxing."

He looked at the blond girl. Her features were more delicate than those of his dark-haired niece, and she must have weighed fifty pounds less. She was probably the one Trevor had been interested in, though Duchamp found his niece to be the more attractive of the two. "You're welcome, dear. Any friend of Sylvie's..." He gestured out over the water. "Don't be fooled by the Gulf of Mexico, though. A sudden storm could raise a fuss in no time, or we could have to run from a waterspout—a tornado on the water. Keep an eye out for white water out here, too; that could indicate a hidden reef, and of course, there are the sharks." He pointed to the horizon, an unbroken line with stacks of white clouds above and the smooth sparkling water below. "No land in sight in any direction, and there are always the sharks."

"Stop, Uncle Raymond. You're scaring us."

"I'm sorry," he said, turning to the blond. "I didn't mean to frighten you, Tami. It's Tami, isn't it?"

"Toni," the blond said.

"I'm sorry, Toni. You're a good swimmer, aren't you?"

"I don't know. I haven't been swimming since I was a little girl."

"Well," Duchamp said, "it's a shame you weren't wearing your life jacket."

"Wait, what?" the girl said. "A shame I wasn't—"

Duchamp bent and locked one hand behind Toni's right knee and grabbed her shoulder with the other. Then, he straightened, suddenly, sending the girl over the polished, brass rail. Her head thunked on the side of the boat as she cartwheeled into the water.

When he turned back, his niece was sitting on the deck, screaming.

"Come along, Sylvie," he said. "You and I need to have a little talk."

TWO

The image from McKinney's computer flickered on the big screen for a moment before it disappeared to display the bright blue background and the message, "Device Not Detected." McKinney fumbled with the cables on the back of the projector while his small audience grumbled.

"Certain lack of professionalism here," one of the men remarked.

"Now Frank, be patient," said another. "After all, this is Chicago." The men chuckled.

McKinney wasn't particularly intimidated by the three men from NASA, and if he hadn't needed the money he would have commented on their rudeness. As it was, he was lucky to have the job. "Sorry about this." He rebooted the computer, took a sip of the coffee he had purchased from a machine in the lab's cafeteria, and grimaced. "It'll just be a minute." While his computer was restarting, he studied his companions in the small conference room. They had flown up from Texas to meet with him at the Walters Research Institute, and they obviously weren't happy about it. McKinney was sure he had solved their problem, so he was a little confused by their less-than-friendly attitudes. All three men wore gray suits, which McKinney judged to be of a fairly inexpensive, wool and polyester blend, and ties sporting the NASA logo. Two wore blue ties; one wore red. *The kind of ties*, McKinney thought, *they probably sell in the space center gift shop.* His lanky, middle-aged frame was simply clothed in khakis and a black t-shirt. He looked more like an aging beach bum than a forensic scientist.

The computer finished rebooting and the screen lit up with a picture of long crystalline shapes, some five sided and some six sided, all with pointed ends. The crystals appeared to be attached to one another, forming constructions that resembled caltrops or jacks from a child's game. On the screen they appeared transparent with a violet hue. "These are your problem," McKinney said.

"What are we looking at?" asked the man with the red tie.

McKinney clicked the computer's mouse and a new image appeared on the screen. This one showed the same type of crystals forming on the surface of a pool of liquid. Superimposed on this image was a picture of a thermometer. "These images are magnified about two hundred times. At forty degrees below zero your lubricant crystallizes. I mounted the microscope slides on a liquid nitrogen cooled stage and slowly brought the temperature down until I got the reaction you see here. I recall your director was concerned that someone was 'putting sugar in your gas tank,' as he put it. Well, I think you can rule out sabotage. You just need to find a synthetic lubricant that can stand up to extreme cold."

"Is that Celsius or Fahrenheit?" asked Red Tie.

"Interesting factoid," McKinney said, "forty below is forty below on both scales."

The lights snapped on, casting a fluorescent glare over the room. In the back, at the light switch, sat a gray-bearded man in a brightly colored Hawaiian shirt. "Gentlemen," he said, "I think Mister McKinney has solved your mystery. Now your space shuttles can lower their landing gear without it sticking."

"That's classified information," Red Tie said, "that you aren't supposed to have." He stood and picked up his copy of McKinney's report.

"Just a guess, sir. What other system on a shuttle requires

lubrication and is exposed to extremes of temperature?"

Red Tie gestured to his companions. "We're through here. Let's go."

As the men filed out of the conference room McKinney called after them, "You don't have to thank me; just remember to pay your bill." He switched off his computer and started unhooking it from the projection system. He nodded to the man in the back of the room. "Hey Mac. What do you suppose that was about?"

"Their shitty attitudes? Simple. They're scientists, 'rocket scientists,' in fact. They were embarrassed that a mere forensic scientist, namely you, was able to solve a problem that had them stymied for the better part of a year. Call it professional jealousy."

Mac Walters was one of the most respected microscopists in the world and a well-known character. He had as many enemies in the scientific community as he had friends. McKinney considered himself fortunate to be numbered among his friends.

"When are you going to go back to work for the Illinois State Police, McKinney? Scrounging around for consulting jobs can't be much fun."

"My case is still in arbitration. The union went to bat for me but my former lab director is in no hurry to welcome me back. I think the day he fired me was one of the happiest days of his life. I appreciate you sending jobs like this NASA thing my way, but I really miss the crime lab."

"Not a problem. Why did the state lab fire you, if you don't mind my asking?"

"No, I don't mind. It was really my own fault. A young, autistic man was on trial for murder, and based on the evidence I analyzed, I thought he was innocent. I made my concerns known to the prosecution and the investigators, but they didn't want to hear it. They thought they had the right man."

"So? That's nothing to fire someone for."

McKinney sighed. "There's more. I became obsessed with the case. It was all I could think about. Nobody was interested in looking at the evidence or helping this young man, so I decided to investigate on my own."

"Oops."

"Yeah, oops. Forensic science depends on objectivity. I've always upbraided scientists who want to be Sherlock Holmes. Those are the sorts of egotists who give forensic science a bad name. Our job is to explain the association of evidence with an event, nothing more, nothing less. It's not our job to determine innocence or guilt, yet there I was, interviewing witnesses and tracking down leads."

"What happened to the young man?"

"The real killer had committed several other murders, leaving behind evidence that compared to the evidence from the original murder. We caught him, and the charges against the young man were dropped."

"So, you were right, and because of you a killer was caught and an innocent person was released."

"Yes, but..."

"I'm not saying the ends justify the means, but what the hell, McKinney. You did what you thought you had to do. I'd bring you on staff here if I had an opening. You're a good microscopist."

⁂

Walking the three flights up to his apartment in Chicago's Wrigleyville neighborhood was an exercise in melancholy for McKinney. He had recently become an empty nester and felt about as lonely as he had ever been. His daughter had decided to go away to college and had moved into a dormitory at Tulane, down in New Orleans. His artist girlfriend was in Manhattan supervising a gallery showing of some of her sculpture. Before she left she told him she needed to take some time off from their relationship. McKinney, the scientist, had suggested they could work out whatever the problem was if she was willing to discuss it. Carla, the artist, explained that it wasn't the type of problem that could be analyzed. "I'm sorry," she said, "but this can't be subjected to measurement or experiment or dissected or looked at under your microscope." McKinney implied she was being irrational, and he hadn't heard from her since. He was feeling abandoned.

The seventy-pound standard poodle that jumped him as he opened the door made him feel a little better.

"Hendrix," he said. "How's my boy?" The big black dog followed him out to the kitchen where McKinney grabbed a beer and a dog biscuit, then back to the living room where they settled together on the couch.

The breakup with Carla came as a surprise. It had taken several years after his wife succumbed to breast cancer before he was comfortable dating. It was a big step for him, and he had somehow screwed it up. That he didn't know how he had screwed it up made it worse.

"My friend," he said to the dog, "when I was a young man, women were a tantalizing mystery, a beautiful puzzle that I longed to solve. These days I just find them bewildering." Hendrix gave him a soft growl that McKinney interpreted as, "Don't bother me; I'm busy chewing."

He finally pushed himself up off the couch and went to his bedroom to change his shirt. He had promised to go to a support group meeting for cancer victims and their families— Live For Today. His wife, Catherine, had dragged him along to the meetings during the final months of her illness. Her oncologist had thought it would help them cope. It had, but not in the way her doctor intended. McKinney and Catherine rarely spoke at the meetings, and when they did it was to offer sympathy or support to other cancer patients or their frightened family members. But in the car, on the way home, they would inevitably break out in fits of laughter, usually at some clueless remark from Beth, the group's organizer and discussion leader. "Oh brother," Catherine would say. "If that chick calls us heroes one more time I'm going to deck her. Hell, all we've done is manage to not die. When did society start confusing survival with heroism? Whatever happened to standards?" McKinney knew that her snarky comedy routines were a way to deal with her own fear and anxiety, but they cracked him up every time. He loved being her audience.

There were only two seats left in the circle of chairs in the basement of the Methodist Church, one next to Beth, the leader, and one directly across from her. He chose the one across from her and sat on a metal folding chair, the least comfortable, he was sure, that had ever been made. Beth was only a few years younger than McKinney but still dressed like a 1960s flower child in a peasant blouse and long paisley skirt. McKinney thought she was attractive with her dark hair streaked with gray and large deep-set eyes. Despite her occasional ditziness, he admired her compassion and her devotion to her group members. He looked around this room he hadn't been in for several years. It looked essentially the same. The walls were concrete blocks that had at one time been sea green but had faded to their present celery hue. Someone had painted a colorful mural of the resurrection on one wall that Catherine used to say looked like Jesus attending Mardi Gras.

He was reluctant to come to this meeting, not so much for his own sake, but for the sake of the other attendees. Beth had phoned and explained that she was organizing a support group for the people whose loved ones had succumbed to their cancers. He couldn't figure out why he had agreed to attend. He knew it would feel strange to show up without Catherine. He thought of her every day of his life. She had made his life better in countless ways. She had made him better. He was thinking of her when he heard Beth speaking to the man sitting next to him, a droopy, overweight guy wearing sweatpants and a Blackhawks jersey. The man's wife, a breast cancer patient, had died last year and the man himself had, incredibly, just been diagnosed with breast cancer.

"You know," Beth said, "breast cancer in men used to be quite rare, but we're seeing many more incidences of it these days, so there's no reason for you to feel odd or peculiar."

McKinney imagined what his wife would have said about that, *If the poor guy didn't feel odd or peculiar before, he sure as hell will now.* Then, without meaning to, and to his own chagrin, he chuckled.

THREE

Raymond Duchamp was not a man who was easily impressed. He often drank expensive brandies and smoked fine cigars, but he had to admit that the 200-year-old Richard Hennessy cognac he had just been served was wonderful. He knew that his host was demonstrating the difference between well-off and filthy rich, but he didn't care. He looked around the large clubroom, with its thick maroon carpet and oak bookshelves, at the fifteen men gathered for the Dauphin Pharmaceuticals presentation. It was an impressive group— some of the most powerful men on the Gulf coast. He settled back into the soft leather of the club chair and focused his attention on the man wearing the hand-tailored Brioni suit and standing at the podium, Samson Edwards.

"We're asking you gentlemen for a rather substantial commitment," Edwards said, "but Dauphin Pharmaceuticals will be the preeminent drug company in the world within five years. We've chosen Mobile, Alabama for its location. The Gulf coast has a cheap work force and a pro-business environment. We've already purchased a facility, one of the many abandoned factory complexes in the area. It will house our offices, laboratories, factory, and warehouse. Most of our development team are Dutch and Swedish, but they're eager to relocate. Right about now you're probably asking yourselves, 'Why should I invest in a startup drug company? There are dozens of successful, established companies out there. Why not buy stock in one of them?' In a moment I'm going to turn the podium over to our chief biochemist, Dr. DeWitte, who will likely bore you to death with details. Let me just say that there has never been a better time to invest in pharmaceuticals.

People are living longer than ever. The number of people living past seventy is at an all-time high, and their numbers are increasing, largely due to advances in medicine. Gentlemen, Dauphin Pharma has recently secured the manufacturing and distribution rights to several important drugs that have expired patents, and we have our eyes on several more. These are drugs that currently have no generic version in the marketplace. We have already started campaigns to brand them. The ROI projections are in the information packets you received as you were seated. You needn't look at them. I assure you that your short-term profits will be impressive, and your long-term profits will make you some of the richest men in the country."

The man seated next to Duchamp pointed at Edwards with his unlit, but well-chewed, cigar. Duchamp recognized him as the owner of several Minor League baseball teams throughout the southwest. "I have plenty of money," he said. "My businesses and investments are doing fine, as, I imagine, are the businesses of most of the men in this room. Why should we invest in, of all things, a drug company, which seems like an iffy proposition, at best?"

"I'm glad you asked," Edwards replied. "As you are undoubtedly aware, heart disease, diabetes, and arthritis are the most prevalent chronic conditions in our society. Looking around the room, I imagine a number of you are currently taking medication for one or more of these disorders. Well, just like any other product, the company with the best marketing, controls the market. Is Coke really better than Shasta? And who in their right mind would choose a Budweiser over a micro-brew?"

There was some laughter from the room, and a couple of the men raised their hands to speak, but Edwards cut them off.

"We will have a team of scientists, headed by Dr. DeWitte, but most of our efforts will be directed toward marketing. Within two years, our line of drug products will be considered essential for the treatment of chronic disease in Europe, Great Britain, and the Americas."

The men who had raised their hands lowered them. A few still whispered and Edwards addressed them specifically.

"Gentlemen, we will not have research expenses. There will be no clinical trials or FDA waiting periods. These drugs have all been approved. They are simply drugs that lacked a vigorous public relations initiative. We will make them household names. They will be the drugs you insist your doctor prescribe, and he or she will be happy to do so. They may not be any more effective, but they *will* be more popular." He looked around the room. "If you've taken the time to count your fellow investors you will note that we have invited fifteen of you today. There are positions in the consortium for ten. We are limiting the number of participants in order to provide the maximum individual profit for each investor. Some of you will, no doubt, decide your money can be put to some other use. Whether you choose to join us in this venture or not, I thank you for your attention and hope you will stay and enjoy lunch with us after the meeting."

Duchamp leafed through the papers in his information packet as a man in a white lab coat approached the podium. He was impressed and excited. He watched as most of the men shook hands with Edwards, congratulating him on his presentation. Only one or two hung back. He really wanted to be a part of this venture. In fact, he needed it. He had squandered most of his inheritance, and the investments that had done so well for him ten years before were tanking. Only one thing could prevent him from becoming an investor, his lack of capital. Duchamp climbed out of his chair and followed Edwards and the others into the dining room.

After the luncheon, Duchamp stood in front of the private club and fumbled with his cell phone. Irritation prevented him from enjoying the view—the lights of the French Quarter sparkling across the Mississippi in the twilight. Before he could dial the number, though, his gold-toned Lincoln Town Car pulled up, cutting in front of the line of S-class Mercedes' waiting to pick up their owners. He stood at the car's rear and waited for his chauffeur-slash-bodyguard to get out and open the door for him. Glancing over his shoulder he saw a couple of men from the meeting staring at his car. When one of them put his hand to his mouth to cover a laugh, Duchamp opened the door himself and climbed in. The giant behind the wheel turned to look at Duchamp over the seat. "How'd it go, Tee Ray?"

Duchamp snorted. "Just drive. And don't call me Tee Ray. You know I hate that name. Dammit, Wayne, I told you to be waiting when I walked out. I even called you before I got in the elevator."

"Sorry. Security made us wait in the parking lot. Said sitting in the circular drive was some kinda fire code thing."

"And why can't you open the door for me like I ask you to? Those stuck-up bastards are laughing at my car, and you leave me standing on the damn sidewalk. This car is a classic, for Christ sake, a '96 Cypress Edition with the full ballistic package. You could shoot at this thing all day and not make a dent." He looked at the back of the big man's head as the chauffeur pulled the Lincoln out of the drive and into traffic, the man's short-cropped black hair standing out against the car's beige interior. "Where's your cap? Come on, Wayne. How many times do I have to ask you to wear your cap? Try to look professional."

"Maaaan." Wayne stretched the word into multiple syllables. "We've discussed the cap before. I don't mind wearing a suit and tie. I'm a bodyguard, right? Got to look good. But I only drive you because you're too cheap to pay for a chauffeur. Mrs. Duchamp drives herself. She's got that little Beamer she likes. I am not wearing that fucking monkey hat."

"Fine. Now please, raise the damn panel."

The smoked-glass divider slid up behind the driver's seat and stuck, two inches from the ceiling. The bodyguard flicked the switch on and off a few times. The panel didn't move.

"What the hell, Wayne?"

"Sorry, Boss."

FOUR

McKinney was wedged between a woman balancing a crying child on her hip and a heavyset man who smelled like fried chicken. Every time the El train lurched one of them would lose balance and bump into him. McKinney was on his way to tai chi class and decided, rather than become annoyed, to use the ride as an exercise. His tai chi practice was important to him. It was more than a hobby. During times of emotional instability, of which there had been many, it was a constant. He bent his legs, tucked his hips to lower his center of gravity, and let go of the overhead bar. The next time the train car swayed, McKinney remained stable. When the woman holding the toddler wobbled toward him, he shifted his weight, rolling back away from her. Surprised by the sudden lack of support, she fell, and McKinney had to hurry to catch her. It was a warm day, and her blouse was damp with perspiration where he touched it, at the small of her back. He was suddenly aware of having broken the social convention against making physical contact with a stranger. Women, he knew, felt particularly vulnerable on public transportation. The alternative, letting her fall, would have been worse. "Sorry," he mumbled. She glared at him for a second, then turned her attention to the child who was now crying even louder.

"Ah, crap," said fried chicken man.

As the train pulled up to the Fullerton Avenue platform McKinney's cell phone rang. He squeezed through the crowd and stepped onto the platform to answer it. He stuck a finger in one ear to muffle the clackety-clack of the departing train and pulled out his phone.

"Hi Dad. How are things in the Windy City?"

"Well, if it isn't my favorite daughter. Everything's fine, Angelina." McKinney hurried down the steps to the street as he talked. How's N'awlins? Hot and sticky?"

"First of all it's pronounced New Orleans. You sound like a tourist. Actually, the weather is fine. We're having a rare cool spell. But Dad, there are bugs down here the size of Chihuahuas."

"In the dorm?"

"No, the dorm's okay, but I've seen them."

"And how's your roommate? You two getting along?"

"That's the reason I'm calling. Madeleine's twin sister, Sylvie, is missing, and Madeleine's really upset."

"What do you mean 'missing'?"

"Sylvie was supposed to meet us for dinner last weekend but never showed up. She's not answering her phone and hasn't been in touch with anyone else in the family for over a week now. Madeleine and I went over to her apartment yesterday. She lives just off Rampart Street, near the French Quarter. Not only wasn't she home but her mailbox was full. It looks like she hasn't been home for awhile."

"Did you check to see if her car was there?"

"I suggested that. Sylvie keeps her car at their parent's house. Madeleine says that's because it's too difficult to find parking in the Quarter. Isn't there something you can do, Dad?"

"Does Madeleine know her sister's friends? Has she talked to them?"

"That's why everyone's so worried. A couple of Sylvie's friends have gone missing, too. I know your next question, 'Have they all gone on a trip together?' I asked that, too, but Madeleine knows one of the friends pretty well and says it's not like her to take off without telling her parents. Oh, yeah, the girl's parents phoned the police, who are being less than helpful."

"Well, I imagine they get a lot of missing persons reports in a city fueled by alcohol." McKinney had continued walking as he talked, down the steps, and now, across a busy intersection. He hurried out of the way of a turning car. The driver gave him a simultaneous horn honk and middle finger salute.

"Are you outside, Dad?"

"Yep, walking to tai chi class."

"I don't suppose there's any way you could take a few days off and come down here, is there?"

"I just happen to be between assignments, honey. I imagine I could drive down and spend a couple of days with y'all southern belles. I surely would love to partake of some crawfish and mint juleps."

"Thanks, Dad. Only please, don't talk like that when you're here."

∽

A backpack filled with black t-shirts and khaki pants was presenting McKinney with a problem. He didn't really want to take anything else to New Orleans, but he knew it would be smart to take some less-casual clothing. He was trying to decide which of his two sport coats to pack when the phone rang. It had been almost a year since he'd last seen Nina Anderson, but he recognized her voice immediately. It was simultaneously shy and sultry.

"Sean, I finally have a consulting job for you that pays something."

"Then I guess I can assume it's not connected to the public defender's office. Unless things have changed, your clients don't have any money."

Anderson chuckled. "True. This is more in the line of a favor for a friend of mine. Tell you what, buy me a drink and I'll tell you all about it."

It was still early in the evening when he walked into Katerina's, a neighborhood lounge walking distance from Nina Anderson's Irving Park apartment. McKinney looked around the room as he entered. It was long and narrow with dark wood and white tablecloths. The bar ran the length of one wall and a small stage with a baby grand piano was at the far end of the room.

Nina pointed to the gin and tonic she had waiting for McKinney as he sat across from her. "I remembered," she said.

He took a sip. "Thanks. How've you been?"

She grinned and waved her hand over the crumpled napkin and discarded swizzle sticks on the table. "Great. Look at this beautiful mess."

McKinney nodded approvingly. Nina was an OCD sufferer whose condition ran to compulsive straightening. The last time McKinney saw her was at her office where she lined up the spines of all the books in her bookcase and straightened several stacks of case files while they talked.

I've been taking yoga classes and meditating for a little over six months now. I haven't got the thing completely licked, but I'm more in control of it than any other time in my life."

McKinney thought of his own peculiarities. His wife had called him a control freak, and he guessed she was right. He'd even disabled the Anti-Lock Braking system in his car because he didn't want a machine making his decisions for him. He held up his glass. "A toast to our successes." He considered inviting Nina to attend tai chi classes with him but caught himself. He didn't know what kind of message that would send. Furthermore, he didn't know what kind of message he wanted to send. He was as attracted to the big, green eyes that peered out from under her blond bangs as he had been the first time they met, but he wasn't really sure what "taking a break" meant to Carla. Were they supposed to be seeing other people? He didn't know, and here was Nina, smiling at him with a smile that lit up her whole face. He was in no mood to grapple with ethical conundrums. He took another sip of his drink instead. It was good gin and chilled just right. He smiled back at Nina.

"How's your family?" she asked. "Last time we spoke you were sending your daughter off to college, right?"

"Yes, she's down in New Orleans. I'm driving down to visit her tomorrow, so I hope this friend of yours can wait until I get back."

"I don't think that'll be a problem. And how's your girlfriend? Carla isn't it?"

"Well, she's in New York for a gallery opening. We've both been kind of busy lately. So, tell me about the job."

"I have a friend," Nina said, "who collects original manuscripts by famous American authors. He owns works by Hemingway, Nathaniel Hawthorne, Kerouac—a lot of big names. Well, he's in the process of purchasing an original poem by Edgar Allen Poe, and he needs someone to authenticate it, so I told him about you."

"Me? I don't know anything about antiques."

"He doesn't need to establish provenance. It belongs to a private party who claims it's been in his family for generations. There's no way to prove or disprove that. Didn't you tell me you did a college internship at the Internal Revenue Service's ink and paper laboratory?"

"I did."

"He wants you to verify the age of the document. You can do that by testing the ink and paper, can't you? I mean, determine whether they were in use at the time the poem was written. If they weren't, if they'd been manufactured more recently, it would be a forgery, right?"

"Yep. When was the poem supposed to have been written?"

"It's called 'The City in the Sea' and it was published in the American Review in 1845, so it would have to have been written before that. In fact, it might be the oldest known copy of that poem. Poe had originally called it 'The Doomed City' but after a poor review in 1831 he reworked it and changed its title." She took a drink of the pale pink liquid in her glass. "I don't know what kind of tests you have to do to find out how old something is, but I'm sure my friend can afford to pay for them, as well as a pretty substantial fee for you. The last Poe manuscript that sold at auction went for three hundred thousand dollars. I think my friend is offering closer to four for 'The City in the Sea.' He probably wouldn't blink if you charged him a few thousand, more if it turns out to be genuine." She set her drink down on the table, and McKinney noticed what he thought was a pattern. The crumpled napkin and the swizzle sticks were laid out in a triangular grid, with Nina's glass anchoring one corner. McKinney wondered if this orderliness was unconscious or if she had merely found a clever way to disguise her OCD.

"What's your friend's name?" McKinney asked.

Nina picked up her glass again and took a long swallow before answering. "Logan Bradley."

"The guy who owns that video game company? What's it called, Brain Drain?"

"That's the one. His most famous game was Cold Cuts

Combat. He's rich and used to getting what he wants. I met him in college."

"Did you date him?"

"Once. Like I said, he's used to getting what he wants. I'm afraid I was a disappointment."

The setting sun cast its light through the bar's front window, framing them in a rectangle of orange. McKinney grinned. He said, "That's nice to know."

FIVE

The file Raymond Duchamp compiled on the Dauphin Pharmaceuticals investors was impressive in its bulk. He had managed to gather an armload of personal and business information about most of the major players: Samson Edwards, current Dauphin employees, and all of the businessmen who had attended Edwards' presentation. There were a few men who were out of reach of his team of private detectives, but he had come up with information about them through his club connections. As he sat in the study of his New Orleans Garden District mansion, combing the files for any actionable items, he was pleased to find that there were several indiscretions that could be used for blackmail. An occasional affair, a hidden bank account, a bribe to a public official—these men were not very careful.

Edwards was the one he really wanted to get some dirt on, but there was hardly any information on the man. Duchamp suspected that he not only paid a bundle for his privacy but had also paid to have all his public records sanitized. Even his high school records from the prestigious Farragut Academy looked incomplete. The only extracurricular activity he participated in, according to the official record, was Drill Team. *Odd*, he thought, *for a man who is listed among the most generous alumni donors.*

Duchamp considered his own high school records. Should anyone decide to look they'd find a litany of detentions and suspensions. On his first day, when an older kid mocked his clothes, he jumped him and had almost bitten the kid's ear off before the two were pulled apart.

It was clear that blackmailing Edwards to get in on the

deal was out of the question. He might be able to blackmail a few of the other investors, get them to drop out so that Edwards would have to take his money to raise the needed capital. He definitely needed to reduce the competition. But, where would he get the money to invest? He was tapped out, in debt up to his ears. He'd be lucky to be able to pay his bodyguard's salary this month. *Where is that damn jailbird, anyway?* Duchamp tossed the folder onto the desktop and pushed a button on the intercom. "Wayne? You in the kitchen again?"

The bodyguard's voice crackled through the speaker. "Just getting a sandwich."

"Well, bring it with you, and meet me in the library. I want to talk to you." He switched off the intercom but switched it back on to add, "And bring me a cold Dr. Pepper."

Getting rid of the competition was a last resort. Raising the capital was the important step, but he had to cover all his bases. As much as he disliked the idea, he'd have to speak to his wife. Maybe her father would loan him the money. Her father hated Duchamp, but if his wife did the asking...

"Here's your soda, Boss." Wayne entered the study from the hallway, shuffling across the antique Persian rug, balancing a plate and two glasses. He set one of the glasses on the desk. Duchamp snatched it up and wiped the desk with his sleeve.

"This is French oak, Wayne. Use a coaster." He set the glass on a magazine. "I got the report back on the rest of the Dauphin Pharma investors. There are a few we can squeeze. What are you eating? It smells good."

"Tuna melt made with brie. I made a balsamic vinegar reduction for it, too. My own recipe. I'm thinking about taking a cooking class. You know, expand my horizons."

"You are something else." Duchamp shook his head.

"If you recall, I was in the culinary arts program up at

Angola."

"Big guy like you should've signed up for the prison rodeo."

"Get stomped by a bull? No thanks. I prefer my beef on a bun."

"Well, Chef Boy-Air-Dee, find my wife and ask her to come into the study, will you? And take the rest of the night off if you want. I won't be needing you."

Wayne clicked his heels and bowed from the waist. In a voice dripping with sarcasm he said, "I believe Mrs. Duchamp is in the television room. I'll deliver your message at once, sir."

❧

Barbara Duchamp had no interest in helping her husband with his financial woes, and she certainly was not going to ask her father for money. Her last word on the subject, before she stalked off to bed, was, "You got us in this fix, and I expect you to get us out. Honestly Raymond, sometimes I wonder why I married you."

Duchamp often wondered the same thing. He knew he had been lucky to find a wife from a rich family, and he didn't want to blow it by pushing too hard. Duchamp's life was predicated on a series of lies. His wife knew about his brief stint in prison, but his wife's family and their friends had no knowledge of his past indiscretions. He'd have to find some other way to raise the money. Nevertheless, he hated being talked to like he was some swamp rat. True, his father had been a fisherman and guide, but he had sent the boys to college. Raymond, however, spent most of his senior year in the Louisiana State Prison at Angola for kiting checks. Barbara rarely missed an opportunity to remind Raymond of his humble beginnings. He picked up his glass to hurl it across the room but thought better of it. He set it in the kitchen sink on his way out to the garage.

His wife's little BMW 435 convertible was more fun to drive than the Lincoln. He peeked back into the kitchen to be sure she wouldn't see him slip her keys off the hook in the mudroom. He took the little car up the 10 to Metairie. He had bought a condo for his girlfriend near the lake. It wasn't a big expense, and at times like this it felt like a necessity. He hadn't bothered to put the top down, but he lowered both windows. Zooming along with the stereo cranked up and the warm, humid breeze in his hair was starting to relax him. Denise would finish the job.

Denise Morreau opened the door with a finger to her lips. "Shhh. I just got Tyler to sleep."

Duchamp kissed her as he walked her back into the hallway, closing the door behind him with his foot. Finally, he released her and held her at arms length to examine her. Her dark hair, streaked with platinum highlights, was pinned up on top of her head and her full figure was barely hidden by cut-off jeans and an old Krewe of Pontchartrain t-shirt. She wore no makeup, but her pouty lips and big eyes didn't really require accentuation.

"I should have told you I was coming over so you could've fixed yourself up."

"I knew you were coming. I've known since yesterday afternoon. I just didn't think this visit warranted a clothing change. We're not going out, are we?"

"No but... Damn it, Didi. I expect a little more than a t-shirt. I swear, you're driving me crazy. Between you and Wayne..."

The young woman dropped his hands and, turning, walked to the couch, rolling her hips as she walked. "Don't compare me to your chauffeur. I'm not your servant, Raymond. I'm your girlfriend, and you will treat me with respect." She shooed an overweight cat off the couch and pushed a clear plastic coffee table to one side with her bare foot. "Why don't you sit here on the floor, and I'll give you a neck rub. You look tense."

Duchamp kicked a pile of toy building blocks to one side, slipped off his loafers and went to sit at her feet. He sighed as the young woman began kneading the stress out of his shoulder muscles.

"What's troubling you, sugar? Tell Didi all about it."

Duchamp closed his eyes and tipped his head back. "Psychic powers on the fritz? I figured you'd know all about it."

"I don't know the why, but I know the what. It's about money, honey."

"I'm almost broke. I've got an opportunity to be part of a deal with some of the biggest venture capitalists in the country, and I don't have the price of admission."

"What about Miss Moneybags? Can't you get the cash from her?"

"Barbara? Her purse is shut as tight as her pussy."

She slapped Duchamp on the top of his head. "Language, Raymond."

"Come on, the kid's asleep. Anyway, I've got to come up with a little over five million dollars to buy in, and I've only got about six months to raise it. And the competition is stiff. There are only ten positions available and there were fifteen interested investors at the invitational luncheon. I may not even get the opportunity to join the consortium unless some of them drop out. My lifestyle is in jeopardy."

"Our lifestyle is in jeopardy," she corrected. "What

---

about that thing with your niece? Weren't you going to get your hands on some kind of valuable artwork?"

"Yes, a painting worth about forty million dollars. That didn't work out so well. Seems I had the wrong niece. Mawmaw Boisseau left that niece some rare coins, which she sold to buy a car. My other niece inherited some antique furniture. I understand the ownership papers for the painting were in the china cabinet. The painting itself is in a museum in Paris. My brother and I argued about it at Christmas dinner."

"But there is another niece, and she did inherit a forty million dollar painting, right?"

"Right."

"Well then..." Didi stroked his hair, and pulled his head in to rest between her ample breasts. "...everything is going to be all right."

SIX

The drive from Chicago to New Orleans was uneventful and relaxing. Around Effingham the traffic thinned, and McKinney lost reception for the jazz radio station he was listening to. Given the choice between country music and talk radio he put in a CD instead. Punching on the cruise control and getting his harmonica from the glove compartment, he accompanied B. B. King on "Night Life." By the time he got to Memphis he was wailing along with Stevie Ray Vaughn's "Pride and Joy."

His neighbor, Mrs. Vladic, hadn't been able to watch Hendrix. She was a devoted Cubs fan and had followed them to St. Louis for an away game. Instead, the big, black poodle was curled up on the back seat. They were staying at The Chimes, a Garden District bed and breakfast he and his wife had stayed at years before. It wasn't billed as pet friendly, but the owners had met Hendrix and were glad to welcome him back. He stopped to eat at a little diner in Mississippi. McKinney lowered the car windows a couple of inches to keep Hendrix cool, then took a seat in the restaurant where he could keep an eye on the car while he wolfed down some catfish and collards. They didn't get to The Chimes until close to midnight. As he carried his bags to his room off the little flower-filled courtyard he felt the damp breeze blowing in off the gulf. The big wind chimes on the front porch of the old Victorian clanged, and he wondered if the neighbors ever complained. He took one deep breath of the night air and went in to sleep.

He slept in the next morning. Breakfast was over, but he grabbed a cup of coffee from the dining room and took it with him to drop Hendrix at the day kennel. Tulane was out on

---

St. Charles Avenue, near the Audubon Park, but rather than let her father see their messy dorm, Angelina and her roommate offered to meet McKinney at a little seafood bar on Magazine Street with vinyl-covered chairs and a tile floor that looked as if it hadn't been washed since the nineteen-sixties. It had only been a few months since McKinney brought his daughter to the university, leaving her in the care of strangers for the first time since she had attended summer camp as a little girl, but for some reason he was nervous about seeing her. He couldn't quite put his finger on it but thought it likely he didn't want to see that she'd grown up. He needn't have worried; the girls were in a silly mood. After hugging McKinney and checking the size of the bald spot on the back of his head, Angelina gestured toward the curly-haired girl standing behind her. "Dad, you remember my roommate, Madeleine Duchamp, don't you?"

The girl held out her hand and McKinney took it. "Of course, I do. Nice to see you again, Madeleine." The girls both wore floppy hats and colorful plastic beaded necklaces. McKinney thought they both looked tan and healthy, like they had been spending time out in the sun. "What's with the beads? Mardi Gras was two months ago."

"They're for you," Angelina said.

"Welcome to New Orleans, Mr. McKinney." Madeleine took the beads from around her neck and was handing them to McKinney when Angelina stopped her.

"Oh no, it's not that easy." She looked at her father. "Show us your boobs, first."

The girls broke into a fit of giggles, and McKinney blushed. "I hope you ladies haven't been lifting your shirts for a handful of beads like some drunken tourists."

Angelina stopped laughing, and her face adopted a stern expression. "Heaven forfend, Pater. We are paragons of taste and propriety. We wouldn't lift our shirts for less than two handfuls of beads."

This started the girls giggling again. They didn't stop until the waitress came with their food. The girls had giant mufeletta sandwiches. McKinney had fried shrimp.

Through a mouthful of sandwich Angelina said, "Still not eating meat, Dad?"

"Fish is meat."

"Hardly. You know, Mom loved prosciutto."

"I'll admit, prosciutto is delicious, but it's made from pigs. Pigs are smart. Pigs have feelings. Anyway, I think she enjoyed it as part of her Italian heritage as much as for the flavor."

While they ate, McKinney managed to ask all the questions that had been worrying him. "Are you getting enough sleep? Are you eating right? How are your classes going? Which professor is the jerk? Are you dating anyone? Are you going to parties? How much do you drink at these parties? Do you have enough spending money? How hard is your homework?" Angelina answered them all calmly and dutifully until Madeleine spoke up.

"We're both serious students, Mr. McKinney. We may take an evening off now and then to relax, but only if we've finished all our work for the week. We really haven't had much time for parties or guys."

"I'm sorry," he said. "I didn't mean to give you the third degree. I just..."

Angelina held up her hand. "I know, Dad. You just worry about me. I'm glad you worry about me, but really, I'm fine. School is okay, and I've got a great roommate." She grinned at Madeleine. "Our only problems right now are studying for finals and finding Madeleine's sister."

After the waitress brought them chicoried coffee and pralines, Madeleine spoke up. "Sylvie and I hadn't been close in a couple of years, but I'm certain she would have told me if she was planning to run off. My parents are going crazy. None of us can think of any reason why she would have left her apartment and her job. The police are stumped. I think my father called the FBI, but I don't know if they've found out anything."

"You talked to her friends," McKinney said. "What did they tell you?"

"We didn't really hang with the same people. Oh, shit." Madeleine covered her face with her napkin and sobbed. "I just talked about my sister in the past, like she's already dead. I mean we don't have the same friends. We used to. We were inseparable when we were kids. We even invented our own language. We called it Complicatish after that Avril Lavigne song, 'Complicated.' We were both skaters."

"Skateboards or..?"

"Yeah, skateboards. I guess we drifted apart in high school. She was more popular than I was. Anyway, the police let Dad and me into her apartment, and we looked around. I found her address book and called some of the people in it. That's how I found out about her missing friends. Our dad gave the address book to the police. He's still paying the rent on Sylvie's apartment." She started crying again. "In case she comes back."

Angelina put her arm around Madeleine's shoulders. "Isn't there something you can do, Dad? Help the cops or look for evidence?"

McKinney watched Angelina comfort her friend and imagined how he'd feel if she were to go missing. He didn't think there was anything he could do that the police hadn't,

---

but he couldn't say no. "I'll have to talk to Madeleine's parents first. If the police and the FBI are handling this I'd just be in the way, but if her parents want my help, I'll do what I can." He patted Madeleine's arm. "Call them and ask if they want to meet with me. I can go to their house this evening or tomorrow after I drop our dog off at the day kennel."

Madeleine nodded.

"You brought Hendrix?" Angelina asked.

"Yep."

"Can I go with you to pick him up? Can we take him to the park for a game of Frisbee? I've missed that dog almost as much as I've missed you, Dad." She winked at Madeleine. "Maybe more."

⁓

After a muggy hour of Frisbee with Hendrix and the girls, McKinney was drenched. He drove back to The Chimes, showered, gave the dog his dinner, and headed back to Tulane. He parked on St. Charles and, as he entered the campus, picked up a copy of the student newspaper, the Tulane Hulabaloo. He skimmed it as he strolled under the ancient oak on the Gibson Quad. Flipping to the Crime Watch column he was relieved to see that the only two entries were "TUPD Vehicle Collides With Pole" and "Burned Popcorn Activates Fire Alarm."

He was also pleased to see that while he was at The Chimes the girls had cleaned their dorm room. The two small beds were made, the floor was free of dirty dishes or unwashed clothing, and one of the girls had dragged a chair in from the lounge at the end of the hall for McKinney to sit on. He sat and looked around at the band posters and family photos on the walls. An electric green skateboard was propped against Madeleine's desk and a picture of her family was taped to her desk lamp.

"Is that your sister?" he asked, pointing to the photo.

Madeleine took it down and handed it to him. "This is from last Christmas. Probably the most recent shot of Sylvie we have. I think Dad gave his copy to the police."

He examined the girl in the photo. She had the same broad features and curly hair as Madeleine. Even their smiles were similar, but there was a hard edge about her that Madeleine didn't have. It took him a minute to figure out the difference. It was, he thought, the way she stood, a little apart from the rest of the family and defiant, a balled fist resting on her hip.

"You can hang on to it if you need to."

"No, thanks. I don't need it just yet. Nice-looking family." McKinney took one more look and handed the photo back to her. "Your dorm is cozy."

"Ah, the realtor's word for teeny-tiny," Angelina said.

"Did I ever tell you about my college roommate? He was a philosophy major. He's the only guy I ever knew who had his bicycle repossessed."

"Your dad's so funny," Madeleine said.

"Maddie! Keep that to yourself. It'll only encourage him."

"Where would y'all lak t'go for dinner?"

"You are not going to use that fake southern accent down here, Dad."

"Can we go to Salu?" Madeleine asked. "It's a Spanish restaurant over on Magazine Street. They have good tapas."

"Is the Mississippi on the way? I'd like to see the river."

"It kind of is," Madeleine said. If we take Tchoupitoulas."

"Why do you want to see the river, Dad?"

McKinney settled back in his chair. Angelina sighed

---

and motioned for Madeleine to have a seat.

"I have a job waiting for me when I get back to Chicago. There's a valuable manuscript of a poem by Edgar Allen Poe for sale, and the buyer wants me to determine when it was written to make sure it's not a forgery. The poem is called 'The City in the Sea.' I checked a Poe book out of the library and read the poem before I left to come down here. It's about a city submerged beneath the sea. There are a lot of ways to interpret the poem. Literally, I suppose, like it's about Atlantis or some ancient lost city, or metaphorically, like it's about the human condition. It made me think of New Orleans after Katrina. Anyway, I thought I'd take a look at some of the levees and the parts of town that were under water. It doesn't have anything to do with my job, but I thought it'd be interesting."

"We'll be glad to show you, Dad, but the levee breaches were mostly on the other side of town. Why are you so interested in the flood?"

"Blame your grandfather. On one of our family vacations—I was probably about seven years old—we had to stop in a little town on the Mississippi River because it was raining too hard to keep driving. He checked us into a little roadside motel thinking that the rain would let up the next day and we could continue on to whatever historic site he was dragging us to. Instead the river breached the levees, the town flooded, and we had to be evacuated in a Coast Guard boat."

"Were you scared?"

"I don't remember very much from when I was seven, but I remember going on that boat. Your grandmother was frightened, but I was exhilarated. I guess I thought my dad would keep us safe. You remember your grandfather; he was a very take-charge guy. I'm sure the evacuation was a horrible thing for the residents of that little town, but it was kind of fun for me."

"Argh! You were even weird as a child."

"Yep. And don't forget, you've inherited my genetic code."

Angelina made a face. "I'm doomed."

"Mr. McKinney, how do you figure out a document's age?" Madeleine asked. "I mean, what kind of tests are you going to do on the poem?"

McKinney was pleased to be asked. "The paper analysis should be simple. First, I'll examine it under a microscope to see what fibers are in the paper and in what ratio. I'll also look for a manufacturer's watermark and check for chemicals like optical brighteners and sizing agents, which weren't in use until the twentieth century. The ink will be more difficult. I won't be able to use any techniques that damage the poem, like taking an ink sample, so I'll probably use some type of light spectroscopy to develop a chemical profile of the ink. That way I can determine if the ink is consistent with the types of inks that were being used at the time Poe wrote the poem."

"Can you compare the handwriting to a known sample of Poe's writing?"

"Someone can, but not me. I'm not a handwriting expert. Besides, a good forger could probably do a pretty passable job of imitating Poe's writing. There are plenty of samples available. You can even find pictures of some of his manuscripts on the internet."

Madeleine hopped out of her chair. "That's so cool! I recently inherited a box of old papers from my grandmother, Francoise." She yanked open the door to her closet and dragged a cardboard box out from under a pile of shoes. "Would you mind looking at some of these and telling me how old they are. A few have dates, but some of the papers that don't could be from the Civil War. They look really old."

"Maddie?" Angelina said.

McKinney smiled at Angelina. "It's all right."

Madeleine pulled a thick sheaf of yellow notebook paper from the box. It was tied with a pink ribbon. "Here's a memoir one of my relatives wrote." She hefted it with both hands. "Look how thick it is. I've only read a few pages. So far, it's pretty interesting."

McKinney took the sheaf of papers and untied the ribbon. "Well, this one is easy, it's loose-leaf, college ruled paper which wasn't available until the twentieth century. I'll take the other papers back to Chicago and test them at the same time as the Poe poem."

McKinney handed the stack of papers back to Madeleine. She picked up the first page and began to read, "I, Justine Marie Boisseau Duchamp, am writing this remembrance at the request of my grandchildren, Claude and Francoise. I would not have done so but, because you children are very special to your old grand-mère, and because I am the last Boisseau who is old enough to remember those plantation days in Louisiana, I will try to recall what I can." Madeleine looked up from the page. "Francoise was my grandmother which makes Justine my great, great or great, great, great; I don't know which, but this looks totally interesting."

SEVEN

I, Justine Marie Boisseau Duchamp, am writing this remembrance at the request of my grandchildren, Claude and Francoise. I would not have done so but, because you children are very special to your old grand-mère, and because I am the last Boisseau who is old enough to remember those plantation days in Louisiana, I will try to recall what I can. I will also attempt to be truthful. Though I have lived a life that would not always be considered Christian, I have always kept the teachings of our Lord close to my heart.

I was born on the Boisseau family plantation on a wet October day in 1873. I know it was raining that day because Mama often told me how the midwife had to wrap her wet hair before she brought me into the world. My parents were Mathieu and Regine Boisseau. My mother's maiden name was Prudhomme. Mama named me Justine after her mother and Marie after Father's aunt, who helped raise him when his own dear mother was taken by the fever.

My most vivid childhood memories are of the sugar harvest, which was always such a gay event, and of my little childhood friend, Betina. Betina was the daughter of Mama's slave, Millicent. Of course, this was several years after the war, so our negroes were no longer slaves, but Father was proud to be able to say that many of them stayed to work the sugar cane long after they became freemen. Millicent stayed with my mother for many years.

As I've said, this was after the war, so I have no personal recollections of that terrible time, but I can tell you a few of the incidents that are well known in our family history. Because the Boisseau plantation was so near the river, as it had to be for the transporting of the sugar and some portion of the raw cane, there were fears that we would be shelled. Yankee gunboats were always coming upriver and shelling the plantations, and a good number of our neighbors were bankrupted by the damage. Father's closest friend, Judge Chauvin, had to leave Louisiana to farm in Texas because of the shelling. Our home was saved because grandfather would line all the negroes up in front of the main house. The Yankees at the canons would shout, "Swing yore hat, Butternut!" as they passed by and grandfather would get everyone to smile and wave their hats in the air.

Another story from that time is how my father was saved from death by witchcraft. Father would often dress himself in his alpaca coat and Panama hat and go into New Orleans to conduct the plantation's business and meet with other planters to discuss the affairs of the day. On one of these excursions he overheard a young soldier insult a woman in the street. I don't recall the nature of the insult, but it was enough to cause my father to strike the man. The soldier happened to be a Lieutenant of the Union General, Benjamin Butler, the man they called the Beast of New Orleans because his rule over our newly conquered city was brutal and, one might say, vengeful. My father was arrested and it is likely he would have been shot. As soon as she heard what father had done, Mama took our old carriage to New Orleans where she paid two dollars to a voodoo priestess. The next day father was released. He and mother returned to the plantation together, neither knowing what sort of spell or hex the witch woman had cast.

The incident that caused Millicent to be so devoted to my mother happened after the war, when her Betina was only five or six years old. My paternal grandfather, a bitter old man whom I barely remember, didn't care for Millicent. One day Mama overheard him transacting with a group of slave traders to sell Betina. Slavery was still legal in Cuba and slavers were able to buy slaves from the plantations since many slaves did not yet realize that they were free. Grandfather felt that taking care of her daughter was interfering with Millicent's duties in the main house. Mama begged my father to stop him, crying, "This is no different than if someone was to take our little Justine from us!" Father ran the slave traders off, and after that Millicent stayed loyally by mother's side, even when the rest of our negroes moved north.

Betina and I were almost constant companions on the plantation. After my lessons in reading, mathematics, the French language, and piano, Mama would let me go outside to play, and Betina and I would run down to the river to watch for boats and pick the wildflowers and horsemint, the leaves of which we would chew for their flavour. At that time, the soles of my feet were almost as tough as Betina's, and I would always leave my shoes behind so we could both run barefoot. Of course, we had to be mindful of snakes, but there was nothing better than standing knee deep in the river on a hot day. I can still picture the little, cornflower blue shift I wore to play in and can smell the fragrance from the dogwood trees. Afterwards we'd go up to the washhouse, and Millicent would give us each a glass of cool water with lemon slices in it. It was around that time that I first learned of the Knights of the White Camellia.

EIGHT

There were a number of large estates with private drives in Covington, but the one Duchamp was looking for had a private road. E. Thomas Ambrose was taking no chances. The rich were getting richer and the poor were getting poorer, and he wasn't about to let the "unwashed masses" take what he had worked so hard to get. It was over a mile on that road to the main house, and Wayne had to stop the Lincoln and identify himself over the intercom at three different, unmanned gates so Ambrose could remotely unlock each one.

"This Ambrose guy must be some kind of nut."

"He's rich as sin, Wayne. He can't afford to be incautious."

The mansion came into view as they rounded a corner inhabited by animal shaped topiary. Some of the bushes were loosing foliage, which made the animals look deformed. Duchamp pointed out a three-legged bear at the entrance to the circular drive. The house was obviously a new construction, but it had been designed to resemble an old plantation house. The pillared front porch, home to a half dozen rocking chairs, was tacked on to an enormous ranch with several bay windows. "Like putting lipstick on a pig," Duchamp said. "Now, that is ugly."

"I told you, man. The guy's nuts."

They were welcomed into the house by an elderly black man in a butler's uniform. He led them into a trophy room with a long, mahogany bar running the length of one wall. He pointed to the bottles and glasses behind the bar. "Mister Ambrose asks that you make yourselves comfortable." He left them surrounded by racks of long guns and mounted animal heads, both common and exotic.

Wayne stepped behind the bar and examined the bottles of liquor. "Drink?"

"Yeah. Make me something with scotch in it. That's what all these guys drink." He pointed at a large oddly-shaped animal head with tusks protruding from its snout. "What the hell is that thing?"

Wayne looked up. "That's a wart hog. They look like something from a horror film, but I hear they taste good."

"Probably tastes like chicken."

"It's a pig."

"I'll ask Ambrose what it tastes like when he gets here."

"Beats the hell, outa me."

Duchamp turned toward the voice. In the doorway was a short, pudgy man in khaki shirt and pants. His upper lip was hidden by a bushy, grey mustache, and on his head was a bill cap from something called Fishtastik Charters.

"I never ate one," he repeated. "Rich food upsets my stomach." He held out his hand. "Duchamp isn't it? Tommy Ambrose. What can I do for you?"

Duchamp took the man's hand. "Thanks for agreeing to see me, Tommy. I'd like to talk to you about the Dauphin Pharmaceuticals project."

"Oh, yeah. Samson's big venture. Your chauffeur can wander down to the kitchen and wait with ol' Clement while we palaver." He tilted his head toward Wayne. "I hear they's some tater pie out there."

"That's kind of you," Duchamp said, "but he needs to stay with me. He's my bodyguard."

Wayne nodded his head. Today he was wearing his black suit with the thin lapels. He also had on a pair of mirrored sunglasses and had stuck a Bluetooth earpiece in his ear because he thought it made him look like a secret service agent. His chauffeur's cap was in the Lincoln's trunk. Ambrose looked him up and down.

"Bodyguard, eh? Reckon I oughta get me one of those. I hate having to wear a jacket in the hot weather, and you can't walk around with your Glock hanging out." He plopped down in a chair upholstered with zebra hide and pointed to a matching chair across from his. "Take a load off. Now, what about this drug business?"

Duchamp remained standing. He walked around behind the chair and leaned his forearms on its back. "Frankly Tommy, I'm worried that there are too many investors. Samson doesn't want to cut the pie into little pieces, and I don't blame him. My concern is that it may take me longer than the rest of you to raise the buy in. I'm a little overextended in some of my other investments, but I don't want to be cut out of the deal."

Ambrose took off his cap, exposing his completely bald scalp, and ran his fingers over the embroidered logo. "Sorry to hear that, Duchamp, but I don't lend money. It just complicates things. I learned that lesson the hard way. My family still won't talk to me."

Wayne set two scotch and sodas on the bar. Duchamp handed one to Ambrose and took a sip of the other. "I'm sorry," he said. "I didn't mean to imply that I was asking for a loan. I agree with your money lending policy, but let's put that in the parking lot." He'd heard that phrase somewhere and thought it made him sound smart, so he worked it into conversations whenever he could. He pointed at the tiger's head on the wall above the bar. "That is a huge cat. Did you shoot him with one of these guns?"

Ambrose pushed himself out of his chair, went to the

gun rack by the door and hefted an elaborately engraved rifle. He passed it over to Duchamp. "This is a Hambrusch Double Rifle chambered for H and H .375 cartridges. It'll stop anything smaller than an elephant. Cost me thirty thousand, but worth every penny."

"What's a double rifle?" Duchamp asked. "You mean it breaks open like a shotgun?"

"Exactly, but instead of shot it fires bullets. Open her up."

Duchamp thumbed the sidelock and dropped the barrel. Two cartridges were pushed out by the ejector. "These are some big bullets. Do you always keep your guns loaded?"

"Sure. It's just me and Clement out here, and I like to be prepared. On the rare occasions when my daughter brings my grandbabies to visit I keep this room locked. She doesn't like to see the trophies anyway. Says it saddens her."

Duchamp reloaded the rifle and snapped the barrels back into position.

"Some folks just don't have the stomach for it. Too bad. You've got some beautiful animals here. I'm especially impressed by the big cats." He pointed to the wall opposite the bar. "And what about this fellow? It's a rhino, isn't it?"

"Ah, the pride of my collection."

"Aren't rhinos on the endangered species list?"

Ambrose looked annoyed. "I have permits for every animal in this room."

Duchamp came back around to the front of his chair and sat, resting the rifle across his knees. "I'm sure you do, but back to Dauphin Pharma. I'm not asking for a loan. I'm asking you to drop out of the consortium."

"Now, why in the hell would I do that?"

"I have a friend who is very good at buying information,

and he recently bought some information on my behalf. It seems that you got your hunting permits by bribing low level clerks. Your rhino, your lion, your tigers—all illegal to hunt, kill, or import. Just off the top of my head I can think of three agencies that would be interested."

Ambrose shook his head. "Whee-oo! I don't know if you've got brass balls or if you're just stupid. Don't you think I figured that would be the way some sharpie would come after me? You're the first, I'll admit, but I've been prepared for this for years. One of my lawyers is a hunting buddy. We've got so many cut outs between us and those bribes that it'd take a team of investigators a decade to trace 'em back to me."

From behind the bar Wayne asked, "What's a cut out?"

"Well, well. The bodyguard speaks. A cut out, friend, is someone who was paid to pay someone else to do something. I paid my lawyer to pay a messenger to pay another messenger, etcetera, etcetera, to bribe some chump into issuing the permits that gave me the right to kill any damned thing I wanted. Makes it almost impossible to trace the money back to its source."

"So, you won't leave the Dauphin Pharmaceuticals deal alone?" Duchamp asked.

"Oh, you might maybe cause me a little inconvenience but not enough to change my mind. Besides, I don't like blackmail unless I'm the one doing the blackmailing. If that's all, I reckon you and Tonto here had best be on your way." Ambrose held out his hand for the rifle.

"Too bad," Duchamp said. He raised the gun and fired. Both men were hurled back into their chairs, Duchamp with a badly bruised shoulder and Ambrose with a half-dollar sized hole at the base of his throat. The body convulsed, and then pitched forward, the head flopping to one side. With Ambrose lying bleeding on the floor, Duchamp could see that the bullet had passed through the chair and the wood gun rack behind it. He stood up, rubbing his shoulder, and turned to Wayne. "How about that, 'Tonto?'"

Wayne stood starring at the still-twitching corpse. "What the fuck, Boss?"

"I told you, Wayne. I need this deal. I've got the goods on a couple more investors, and if they aren't willing to drop out they'll have to be disposed of too. If you haven't got the guts for this kind of business, let me know right now."

"I just want to go to cooking school."

"Stick with me, Wayne, and I'll make that happen."

The big man looked down at Ambrose, and then at the gun in Duchamp's hand. "All right, but let's get out of here before someone finds us."

"You're forgetting something, Wayne. We have to get the recordings from the security cameras. Besides, the butler knows we're here. I've got another bullet in this little canon, so let's find the old boy and eliminate the only witness."

Duchamp crossed the room and was reaching for the doorknob when the door opened inward. Clement stood in the doorway, looking into the room with a worried expression on his face. "Excuse me, Mister Ambrose, but I thought I heard a noise. Is everything all right?"

NINE

McKinney woke in time for breakfast at The Chimes. He was starting to have doubts about his decision to stay there. He'd thought of it as a way to get in touch with the memory of his wife. He and Catherine had had an almost sybaritic relationship with New Orleans. They ate and drank their way across town. They went to the most out-of-the-way jazz clubs they could find, always sitting in dark corners, holding hands and kissing like newlyweds. Those were images he called up often when he thought about her, and he was afraid of trivializing them, turning them into nostalgia—vacation memories. He fed Hendrix then walked across the courtyard to the main house.

The proprietress, Jill, was sitting at the dining room table with the other guests. Though the table could seat a dozen it didn't begin to fill the Victorian's enormous dining room. Jill was talking about swamp tours with a British couple. The woman was nervous about going, and Jill was trying to reassure her.

"It's very safe, really. You're in a boat with a dozen other tourists and a guide. People do it all the time."

"But he's crazy." The woman pointed to her husband. "He'd jump out of the boat and wrestle one of those things, those alligators." She punched the man in the shoulder. "You know you would. You're crazy."

Jill turned to the man. "Would you?"

"Aye. I would." He grinned as he said this, and his grin did look crazy.

McKinney would like to have listened to the conversation, but he had to drop Hendrix off at doggie day care before picking up Angelina and Madeleine. Madeleine's parents lived out in Lafayette, near the country club, and he estimated it would take over two hours to get there from Tulane.

The Duchamps' home was a large, Acadian style surrounded by a manicured lawn dotted with live oaks. Mrs. Duchamp welcomed them with a tray of lemonade and showed them through the house to the screened-in porch. A smallish woman with a voice so soft that McKinney had to strain to hear her, she had a ruffled apron tied around her waist, something he thought women no longer wore. Mr. Duchamp, on the other hand, greeted McKinney with a booming, "Come on in!" He was sitting in a wooden glider, drinking something in a highball glass but hopped up as soon as he saw his daughter. He wrapped his large, walnut-brown arms around Madeleine and squeezed. His dark skin made his gray hair look unnatural, but McKinney noticed that the man's eyebrows were gray, too. He couldn't estimate his age and figured it to be anywhere from forty-five to a robust sixty. Finally, Duchamp released his daughter and extended his hand to McKinney.

"Hervé Duchamp. Glad to see you Mr. McKinney. Friends call me Harve."

"Thank you for meeting with me, Harve. Our daughters seem to have struck up quite a friendship. A lucky thing since they're sharing a dorm room."

"Well, we figured Tulane was too far for our girl to commute but close enough for her to come home on weekends. And she has nothing but good to say about your Angelina." His tone sobered. "She also tells me that the two of them asked you to help find her sister."

McKinney noticed Mrs. Duchamp set the tray down and hurry from the room at the mention of her missing daughter.

"Well, I'm not sure how much help I can be, but I'm certainly willing to discuss the problem with you, maybe offer some suggestions."

"Fine," Duchamp said. "Maddie, why don't you take Angelina in and keep your mother company while her father and I kick this around." He pulled a chair up to a wrought iron table and gestured for McKinney to sit across from him. "I'll be honest with you, I don't think we're going to find her. She's been gone over a month. The NOLA police searched Sylvie's apartment, and there was no indication of any kind of a struggle. There was no break in. The doors and windows were locked. When I realized the police were spinning their wheels I got in touch with a friend in the Justice Department. He put me in touch with an investigator who contacted all her friends and neighbors, including every name in her address book. The only thing he came up with was that she had asked some of her friends if they wanted to go on a boat ride, but none of them knew on whose boat or when they were going."

"The girls said a couple of Sylvie's friends were missing, too. Have they turned up?"

"Not to my knowledge. For a while the theory was that they all went out on some boat together, but the police checked all the reported boating accidents in the area. Sylvie and her friends weren't involved."

"What about men? Was Sylvie seeing anyone?"

"We don't know, and it's my fault that we don't. I was strict with the girls. I set boundaries and dealt harshly with violations. Children need boundaries. Madeleine benefitted from them. Sylvie did not. Rather than disappoint me she became secretive. Her mother believes that if I'd been more even handed, less rigid... Well, she thinks if Sylvie had been able to confide in us..." He was silent for a moment, then looked out through the screens and pointed to a lone pecan tree standing in the middle of the yard. "Deer used to come into the yard to get at those pecans. When the girls were little they'd hide over there behind the glider to watch. You know, when the girls moved out the deer stopped coming into the yard. Isn't that the darnedest thing?" He finished the last of his drink, tipping his head back until the ice clicked against his teeth. "Pardon my asking, McKinney, but exactly what is it you do? Maddie said you used to work for the police up north, but she didn't say in what capacity."

"I'm a forensic scientist. Currently, I'm on my own, consulting. Frankly, I'm not sure what good I can do you. Forensic science is based on comparison. I compare evidence from a crime to a known standard. Fibers, for example, that were found on a victim might compare to those in a shirt the suspect was wearing. You're not even sure that a crime took place. I certainly hope it turns out your daughter's unharmed, that she just needed to get away for a bit." McKinney was watching the other man's face as he spoke. He noticed his mouth turn down at the corners. "How about this. I know the police have been through your daughter's apartment, but it never hurts to have an extra pair of eyes. Madeleine says you're keeping up the rent there. Let me take a look around tomorrow afternoon. Years of examining evidence have given me a pretty good eye for detail."

"You say you're a consultant. How much do you figure to charge me for this consultation?"

McKinney wasn't sure how to answer. Charging the man had never entered his mind. "I'm a father, Harve, and Madeleine is my daughter's friend. I wouldn't accept a fee if you offered it."

Duchamp stood and fished a ring of keys out of his

pocket. "Don't be insulted, McKinney. I just like to know who I'm dealing with. It's kept me out of the poor house." He tossed McKinney the keys. "Madeleine can take you to the apartment tomorrow. I'm afraid I don't have the heart for it."

∽

They parked in a lot on Chartres and walked up Frenchmen Street, past the now-empty bars and nightclubs, to Rampart. An old man was sweeping plastic drink cups into a pile in the street. The air still held the scent of beer and vomit. McKinney ruffled Angelina's hair then let his hand rest on her shoulder as they walked, something he had done hundreds of times since she was old enough to walk next to him. With his first look at her, on the day she was born, he knew she was the most beautiful thing he had ever seen. That his DNA had contributed to her existence was incomprehensible to him. When she was just a little girl he had routinely taken her hiking in the woods or exploring Chicago's diverse neighborhoods, lecturing her all the while on the complexity of the world around them, helping her to make sense of it the way one makes sense of a jigsaw puzzle with some of its pieces missing. Teaching her to look, not only at what she can see, but also at how what she sees can help define the nature of things that can't be seen. He tried to teach her logic. It was her mother who taught her joy.

McKinney's wife, Catherine, was the playful yin to his sober yang. She had worked hard to get him to loosen up, and she wasn't going to let him turn Angelina into a thinking machine. She had devoted much of her life to helping her family appreciate the value of fun. It was Catherine who insisted they get a dog. McKinney remembered the day she brought the big poodle home from the pound. Angelina, still in grade school, was waiting in the middle of the living room holding a squeaky, rubber fire hydrant. Hendrix launched his bulk across the room, knocking Angelina on her butt, to get at the toy. The fall barely fazed her and, instead of crying, she hopped up and chased after the dog. They had played keep away all that day, finally curling up on the floor together for a nap. McKinney smiled at the memory and gave his daughter's shoulder a squeeze.

He brought Hendrix along on the search of Sylvie's apartment so Angelina could spend a little more time with him, but he had no illusions about the dog's nose skills. Hendrix wouldn't be any help unless there was a hidden box of dog biscuits.

The ancient apartment was a one bedroom, but it wasn't much larger than a studio. They propped the front door open and raised all the windows; even so, the air inside was stifling. McKinney was shocked by the mess. Boxes of cereal had been emptied into the sink and the refrigerator door stood open. Books and magazines were scattered across the living room floor, and the couch cushions had been slit and the stuffing pulled out. The place was a shambles.

"I don't know how they work down here, but this can't be the result of a police search."

The girls stood out on the wrought iron balcony, holding Hendrix and peeking in through the door. Angelina asked. "You think the place was robbed, Dad?"

McKinney looked at the flat screen television. The back had been pulled off. "Well, searched anyway. You girls stay out here with Hendrix, maybe have a look in the kitchen. I'll check the bedroom." He carefully stepped over the piles of trash on the floor. The bedroom was in a similar state of disarray. Clothes were strewn around the room, and the dresser drawers had been removed and tossed in a corner near the window. The bed was a simple futon on the floor that looked like it had been turned over, the sheets and blankets lying underneath. McKinney sifted through the clothing and peered behind the dresser. He didn't expect to find anything after the thorough search someone else had already conducted, and fifteen minutes later he decided to move on to the bathroom.

The bathroom looked like a room in a museum with yellowed porcelain fixtures and a water tank fixed high up on the wall. The toilet flushed with a pull chain. McKinney took a toothbrush out of its rack and used it to poke around in the pile of jars and bottles that had been left in the sink. He looked behind the old claw-foot tub and noted that the tiny bathroom window was painted shut. Like the bedroom, this appeared to be a dead end, but when he opened the mirrored door of the medicine cabinet he felt the whole thing shift slightly in the frame. He braced the top of the cabinet with one hand and pulled the bottom outward. The unit slid out, and he carefully set it in the tub. Inside the wall, wedged between two pipes, were a mason jar and a small book. McKinney pulled them out and dusted off the book. It was a child's diary—pink, with a cheap little lock on the front, presumably to keep out nosy little brothers. He held the jar up to the light. It was filled with hand-rolled cigarettes, probably marijuana. He had just popped the lock on the diary with the toothbrush when he heard Hendrix barking from the other room. He put the jar back in the wall, replaced the medicine cabinet, slipped the diary into his back pocket and went to see what the commotion was.

By the time he worked his way back through the debris that covered the living room floor Hendrix had stopped barking and was lying on his back enjoying a belly rub from a young woman with long blond hair. McKinney didn't fail to notice that her cut off jeans revealed shapely tanned legs. "Dad,"

Angelina said. "This is Erin, Sylvie's next-door neighbor." The woman looked up and waved at McKinney. "Hello, 'Dad.'"

McKinney smiled. "Looks like you've made a friend."

"Yeah, animals and old ladies love me." She scratched Hendrix behind the ear and stood up. "What a mess, huh? The girls were just telling me that Sylvie's missing. I was out of town visiting my folks for a couple weeks, so I didn't know. Any idea what happened?"

"No. That's why we're here. We're trying to figure it out. The family's pretty upset."

"I bet." She gestured toward the mess on the floor. "So, what's up with this?"

"I don't know, a robbery, maybe. Mind if I ask a few questions?"

"Sure. I'd invite you to my place, but I don't think my cats would approve of your dog. Guess we'll just have to stand."

McKinney tossed a pile of coats and torn cushions aside, to clear a space, and sat on the floor. The blond sat down, and Hendrix trotted over and lay on the floor next to her. Angelina and Madeleine joined them. Angelina ruffled Hendrix's fur. "Traitor," she said.

"Were you and Sylvie friends as well as neighbors?" McKinney asked.

"Well, I don't know about friends. We'd chat, and a couple times we smoked a bowl together, but we weren't tight."

McKinney thought she hesitated a second before answering, like she had to think about whether or not she and Sylvie were friends.

"So, you were just neighbors?"

"Well, I'm a few years older, y'know."

"Was she a good neighbor? Did she feed your cats while you were away?"

"No. My partner... My girlfriend fed them."

"Did she say anything to you about going away or mention any trips she was planning?"

"Not a word. The only plan she mentioned to me was some party at Tipitina's she wanted me to go to. It was while I was away, so I couldn't make it."

"Do you remember the last time you saw her?"

"Sure. That was the day before I left. She knocked on my door and asked if I wanted to go for a boat ride. She had some old guy with her. I think it was her dad."

Madeleine looked surprised. "Our father? He didn't tell me he was here visiting."

"Do you remember the date?" McKinney asked.

"April fifth. I left on the sixth. It was a nice day to go out on the Gulf, but I was busy packing. Besides, the old guy gave me the creeps. He kept checking out my ass and asking if I was sure I didn't want to 'ride on his boat.'"

"That was not my father," Madeleine said.

"Well, whoever he was, he seemed to think I was easy. I suppose New Orleans deserves its reputation, but I don't think we're any more or less sinful than anyone else. Maybe it's just that living under water, like we do, makes us aware that life is short."

McKinney took out his smartphone and opened the calendar app. "What did the man look like?" he asked.

"He was a tall, white guy but really tan. And built. He looked like one of those guys who spends a lot of time looking at himself in the mirror at the gym."

"If it was April fifth it was within a day or two of when Sylvie went missing. It might even have been the same day,"

McKinney said. He made a note on his calendar. "Are you sure they were going out on the Gulf and not Lake Pontchartrain or somewhere else?"

"Yeah. I'm pretty sure 'cause they said they were driving down to Grand Isle."

Madeleine said, "That was not my father."

"Well, whoever he was, he creeped me out."

McKinney dropped the girls off at their dorm. Madeleine had pleaded with him not to tell her parents about Sylvie's hidden pot. "Please Mr. McKinney, my mother would be devastated." Against his better judgment, he left the mason jar hidden in the wall. He drove back to The Chimes to walk Hendrix and give him his dinner. He stretched out on the bed and flipped through the little pink diary while the big poodle ate. It was Sylvie's all right. She had begun the diary while still in high school but had written so infrequently that there were still a few empty pages. McKinney skipped past the descriptions of boys and the frustrated rants about Sylvie's family to the most recent entries. There was one dated March twentieth that appeared to be a guest list for the party at Tipitina's. He could compare this to the list of friends in Sylvie's address book to see if there was anyone who hadn't been contacted by the police. After that was a list of April Fools Day pranks that Sylvie either played or had had played on her. One of them read, *Pee in Bobbie's shampoo bottle.* McKinney hoped she had instead chosen the less obnoxious, *Dog food burgers!*

The last eight pages were written in code. Small groups of letters and numbers were separated by dashes, presumably to represent spaces between words. Some groupings only contained letters. McKinney thought it might be a substitution code, replacing letters of the alphabet with other letters and numbers. He took out his cell phone and searched "most frequently used letters in the English language" coming up with A, E, N, O, and T, with E being the standout by far. He thought perhaps a simple frequency analysis would help him break the code quickly. He scanned the first page of code for letters that repeated. There were thirteen Ts. *Probably*, he thought, *the substitute for E.* He grabbed a pen and the stationary The Chimes had supplied and wrote out a key for a simple sliding substitution code, one that starts the alphabet a certain number of letters along the row from A. He picked a letter grouping from the diary that appeared more than once—TKOF. *In a simple sliding substitution code, if T replaces E then TKOF would spell...* He copied the letters from the code key he had devised—EVZQ. That seemed unlikely. He remembered Madeleine mentioning a language she and Sylvie had invented when they were young girls. He'd show her the diary that evening at dinner. Perhaps the code was Complicatish.

TEN

The Knights of the White Camellia had been around since before I was born, but it wasn't until I was in my teens that they made an appearance at our little plantation. I should say that I hadn't previously been aware of their presence, being a young girl whose preoccupations were her studies and her toys. I understand now that they had been instrumental in the return of some of our runaways and that Father, though he disapproved of their methods, sympathized with their efforts to oust the Republicans who had made such a mess of things after the war.

Though I had spent the entire year leading to my sixteenth birthday lobbying Father for a cotillion, I knew that we were no longer able to afford such an extravagance. He was equally opposed to my attending one of the debut balls in New Orleans as I was still his "jeune ange." It is to my shame that I was not able to accept this more graciously, but I was young and headstrong and possibly a bit spoiled. My mother did her best to cheer me, gathering the family and inviting a neighboring planter, Monsieur Grennon, and his family for a small celebration. They all came dressed in their fine clothing. Madame Grennon had not yet adopted the bustle, however she must have been wearing at least five petticoats under her beautiful satin dress. Mother simply wore a cotton tea gown as she had spent the morning cooking. She and Millicent baked me a beautiful cake and filled the house with flowers, and everyone gathered to sing, "Nos voeux les plus sincères. Que ces quelques fleurs. Vous apportent le bonheur. Que l'année entière." Rather than thank them, I brooded over my situation for, as I saw it, any young lady of style deserved a cotillion.

I ran from the house crying. Father called after me, "Justine Marie," but I flew down the front steps and would have run clear to the river if I hadn't run into Oncle Joseph.

Oncle Joseph was the oldest of our negroes. He was ancient but massive, and he walked slowly due to some injuries he had suffered as a youngster. Blinded by my tears I ran smack into him. The impact had little affect on the large man, but I fell to the ground at his feet.

"Where you goin' in a big hurry," he asked, and reached down to help me to my feet.

"Oh, Oncle Joseph. I'm so unhappy."

We sat on the steps for a bit, and he listened while I told him all my silly problems. When I was finally through unburdening myself he patted me on the knee and said, "Miss Justine, I've watched you grow from a tad and seen you at play with little Betina, and you always gived me a smile. I 'specially liked to watch how you girls played like you was tough as boys, climbing trees and running barefoot. They was times when you'd fall down and bang your shins, and 'stead of crying you'd just get up and keep on playing. Well, now youse a young lady, and here you is crying over some party." He slowly shook his big head. "Somehow, it just don't seem right."

His words cut straight through my petulance, and I felt ashamed. I looked up at him to apologize and, as I did, he removed the red kerchief he always wore about his throat and wiped the perspiration from his forehead. That was when I noticed, for the first time, the horrific scar on his neck. It was in the shape of the letter B, and the skin around it was shiny and puckered so that I knew it was from a burn.

"Oncle Joseph," I asked, where did you get that terrible burn?"

"Child, don't you know? You're granddaddy Boisseau give me this the very first time I ran away. Them White Camellias brought me back and held me down while the old master did the branding."

He winced a little as he remembered it. I don't know what came over me then, but I reached my hand up and touched his poor, marked skin. It was cool to the touch and felt like wax under my fingertips. That started me crying all over again. "I'm so sorry," I said.

"Ain't your fault. All this happened before you was born."

He handed me his kerchief to dry my eyes, but instead I clasped it with both hands and ran indoors to my parents. They were still seated around our big, oak dining table while my mother stood, cutting slices of cake and handing them around to the guests. I laid the kerchief on the table and pointed to it.

"This is Oncle Joseph's," I said. "It is what he wears to cover the wound that was inflicted on him by grandfather." I looked at my father. "Do you know of it?"

Father looked at my mother and the other adults in the room and sighed. Then he sat back in his chair and stared at the red kerchief which, on my mother's white tablecloth, looked more like a stain than a piece of cloth. Finally, he spoke up. "Your grandfather was a man who valued money above all else. He thought of the slaves as his property, the same as one would think of a goat or a chicken. If one of them ran off, his point of view was that the runaway was stealing his property."

"But Oncle Joseph is a man," I said.

"Yes, an old man who is no longer able to do his share of the work here, and yet he has food to eat and a roof over his head for as long as he likes. Times have changed, chere, and I am not so cruel as my father."

This explanation would have pacified me, for I loved my father and barely remembered my grandfather, but then Monsieur Grennon spoke up.

"You youngsters don't appreciate that running a plantation involves certain economic realities. Most owners did not mistreat their slaves, if for no other reason than that an injured slave could not perform his or her duties. A sugar plantation requires hard work from everyone. If the cane sits in the field too long or the boiling is not begun on time, all profit will be lost. The North has destroyed what may well have been the foundation of our business."

"Please, Grennon," my father said, "spare her your lectures."

"Boisseau, we have been done a terrible injustice, and it is time she understood its consequence. The Knights of the White Camellia are organizing again. We shall have reparations."

"Monsieur, she is only a girl, and today is her birthday." Father picked up the offending kerchief from the table and handed it to me. "Return this to Oncle Joseph, then come back inside. Your mother has made you this beautiful cake, which I'm sure is quite delicious." He picked up a piece of the cake, wrapped it in a serviette, and handed it to me. "Take this to the old fellow. He might enjoy a sweet."

I took the package, but before I went out to the yard I looked directly at Monsieur Grennon. "I may be only a girl," I said, "but I am old enough to know that a bit of cake cannot amend the wrong that was done to Oncle Joseph."

ELEVEN

Raymond Duchamp couldn't figure out why he was nervous. He hadn't felt nervous about anything since his parents sent him to the high school in town. He and his brother had been the only kids bussed in from the fishing camps, and the town kids had let them know they weren't welcome. He remembered getting into some kind of fight almost every day until he started high school, when his father sold a parcel of land he had inherited from his father and moved the family into New Orleans. He had hated school. His fondest childhood memories were of the fish camp out in the swamp. He and his brother had gone out with their father early in the morning, combing the Gulf for tuna but mostly catching redfish and bonita. In the afternoons they'd sort the fish and ice them, then check the crab traps in the river while their father cleaned the boat. He enjoyed being a swamp rat, and he didn't understand why the town kids made fun of him. He still got angry when he thought of it.

Now he was meeting with his niece, and that he was nervous about this puzzled him. He assumed it was because she would undoubtedly mention their meeting to his brother. He tapped his coffee cup on the shiny white table top while he waited for her in the Lavin-Bernick Student Center at Tulane. When he finally saw her working her way through the throng of students, he knew why he was nervous. *Dark wavy hair, broad features, athletic build—she's a dead ringer for her sister.* The term dead ringer made him smile. He got up from his chair, and opened his arms, wide. "Ma chere!"

Madeleine shrugged a powder blue book bag off her shoulder, set it and her skateboard on a chair, gave Duchamp an obligatory hug and sat down at the table. "Good to see you, Uncle Raymond. My God, look how blonde you are! You had dark hair at Christmas."

Duchamp self-consciously touched his hair. "My concession to mid-life crisis."

"How's Aunt Barbara?"

"Fine, fine. She sends her love. Can I buy you a coffee?"

"No, thanks. I have class in a few minutes. What did you want to talk to me about?"

"You recently inherited some papers from your grandmother. They were in her china cabinet, I believe. I've started working on our family's genealogy, and I'd like to borrow the papers for my research."

"Oh, well sure, but I don't have them here, not all of them anyway. I loaned the really old ones to my roommate's father. He's a scientist. He's going to study them and tell us when they were written. I've still got Mawmaw Boisseau's journal, though. That ought to help you, but I just started reading it. I can loan it to you when I finish."

"That's fine, thanks. Any chance we can get those papers back from this scientist fellow? I'd really like to get started on this."

"Not right away. He lives up in Chicago. My roommate asked him to come down and help out with Sylvie. I guess you heard that she's missing."

Duchamp set his coffee down and put his hands in his lap. They were shaking. "Yes, a terrible thing. Of course, I'm very upset. How're your parents holding up?"

"Not well. Mom hardly talks anymore. She just sits and stares out the window."

"Sad. Give them my love. What does this scientist have

to do with it? I mean, how can he help?"

"He used to work for the police—some kind of scientific investigator or something." She pushed her chair back and stood up. "I should get going, Uncle Raymond. I can't be late for class."

"Did you ever find your great-grandmother's painting? It was a seascape. It hung in her dining room. I remember seeing it when your father and I were children. We discussed it at Christmas; remember?"

"I remember Dad said it was a photograph or a reproduction."

"He thinks being the older brother means his memory is better, but I remember Mawmaw Boisseau talking about getting the painting when she lived in Italy."

Madeleine picked up her skateboard and book bag. Duchamp held onto the bag's strap until she looked him in the eyes. "Don't forget about those papers. I really want to borrow them."

"I won't forget."

"That's fine," he said, releasing the bag. "You have a nice class, now." He watched as Madeleine walked away, looking unsettled. He called after her. "Come for dinner sometime. Your aunt would like to see you, too."

When she was out of sight he took out his cell phone. "Wayne? Pull the car into that circular drive on St. Charles Street. I'll be out in a minute." He hurried back across the quad, past a giant magnolia tree and several of the steel sculptures that lined the sidewalk. He paused just long enough to marvel at one of them and thought, *I'll bet they paid somebody good money for that rubbish.* The big Lincoln was idling in the drive. Duchamp slid into the front passenger seat.

"How'd it go, Boss?"

"Lousy. I need you to search her dorm room. She just went to class so you've got about an hour. I want you to find a couple of things—her roommate's home address up in Chicago and an old manuscript. In fact, just grab any papers or books that look old."

"Don't these dorms have guards or something? Anyway, I don't know which building it is. How am I supposed to find her room?"

Duchamp pulled a map of the campus and an official-looking envelope from the interior pocket of his sport coat. "You have important papers to deliver that can only be signed for by Madeleine Duchamp." He handed over the envelope. "This is just some bullshit from my broker. Keep your finger over my first name on the envelope. If you have to show it to anyone they'll just see the name Duchamp. And, try wearing your damn cap for a change. You'll look more like a messenger. Now, move out. I'm taking the car."

"What do you mean you're taking the car? How'm I supposed to get home?"

"Take the street car. It's only a couple of miles. Hell, you can walk it in less than an hour."

"But it's hot out. Look!" He held up one arm to show the sweat stains on his shirt. "Man, this's bullshit."

TWELVE

McKinney parked under one of the live oaks in front of Harve Duchamp's big ranch house at a little after eight in the morning. He had hoped to get on the road back to Chicago early, but he needed to give the man his daughter's diary.

The previous night, over a Sazerac and a big plate of boiled crawfish, he had shown Madeleine her sister's diary. He opened it to one of the coded pages as he handed it to her.

"Is this the language you and Sylvie invented?"

Madeleine took the book and dabbed at her eyes with her napkin. She sniffled. "No. I don't know what this is. Complicatish is just like Pig Latin except instead of A-Y you use O-M-P. Igpay atinlay would be igpomp atinlomp and like that."

McKinney took photos of all the coded pages with his cell phone before he went to bed that night. He'd have to work on the code when he got home.

Duchamp greeted him on the lawn, handing McKinney one of the mugs he was holding.

"Chicory coffee," he said. "Kind of a tourist thing, I guess, but I got used to it as a boy. I'd like to talk out here, if that's all right. My wife is still pretty upset."

McKinney let Hendrix out of the car and the three of them strolled across the lawn, sticking to the shady patches under the trees; it was already muggy. McKinney handed over the little pink diary.

"I don't know that there's much here that you and the police haven't already covered, Harve. She mentions a party at Tipitina's that might be worth looking into. Maybe compare the guest list to the list of friends you've already contacted.

There might be a few more names. I spoke to Sylvie's next-door neighbor, a woman named Erin, but she was out of town when Sylvie went missing. She mentioned meeting an older man at Sylvie's, but couldn't remember his name. Because of his age she assumed he was her father. All she could recall about him was that he's tall and muscular."

"I have no idea who that could be. Like I said, Sylvie didn't confide in us much. I'll ask her sister if she knows who it is."

"She doesn't. In fact she was a little upset that the neighbor thought it might have been you. Apparently this guy was a bit of a lech."

Harve Duchamp said, "Oh, lord." He set his coffee cup down on the grass, opened the diary and flipped through it.

McKinney took a sip of his own coffee. "I hate to suggest this, Harve," he started.

"Go ahead. I want to make sure we're doing everything possible to find my daughter."

"You've said that Sylvie had fallen out of touch with you, stopped communicating. Is it possible that her relationship with her mother was less strained? I know your wife is upset, but she might have some knowledge or insight that you and Madeleine don't."

The man looked back at his house. McKinney followed his gaze and saw the living room curtain close. "My wife is not a strong person, McKinney. Your suggestion has merit, but I need to find a way to talk to her that won't set her off. She's always had emotional problems. She's been seeing a doctor, a therapist, since Sylvie disappeared." He thought for a minute. "I'll talk to her a bit after you leave, but maybe the best way to handle it is to get Maddie to come home for the weekend. Then we can all sit down and go over this as a family. That way it'll seem like less of an interrogation."

"Maybe Sylvie confided something to one of them. She might have said something to your wife that doesn't seem important. Some offhand remark or a mention of the guy Sylvie's neighbor met."

The man looked down at the little pink book in his hand. His shoulders were slumped, and for a second he seemed smaller, shrunken. Then he held out his hand. "Thank you for your help, Mister McKinney."

"Good luck to you, Harve. Keep me informed, please." McKinney took the man's hand. "I certainly hope Sylvie turns up." He left him standing on the lawn, looking like the last thing he wanted to do that morning was go inside to talk to his wife.

McKinney drove east to 59, then headed north, going through Mississippi, so he could see some of the surrounding country. Spring came earlier there than it did in Chicago, and the green countryside slipped past as he thumped his palm on the steering wheel in time to a CD by his latest find, bluesman Guitar Slim. Just past Meridian, 59 turned into 45, and the tree-lined corridor narrowed. McKinney clicked off the CD player and opened all the windows. The oxygen-rich smell of damp vegetation transported him back to his early teens. An older girl, LuAnn, had taught him to drive when he was fourteen. Every weekend for a month she had driven him out of town to a rural Midwest road and let him take the wheel. As soon as he got his learner's permit he was off on his own, cruising country roads and exploring all the little towns between Chicago and Dekalb. He always drove with the windows down so he could smell the country he was driving through—chlorophyll and hot dust in the summer, snow and cold that froze the hairs in his nose in the winter. He let it all in. It excited his senses. What he most enjoyed was driving alone over roads that dipped and rose across hills and snaked through woods or cornfields. He was sure that right over the next hill would be something amazing. His teenage excursions had scared the hell out of his parents, but to McKinney driving meant freedom and possibility.

When the road narrowed to two lanes up around Tippah County he decided to look for a place to spend the night. A sign advertising Cabin Rentals netted him a little cabin on Sandy Creek, a branch off the Tennessee River. He grabbed a handful of tourist pamphlets as he left the rental office and flipped through them as he and Hendrix walked down to the creek. The Cherokee Nation's Trail of Tears, the Civil War battlefield at Shiloh, and the museum commemorating Sheriff Buford Pusser of *Walking Tall* fame were all nearby. All of these sights would have interested his father, an amateur historian who dragged the family from one historic monument to another on their summer vacations, but none attracted McKinney. What he was interested in was the Pickwick Reservoir. Just up the road from his cabin, this was a manmade lake created in the 1930s when the Tennessee Valley Authority built a hydroelectric dam, flooding the surrounding area and submerging the towns of Riverton and Waterloo, Alabama. This seemed to dovetail perfectly with his interest in the flooding of New Orleans and "The City in the Sea" poem.

He and Hendrix dined on the contents of the cabin's small kitchen, a few groceries supplied by the cabin's owner. McKinney ate fish sticks and canned corn while the poodle devoured a can of beef stew. He had brought a Tribune along and scanned the paper while he ate, looking for stories about any interesting crimes he might be missing now that he was no longer working for the Illinois State Police Crime Lab.

As much as he disliked the lab's director he had to admit, he missed the job.

Afterwards, he started to look through the box of papers Madeleine had given him, but Hendrix wouldn't leave him alone, smacking him in the leg with his favorite toy, a plush Capone-esque mobster doll Angelina had bought for him one year at Christmas. McKinney set the box aside and took the doll. For a while he had worried that he would start to think of his daughter as a link to Catherine. That he would relive all the experiences they had shared as a family whenever he saw her, turning her into a talisman. Seeing her as a college freshman had dispelled that notion. She had always been her own person—smart, and funny, and strong-willed. Her personality was too strong to be subsumed by the memory of her mother, now more than ever. He looked at Hendrix and swore the dog was smiling. He waggled the gangster doll in front of the dog. "You want this?" He ran around behind the little couch. Hendrix chased after him, barking and jumping after the toy. "Oh, you want this?" McKinney circled the couch again, and the dog followed, barking and springing after him. They played until they were exhausted, then slept together in the cedar log bed, the dog on top of the covers but with his head pressed firmly against McKinney's leg.

In the morning McKinney practiced tai chi down by the river. Parting the wild horse's mane, the white crane spreads it's wings—the flowing river paralleled his graceful moves as McKinney performed the colorfully named combat techniques. Back at the cabin he and Hendrix shared some toaster waffles, then drove to the dam. Along the winding road they passed a half dozen Baptist and Pentecostal churches, a gun shop, a diner advertising outdoor karaoke, and a state park. They also passed the Pickwick Paper Company, which, despite its nod to

Charles Dickens' first novel, caused McKinney to raise the car windows to fend off the noxious smell it emitted.

The dam itself was disappointingly sparse. There were a couple of fishing boats out on the river, but the road was deserted. McKinney turned in at the gravel track running alongside the dam and parked. He walked along the dam, looking down at the water in the reservoir. It was dead still, flat without a ripple, but the sun made the green surface sparkle. The banks were lined with trees and not much else. He imagined the buildings beneath the water, a few houses, a church, maybe a store. He knew all the people had been evacuated before the valley was flooded, but it was still eerie to think of those empty structures, deserted and submerged. Were there cans of food still sitting on pantry shelves? Was there a dress in a closet, left behind to sway in the current?

He knew he was near the spot where Tennessee, Mississippi, and Alabama meet, but he wasn't even sure which state he was currently in. He drove to the state park on the west side of the river and tried to get information from the lone employee in the visitor center, a doughy-looking young woman in a plaid shirt and jeans.

"Honestly mister, I've never heard of any underwater towns, but I know that Waterloo still exists. Problem is, it's clear over on the other side of the river and South a ways. Take you almost an hour to get there. It's a real pretty drive, but there ain't nothing over there."

"Why's that?"

"Unless they farm, most folks in Northern Alabama live close to Huntsville, just like most Tennesseans around here live within commuting distance of Memphis. If they do farm they're likely just scraping by because they work on contract for some big agri-company."

"On contract? You mean like share croppers?"

"Not quite. The farmers own the land and do the work, but the companies own the crops or chickens or whatever. The smart farmers buy crop insurance, 'cause they're liable for any losses. There was a big stink over contracts in Alabama with the chicken farmers awhile back." The woman laughed at her unintended joke. McKinney looked confused. "Big stink?" she said. "Chicken farms? Get it?"

McKinney chuckled politely, thanked her, and decided to get back on the road. He drove along more small winding roads for several hours before hitting Highway 57. As he drove he passed several pickup trucks, some shiny new, pulling big bass boats on trailers. A few were antiques that looked like they were held together with bailing wire and duct tape. He thought about farmers who no longer owned their crops. He thought about New Orleanians who had taken pennies on the dollar for their homes when developers descended on the city after Katrina. Maybe he'd found the real underwater city. It wasn't the towns flooded by the reservoir; it was all the people who'd had faith in a system that had sold their rights to the highest bidder.

∽

He had just tossed his backpack on the couch in his apartment when his cell phone rang. He carried it to the kitchen as he answered so he could refill the water bowl for Hendrix.

"Dad, I think we've been robbed!"

"Hi honey, what do you mean you *think* you've been robbed?"

"I tried to call you before, but you didn't answer your phone."

"I probably wasn't near a cell tower. I just got home. Slow down. Take a deep breath, and tell me what happened."

"We came back from classes and found our room all messed up. Stuff was dumped on the floor and everything was out of place."

"What did they take? What's missing?"

"Nothing. Well, I don't know, yet. We called the campus police. They came by and looked at the room, but I don't think they're going to do anything about it."

"Well, unless there's something missing or the thief left some kind of evidence behind, there's not a lot they can do. Most burglaries go unsolved."

"Shouldn't they dust for fingerprints?"

"That would be up to the city police, and unless something valuable is missing they probably won't take the time. You girls haven't made anyone mad have you? Is there a jilted boyfriend in Madeleine's past?"

Angelina chuckled. "Jilted? What century are you living in? I don't know about her boyfriends. I'll ask her later. Sorry I sounded so panicky, but it's pretty scary to open your door and find your room turned upside down."

"Don't apologize. I'd be upset, too. Any word on Madeleine's sister?"

"Nothing. She said you gave her dad that little diary. They're going to check the people Sylvie mentions in there against the ones in her address book to see if the police missed anyone."

McKinney kept the phone to his ear and opened the refrigerator for a beer. In the back he found the last bottle of Negra Modello. "I'm going to start working on the coded pages from her diary, tonight. Maybe we'll get some hint to what she was doing, though I'm betting the pot was part of it. Have you or Madeleine told her parents about that hidden jar of joints?"

"No. That's Maddie's decision."

"For now. If it looks like the pot had something to do with Sylvie's disappearance, though, we'll have to tell them. Her father, at least."

"Do you think it does?"

"I have no idea. Let me know if you find something missing from your room. I worry about you down there. Isn't your dorm supposed to be locked? I think I should call the campus police."

"The dorm is locked at night. It's open during the day, but there's usually someone at the desk. Non-residents have to sign in and out."

"Well, you be careful, honey."

McKinney carried his beer into the living room, picked up his unread mail, and plopped down on the couch. He hadn't let on to Angelina, but he was worried about her. She might not be directly involved with her roommate's family problems, but he didn't want her to become collateral damage. It had taken him years to learn how to live with Catherine's death. He knew he'd never really get over it, just as he knew he couldn't learn to live with it if something happened to his daughter.

Hendrix trotted in from the kitchen and wiped his nose on McKinney's pant leg before stretching out on the carpet for a nap. McKinney was sorting through the mail when his phone rang again. He recognized the voice as Carla's and the tone as distant.

"Carla! How's New York? How's the sculpture exhibit going?"

"It's fine, Sean. I've sold several pieces, one to a museum. This is a pretty exciting time for me, career-wise, I mean."

"That's great. I'm sorry I couldn't be there to support you." He regretted the words as soon as they left his mouth. It had been Carla's request that he not go to New York. He didn't want to sound petty.

"That's why I'm calling. There's been a development." She paused.

Development? "Go on."

"I've met someone."

There it is. He let her continue.

"I didn't come here with the intention of meeting someone. It just…"

"I know. It just happened."

"Don't be cruel, Sean."

"Then don't speak in clichés. How'd you meet him? Is he an artist, too? Give me the details."

"He owns a little gallery in the Chelsea neighborhood. He bought one of my figurative sculptures, the woman in the raincoat carrying the shopping bags."

"He's got good taste. That's a nice piece."

"Thanks. I'm coming back to Chicago next week to put my furniture in storage and pack some things. I'm moving out here."

"That's nice." *That's nice?* "Sorry. Well, good for you. If you need help moving your stuff…"

" Probably not a good idea. I appreciate the offer, but I think it would be too difficult, you know, considering."

"Too difficult? You mean for me? Not at all. I'm happy for you. Springtime in New York. Love in bloom. Increased neuronal dopamine production."

"Goodbye, Sean."

He tossed his cell phone onto the couch next to him, took a swig of beer and picked up his phone, again. This was as good a time to work on Sylvie's code as any. He needed something to do. After five minutes he put the phone down. He couldn't concentrate. He was irritated. She had a lot of nerve to think that he would be so devastated over this breakup that seeing her would be "too difficult." It dawned on him that, despite being angry, he wasn't particularly hurt. He liked Carla. She was fun to be with. She had made him feel good about himself again, and she had gotten him back into the world after years of being immobilized by grief. He wasn't, however, in love with her. He thought about Catherine and how his love for her had bordered on mania. He remembered a letter he wrote to her when they were dating. In it he had included a poem from the thirteenth century poet Rumi: *From far away, you keep ordering me to dance. But I don't know how to dance without your melody.* Suddenly, he felt very lonely.

⁂

There was just a small group in the basement of the Methodist church, a skeleton crew. McKinney had found a Live For Today pamphlet in the stack of mail that was waiting for him when he got back from New Orleans. Beth was indeed persistent. There was a meeting that very night, and McKinney went, needing company but determined not to say anything.

The chairs were in the usual circle, but one of the members had pulled his chair back to sit behind a woman who was probably his mother. The young man was tall and thin, so McKinney wasn't sure of his age. He guessed late teens, but realized he could be off by a few years in either direction. The woman was squat and spoke with an Eastern European accent. Her husband had died of a brain tumor, or as she liked to put it, "suicide by brain tumor." He had been a photographer and the tumor rested on his optic nerve. The surgery and radiation had blinded him, so when the tumor grew back he refused treatment. "He say we are not enough for him. His pictures was everything to him, so he rather die. Imagine how that make us feel." She jerked a thumb at the boy sitting behind her. "If not for him maybe I suicide, too." The boy peeked around his mother and grinned at the small assemblage. He held a small dog in his lap, which he petted continuously with a stiff, flat-handed motion.

Seeing the empathetic nods from the other group members made McKinney almost ashamed to admit that he had never considered suicide. He would like to have attributed that to having a daughter to raise, but he knew that wasn't the only reason. He had spent the two years following his wife's death in a zombie-like state, unable to think or act. His only feelings had been sorrow and anger. Despair hadn't had a chance. The truth was, during that time he hadn't thought enough about being alive to consider the alternative. By the time he became involved in living again it was too late. He thought, *I guess life had a grip on me.*

He turned his attention back to the woman and her son. She was just finishing speaking. "Easier to be alive when helping other people." She pointed to Beth. "Like you. Maybe I call the hospital. Apply for volunteer work."

Beth smiled at the woman, then ended the meeting as she always did, by reciting the famous passage from Ecclesiastes, "To everything there is a season and a time to every purpose under heaven." After the meeting, she approached McKinney and put her hand on his arm. "How are you doing?" she asked.

THIRTEEN

After my sixteenth birthday I determined to leave the plantation and attend school in New Orleans. I began a campaign of begging Father and Mother to send me to the same school attended by my cousin, Pauline, whom I adored. This was a school for young girls, and it was adjacent to the Vieux Carré and very fashionable. Mother agreed that plantation life was not conducive to a young lady's cultural growth, but we had a difficult time convincing Father, who saw it as an unnecessary expense. Finally though, after months of coaxing and cajoling, Father relented. My bags were packed and I was taken to Madame Broussard's.

Cousin Pauline was a year or two ahead of me, so we weren't allowed to take classes together or room together, but I saw her often, mostly on the weekend. My roommate was a girl named Lisette, and when I was first introduced to her I feared that we would not get along. My mother accompanied me to my room while Father remained in the office, chatting with the headmistress and, I'm sure, giving her instructions for my care. One of the older girls helped with my bags, and it was she who opened the door to my room. Fortunately, Mother was standing behind us, so she failed to notice that Lisette had been sitting by the open window and smoking a cigarette. When the door opened she tossed the cigarette out the window and waved her arms in the air to dispel the smoke. I was rather appalled to see the girl with whom I was to share quarters so blatantly breaking the rules, but it wasn't long before I was mad about both Lisette's independent attitude and the Fragrant Rose cigarettes she smoked.

School was both a delight and a trial. I took classes in English and French composition, elocution, history, arithmetic, piano, and my favorite class, solfeggio or sight singing. This is the method of reading music that assigns syllables to the different notes; do, re, mi, and so on. My teacher, Mlle. Dunnewold, was a beauty with a ready smile and a voice like an angel. At least once a week she would take Lisette and me and a few of the other girls to the French Opera House on Bourbon Street. I don't know if I learned much about music from those excursions, but I loved the splendid décor and performers' elaborate costumes. Often we would stop at one of the cafes for some small refreshment after the performance.

Even though we were with our chaperone, the young gentlemen in their long coats would try to make our acquaintance in the lobby. They almost always approached Lisette first. Lisette had a milky complexion and fine hair, and the young men buzzed around her. I had my share of followers, but my curly hair and brunette complexion attracted a different kind of attention. Many of my potential suitors were recent immigrants from Sicily. Lisette and the other girls looked down on the Italians. Many of them were quite wealthy, yet they were considered to be lower class. Of course, we were forbidden to speak to any men, and Mlle. Dunnewold would have had a conniption if she had caught us, but we always managed to find some way.

I remember when I met my first beau, Peter. We had just seen Le Tribut de Zamora and were gathered in the lobby. I wasn't feeling as jolly as the other girls who were giggling about some of the scandalous costumes the singers had worn. There had been a scene in the opera of a slave auction, and though it was a Moorish auction, the sight had made me a bit morose. I was standing apart from the group when a young

---

man sporting a thin, black mustache approached me and extended his hand. Because I was distracted by my thoughts I was caught off guard and gave him my ungloved hand. He bent from the waist and touched the back of my hand to his lips. That brief caress sent a tremor through my limbs that was quite unsettling. When he straightened he was smiling. I thought that I had never seen anyone so handsome.

"Pietro Monasterio," he said. "May I have the honor of knowing your name?"

I looked across the room at Mlle. Dunnewold. Fortunately, she was engaged with the task of gathering her little flock for the walk back to the dormitory. "I'm afraid that would be imprudent, don't you agree? We haven't been introduced."

"An oversight that can be easily remedied." He grabbed the elbow of the young man standing behind him. "Matrangas, introduce me to this lovely creature."

His friend looked confused. "I don't know her."

"You know me," Peter said, "and that's sufficient."

"Fine," the man said. His look of confusion was replaced by one of annoyance. "Peter, this is some girl. Girl, this is Peter."

"That was hardly a proper introduction, and anyway, I see my classmates are leaving." Lisette was waving to me, and the other girls were filing out into the hot, afternoon sun. I turned to leave, and Peter let out a little gasp. His hands flew to his chest, mocking a wound to his heart. I couldn't help but laugh at this charming foolishness, so over my shoulder I whispered, "My name is Justine," as I hurried to catch up to my classmates. I hardly noticed the heat or the foul odors left by the horses as we walked back to school. In fact, I paused in front of the Pareti brothers market to admire the bananas, plums, and other fruits on display. An old woman selling cala cakes ambled by, balancing her basket on her head. The deep-fried rice cakes smelled so good I bought two on the spot.

Back in our room I sat on our little footstool by the open window, trying to catch a breeze, while I told Lisette of my adventure. It was obvious that she didn't share my opinion of Peter, but she definitely approved of flirting with men. In an imitation of Mlle. Dunnewold she chirped, "Young ladies do not associate with strange men, particularly those to whom they have not been introduced."

"Oh, Peter was introduced to me by another young gentleman."

"And do you know this gentleman's name? You do not. For all you know they may be thieves or highwaymen. Worse, they may be vegetable merchants."

"I've nothing against vegetables."

"Well then," she said, giving me a salacious wink, "do be careful of his carrot."

FOURTEEN

It was a perfect day for boating on the Gulf of Mexico. The sun drifted in and out of a bank of fluffy non-threatening clouds and the water was calm, just a few small whitecaps giving evidence of a breeze. Raymond Duchamp carried a planter's punch out to his wife, who was sitting on the little dive platform attached to the rear transom of their forty-foot motor yacht. Duchamp had thought the boat a little small when he first saw it in its slip, but his wife, Barbara, had oohed and ahhed over the teak built-ins and the large master stateroom. She had seen one like it in Italy when she was there on vacation, and it was, after all, her money.

Duchamp reached down and handed her the tall glass. "Something cool for you, ma chere."

"Thank you, Raymond. What a nice surprise this day has been. We haven't been out on the Fleur De Lis in ages. I'd almost forgotten how much I love being on the water."

"And I'd almost forgotten how much I enjoy spending time with my wife. We've been at odds a lot lately, and I blame myself for that. I thought maybe we could talk things out."

"That's very sweet, but let's not spoil the day. I just want to soak up the sun and enjoy the motion of the waves rocking us to and fro." She looked out to the empty horizon. "It's almost like we're the only people left on earth, and this little boat is our ark."

Duchamp climbed out onto the dive platform and sat down, taking his wife's free hand in his own. "What a romantic image. I like that. I need to discuss something with you, though. I wouldn't bring it up, but I've been under a lot of stress lately."

"Really, Raymond? Stress?" Her tone was sarcastic. "What have you possibly got to be stressed about? My money pays the bills, even the salary of that silly, unnecessary chauffeur, or whatever he is."

"I know, and I'm grateful. I've tried to contribute, but my investments haven't done well, lately. In fact, we're almost broke. Except for the house and this boat we no longer own much of anything."

"That's why there're in my name, along with my car and our two mutual fund accounts. You're not a businessman, dear. I've known it since before we were married."

"Hence the pre-nup," Duchamp said.

"Yes, hence the pre-nup. You're an ex-swindler, and you have no head for business. I've no intention of letting you blunder us into the poor house."

Duchamp held his temper. "I currently have an opportunity..." He stopped and rested his palm on his wife's chin, turning her head to look at him. "*We* have an opportunity to join an investment consortium that's backing a new pharmaceuticals company. It requires a pretty steep buy-in, but the return on investment will make us fabulously wealthy."

"What if I don't want to be fabulously wealthy?" She gestured at the boat and the expansive waters beyond. "What if this is enough for me? Why can't it be enough for you, too?"

"You said it yourself. I'm an ex-swindler. I tried a scheme to make a lot of money fast, and it didn't work. This isn't like that. The guy heading up this venture, Samson Edwards, is an entrepreneurial genius. The man reeks of success. Your family thinks I'm a bum. Your father barely speaks to me. I can't stand being the failure they all think I am. I can be a success if you're willing to help me. I need this, Barbara."

"Have you considered getting a job? I mean, if you

want to feel like you're accomplishing something maybe you should work. Heaven knows I don't want to work. My stint in retail while I was away at college cured me of that, but you might take to it. I'm sure my father could find you something at one of his firms."

He ignored the taunt. "This isn't some get-rich-quick scheme. The consortium is made up of some of the wealthiest men on the coast. Like I said, the buy-in is large, but I can get us in on a contingency basis for quite a bit less."

"How much?"

"Five hundred."

"Five hundred thousand? Half a million dollars?" She laughed. "You must be out of your mind."

"Look, once we're in I'll figure out some way to get the rest. I told you; the ROI on this thing is huge. In two years we'll be taking in ten mill a year."

"And how much is the full buy-in?"

"Close to five, but your father…"

"I'm not asking my father for five million dollars."

"It would just be a loan. I'd pay whatever interest he wants. I can't go to the banks. My credit is bad, and I haven't any collateral."

"Even if I wanted to help you, which I don't, my father would say no. He doesn't like you."

"You could say it was your idea."

"No."

Duchamp took a deep breath. "Okay, let's sell the Fleur De Lis. We paid almost five hundred for her."

"I'm not selling this boat. Besides, she's old in boat years. We bought her used; remember? We'd be lucky to get two hundred thousand."

"But she's insured for the replacement value. If she sank

we'd get the five hundred thousand." Barbara looked at him as though he was crazy, but he ignored her and continued. "Every appliance on this boat uses propane, the heater, the stove, the hot water, the little clothes dryer you had installed. I put the inflatable dinghy on board before we left the dock. All we have to do is nick a hole in one of the propane lines, light a candle, and climb into the dinghy. The boat has a wood hull. It'll burn to the waterline, and I'll row us to shore. Simple, really."

"Even if I was willing to entertain such an insane idea, which I'm not, there are two good reasons why it won't work. A close look at our finances would be all the insurance company would need to start an investigation."

"And the other reason."

"The Fleur De Lis isn't paid off, yet. I didn't tell you, but I didn't buy her outright. After you started losing money hand over fist, I decided it wasn't smart to have that much of my trust money tied up in a boat. I've been paying her off on time."

"How much do you still owe?"

"More than her resale value. These boats depreciate quickly. What's that term they use for when you owe more on your house than it's worth?"

"Under water?"

"That's it. This boat is under water. Hah! Pretty funny."

"Yeah. Funny." He got up, walked forward to one of the boat's lockers and came back with a dive mask and fins. Resting his hip against the transom for balance, he pulled on the fins.

"Don't be mad, Raymond."

"I'm not mad," he said, "but you've put me in a spot. You won't help me get the money for this investment, and our pre-nup ensures that I get no money if we divorce. I'm afraid the only other source of capital I have is your life insurance. It's not five million, but it's enough to get me into the consortium. Your will leaves me the house, too, so..." He slipped the dive mask on and grabbed the straps of her swimsuit at the shoulders. "Here we go!"

He dove over her head and off the platform, pulling her in with him. His legs slammed into her back as they entered the water. Duchamp plunged straight down, kicking hard and dragging her along with him. She tried to pull away, twisting her body in the water, working to get upright. She got one foot against Duchamp's shoulder and started to push, but he shifted his weight and her foot slipped off. He was amazed at her strength. She grabbed one of his wrists and pulled herself toward him, clawing, trying to bite him. He released that strap and switched his grip to the other strap, both hands on the one strap, pulling her deeper.

He was out of air by the time she quit struggling, but he held her under a few more lung-searing seconds to make sure. Then, he surfaced, gasping and coughing, but keeping hold of her swimsuit. He towed her back to the boat and slipped a loop of rope from the dive platform around her ankle. He didn't want her drifting off while he napped. She hovered there, face down, her hair rippling out around her. That would be his story. They had had a little too much to drink, and he had taken a nap while she went for a swim. He didn't even know she was gone until he woke up and saw her floating in the water.

He climbed aboard and tossed the mask and fins aside. He truly hated having to kill her. He had loved her once. He thought about the fun they had had when they were dating and how she had stuck up for him when her snooty mother suggested she could "do better." Then he lay down on the deck and closed his eyes. He would need to get a good, dark sunburn to corroborate his story.

FIFTEEN

McKinney glanced through the papers in the box Madeleine Duchamp had given him. There were a few newspaper clippings and some official-looking papers, but most of it consisted of old letters. He would be able to do ink and paper analysis on those. Now though, he wanted to get to work on Sylvie's code. He turned on the WiFi on his cell phone and opened the photos of the pages from her diary, then connected to his printer and printed copies to study.

The arrangement of letters and numbers still looked to him like a simple substitution code. If it was a sliding substitution code he simply needed to find the starting letter, the one that substituted for A. He tried a variety of possibilities. He wrote the alphabet backwards, substituting Z for A. He started with Sylvie's name. He used her birthday, and then her address swapping the digits for their equivalent numbers, one through twenty-six. After an hour of this he was no closer to finding Sylvie's Rosetta Stone than when he started. He had been using his laptop computer to type in the lines of letters for comparison. He looked down at his keyboard, and something jelled. *QWERTY, of course*, he thought. It *was* a simple substitution code–a QWERTY code, based on the arrangement of letters on a standard keyboard. Q substituted for A. He typed out the pages using the keyboard substitutions. The meaning was still a little unclear, but knowing that it had been hidden with a jar of reefer helped him make sense of it. O-GVT-TKOF-400R became I-OWE-ERIN-400D. The combination of letters, TKOF, popped up often. Sometimes the references to Erin said GQOR-TKOF and a number. This translated to PAID-ERIN. If the D meant dollars, Sylvie was into Erin for a lot of money. Lesser amounts were associated with entries like WQKW-10P-80R, which McKinney thought likely meant BARB-10J (joints)-80D (dollars). So, Erin was supplying Sylvie with pot, which Sylvie would then roll into joints to sell to her friends. McKinney didn't know if Sylvie had coded the dollar amounts, but they seemed to reflect what little he knew of current market prices for marijuana. If the numbers weren't coded he might be able to get some sense of her activity before she disappeared, since there were, what appeared to be, dates in front of many of the entries. He looked at the final entry on the last page. It read 04/04-ZKTCGK-5P-40R meaning 04/04-TREVOR-5J-40D. So, on April fourth she sold Trevor five joints for forty dollars. April fourth was probably the day before she disappeared. Trevor was someone worth talking to. So was Erin. He hoped Harve Duchamp still had the investigator his Justice Department friend had recommended. If not, he'd have to go back to New Orleans himself, which might be a problem. He hadn't been paid for the NASA job yet, and funds were scarce. McKinney picked up his phone and punched in Harve's number. He'd have to tell him about the hidden pot after all.

∽

McKinney had thought that the owner of the Poe manuscript would want him to work on it in his home, or at least someplace where he could keep an eye on it. He was surprised when Nina told him she had been entrusted with the poem and could deliver it to him whenever he was ready to start working on it. She suggested they again meet for a drink. He suggested they meet for dinner. "Okay," she said, "but not Italian. I don't want to get marinara sauce on 'The City in the Sea.'"

They went to a little seafood place on Montrose, just a

block from the El platform. There was a line ahead of them, so they ordered wine and stood out on the sidewalk while they waited for a table. McKinney refused to open the package containing the manuscript.

"I'll wait until I'm in a clean safe environment."

"Aren't you even curious? I am. I've never seen a four hundred thousand dollar poem before."

"And you're not going to see one tonight, either."

Finally they were seated, and after too many garlicky muscles and just enough wine, Nina addressed the elephant in the room. "I asked you about your girlfriend the last time we got together, and I felt like you kind of glossed over the answer."

"I wasn't too sure about the status of that relationship, then. We had been having problems and had agreed to take a little break." He sipped his wine. "That uncertainty has been cleared up. We are no longer an item." He still felt odd talking about Carla, so he steered the conversation in another direction. "How are things at the Public Defenders office?"

"I transferred to the juvenile division. I initially thought there was less chance of one of my clients killing someone on release than when I worked defending adults. I was wrong." Nina turned her spoon so it was parallel to her knife and fork and moved her water glass an inch to the left. "Oh, hell," she said. She snatched up the tableware and let it drop, destroying the neat pattern. "Sorry about that. I mean, that you and Carla... and this damn OCD... and I hate my job. Everyone accused of a crime has a constitutional right to legal defense, and they should. Most of my clients are basically good kids who can turn their lives around, but some of them are just rotten punks. The police mess up the arrest, or I'm just a little more persuasive than the prosecution, and they get released so they can go and shoot someone else." She pressed her napkin to her eyes with both hands. "Sometimes I just want to lock them up and throw away the key myself. What kind of defense can I give a kid if I hate him?"

McKinney understood. "I had similar feelings when I was working for the State Police Lab. Forensic science is based on objectivity. When I'm analyzing a piece of evidence the circumstances of the case should make no difference to me. In fact, the integrity of the analysis depends on my being entirely impartial. But, humans don't work that way. We want to find truth, see justice done. Some bias is bound to creep in."

"I know. It's just…" She gave a little laugh. "When I was in law school I thought our justice system was the best in the world. It was designed to punish the guilty while protecting the innocent. I've seen plenty of instances where the result is the exact opposite."

"Yeah, sometimes it doesn't work, but I think it's the best we've been able to come up with. It's like one of those wacky Rube Goldberg machines from the nineteen thirties, a complex mechanism that requires every part to function in order to yield its less-than-spectacular result." McKinney turned his fork askew in a gesture of solidarity. "And, I'm surprisingly okay with Carla ending our relationship, and your Obsessive Compulsive thing bothers you more than it does me."

Nina looked down at the bowl of empty muscle shells on the table, then peered out from behind her hair. "Sean? Is this a date?"

McKinney thought for a minute before answering. He certainly liked Nina, but how in touch was he with his emotions? Years of pain followed by emotional numbness had left him confused. Why hadn't he been more upset when Carla ended their relationship? Wouldn't his confusion be unfair to Nina? What would be fair to Nina? She was, he decided, an adult. She had to be responsible for her own decisions. "I'd like this to be a date, but we could call it a pre-date or a date lite. Maybe this is a good time to decide whether or not to go on a date some time in the future."

Nina smiled. "Screw that nonsense. This is a date."

After they ate McKinney walked her the five blocks to her apartment. During the last block of their walk he began to wonder if kissing a woman with OCD would somehow be different. Would her kiss be more structured? Would she insist on just the right angle of head tilt? How would the tongue come into play? He almost chickened out. He wasn't sure he was ready to find out. He wasn't sure kissing on a pre-date was appropriate. When they stopped in front of her brownstone she only paused a second before pulling him into a kiss. He wasn't disappointed.

∽

McKinney wanted to dig into the Poe manuscript, but he knew working on it at home was a bad idea. Anything with the potential to be worth four hundred thousand dollars ought to be examined in a more professional environment. He had already arranged to use one of the labs out at the Walters Institute in the morning. Tonight he'd go through Madeleine's papers.

He cleared off the kitchen table, laid down a fresh sheet of white butcher's paper, and took a compound microscope from one of the kitchen cabinets. There were more analytical instruments and reagent bottles in his kitchen than food. He pulled on a pair of clean, white cotton gloves, took the documents from their box and separated them into three stacks—newspaper clippings, personal correspondence, and official-looking documents. Some of the newspaper clippings were about various Civil War battles and appeared to be from that era. The rest of the clippings were recipes for deserts and pastries. He picked out a cake recipe and noticed that it contained lard. "No, thank you," he said, and put the recipes back in the box.

The personal correspondence was more interesting. There were a number of envelopes with confederate postage stamps, most displaying the likeness of Jefferson Davis, and a few international letters postmarked from Italy and France. He selected one and carefully unfolded it. Looking at it under the microscope he was able to see the fiber makeup of the paper. It was mostly cotton, a good indication of its age since most twentieth and twenty-first century papers contain a high percentage of wood fibers.

The official documents were the most interesting. He quickly shuffled through a stack of utility bills, but mixed in with them was a bill from a milliner. Justine Duchamp had paid almost a hundred dollars in 1928 to have a hat made. There was a photograph of the hat attached to the bill. It was a hideous thing covered in feathers and beads with a dark mesh veil that could be pulled down over the eyes. An enormous peacock feather stood straight up from the back of the hat. There were letters from New Orleans merchants demanding payment for items as varied as sacks of rice to cases of champagne. There was even a deed to a small oil well in Texas along with a letter from the drilling company saying that the well had dried up and was no longer being worked.   McKinney opened a heavy manila envelope, postmarked in August of 1937, from a Parisian art gallery. Inside were several letters, one from the Museo Correr in Venice, one from Paul Rosenberg, the owner of the gallery at 21 rue La Boétie in Paris, and the other from

Rosenberg's attorney. There were sheets with English language translations attached to each letter. Also in the envelope was a photograph of a painting. McKinney looked at the photograph first. The painting was on a large square canvas and showed a ship being tossed by the waves on a stormy sea. There were people in the water near the boat. The painting was done in, what McKinney thought was, an impressionist style with vibrant colors, at least as far as they were represented by the old photograph. He turned the photo over. Written in pencil on the back was the title and the artist's name, Massacre on the Zong by Joseph Mallard William Turner.

While they were dating, Carla had attempted to give McKinney some insight into, and appreciation for, painting and sculpture. It had worked, and now it wasn't unusual for him to spend an afternoon alone at the Art Institute of Chicago, just wandering around soaking up the art. There were two Turner canvasses at the Art Institute, and he recalled seeing them. The style of the painting in the little photograph was similar.

In addition to an appreciation for art, Carla had given McKinney a series of books about art and artists. He pulled one from the enormous, overfull bookcase in the living room and leafed through until he found a chapter on Turner. The author considered Turner's work "somewhat impressionistic" even though most of it was done before Claude Monet was born. Turner was British but traveled to Venice on several occasions, producing dozens of sketches and paintings of the floating city. McKinney flipped to the index, and sure enough, under Turner's name was the entry The Slave Ship. He flipped back and read the text. The painting was Turner's representation of a real event. In 1781 the captain and crew of the slave ship Zong threw one hundred and forty-two African slaves into the sea. Some had died of disease and some were sick, but many were simply thrown overboard to drown. McKinney looked at the image on the facing page. The Slave Ship and Massacre on the Zong were two different paintings, but both had been painted by Turner, and both chronicled the same event.

According to the English translations of the letters Madeleine inherited, Massacre on the Zong was on long-term loan to the Museo Correr in Venice from Justine Marie Boisseau Duchamp. She had been the owner of the painting, a benefit that, apparently, now went to Madeleine. The painting had been brought to Paris in 1937, with the owner's permission, by Paul Rosenberg for an exhibition. That it had been on loan since the 1930s wouldn't matter; the painting was legally Madeleine's. McKinney phoned the girls with the news. In the morning he would swing by the bank on his way to the lab and put the letters and photo in his safe deposit box.

The Poe poem required a little more care. The lab McKinney had reserved at the Walters Institute was attached to a clean room, a well-lit room with HEPA-filtered ventilation, devoid of furniture with the exception of a large table in the center of the room. McKinney, dressed in a lab coat and disposable gloves and booties, covered the table with a large sheet of white butchers' paper. The room was equipped with several microscopes and a forensic light source capable of projecting light in a number of different wavelengths. On one wall of the clean room a window looked out into the rest of the lab.

He examined the manuscript and considered the best way to analyze the ink. This presented a problem. The techniques McKinney would normally use for ink analysis, such as thin layer chromatography, were destructive, meaning that a small sample of the ink would have to be removed from the paper, something he couldn't do with a valuable antique manuscript. Thinking the ink would probably be iron-gall ink, which was in common use in the 1840s, he thought a good bet for a non-destructive analytical technique was Raman spectroscopy. He knew conservators of fine art often used it to analyze inorganic pigments in paintings. If he could identify the components in the ink he'd be a step closer to determining the type of ink and, subsequently, its age.

He decided to concentrate on the paper first, and an hour later he had filled several pages of his notebook with his observations. He began by looking at it under oblique lighting. There were no unusual impressions in the paper and no under-writing. A microscopical examination showed that the paper was wove rather than laid, and that it was composed of a mixture of cotton and wood fibers. The presence of wood fibers hinted at manufacture after the late 1860s when rag shortages forced paper manufacturers to begin using wood pulp. The most significant observation, though, was that the paper fluoresced under ultraviolet light. This was an indication of the presence of optical brighteners, an additive of modern papers. However, there was no watermark, which would have helped him identify the manufacturer. The paper, he concluded, was manufactured well after the 1840s.

He thought of calling Nina to tell her but decided to wait until he had more information. He was suddenly aware of being sorry that he had decided not to call her. He liked Nina and knew, without knowing how he knew, that they would wind up in bed together. He savored the anticipation. He hadn't had much to look forward to lately.

SIXTEEN

It was several months before I saw Peter again. I hadn't found my schoolwork to be particularly difficult, and so more of my time was devoted to learning about life off the plantation. I rarely saw Cousin Pauline any more and, in truth, probably avoided her in order to keep my extracurricular activities hidden from my mother and father. Instead, I enlisted Lisette as my mentor. She taught me how to smoke without inhaling, how to drink alcohol without becoming ill, and how to make myself attractive to men without indulging their appetites. As our room at Madame Broussard's was located on the ground floor it was a simple matter for us to slip out after the evening room check. For a time our regular destination was the Chenes Verts, a restaurant out on Dumaine Street that was well known for entertaining a young and fashionable crowd. Women were not allowed at the bar, but when we were seated at table we never lacked companions. Occasionally we would indulge in a friendly wager.

Lisette was proud of her ability to persuade young gentlemen to pay for our refreshment, and I must admit she was quite an adept. Of course, her natural beauty was what drew the men to our table, but it was her skill at flirting that opened their pocketbooks. I observed her for a time and then began to mimic her art—the hooded eyes, the half smile, the pout, and especially, the over-the-shoulder glance. To this arsenal I added a technique of my own. My hair, though having more curl than Lisette's, was cut quite long and fell over my shoulders when I wore it down. I found that twisting a strand around my finger and peeking out from behind it would almost always improve the quality of our fare. A man who had started buying us sauternes often found himself paying for champagne.

"The mustachioed gent wearing the maroon tie," Lisette would say.

"I see him."

"I believe he's good for a couple of glasses of sherry."

"I'll see your sherries and raise you a full dozen oysters."

In the beginning of course, I would lose every wager. Lisette might have remained as motionless as a mannequin and still won our bets. This was hardly a disaster as the stakes were simple—finishing the other girl's mathematics lessons, for example. As I grew more sure of my abilities I won more of our little games, and to her credit, Lisette applauded my new confidence. In truth, it was my transformation from barefooted plantation lass to young sophisticate that enabled us to attend my first quadroon ball.

One evening, at the Chenes Verts, we noticed a rather boisterous crowd gathered around a table across the room from ours. Lisette recognized a number of well known members of the business community. They were surrounded by elegantly dressed women vying for the attention of someone seated at the head of the table. That person was hidden from our view by the crowd, but eventually the sea of fashionable gowns parted, and we were able to glimpse a stocky, red-haired man in a vest of bright blue silk decorated with gold braid. Even I recognized Mr. Tom Anderson, the unofficial mayor of the crib district, which was later called Storeyville, holding court. As soon as I saw him I realized that the women surrounding his table weren't the cream of New Orleans society but crib girls, those women who work in the pleasure houses offering sexual favors for money. I was so fascinated by this scene that I barely noticed the men who sent food and drink to our table. I'm afraid that I was caught staring because finally Mr. Anderson himself approached our table.

"Good evening, ladies." He gestured at our collection of uneaten pastries and, speaking directly to me, said, "You don't appear short on food, but can I offer you a bottle?" He handed some money to a passing waiter.

I confess I was too shy to speak up and fell back on one of the looks I had learned from Lisette. I don't recall which one, but I know I must have blushed as I could feel the heat in my cheeks. Mr. Anderson smiled at my shyness and handed me a printed handbill.

"I'm promoting a little entertainment next week. I hope you'll grace us with your presence." He winked at me and walked back to his table.

"Now that," Lisette said, "is a vest. Somewhere there is a window drapery missing several feet of fabric."

The handbill was an advertisement for a grand soirée two days hence, a quadroon ball presented by The Two Well-Known Gentlemen, though of course they were not well known to us. The handbill didn't refer to the dance as a quadroon ball, and even if it had I wouldn't have understood what that meant, but Lisette enlightened me.

"I will gladly attend this ball with you, but I did notice that Mister Anderson handed the invitation to you."

"I noticed, too. Why do you suppose he did that?"

She looked at the invitation. "This is a quadroon ball, and you are that most desirable of guests, a creole with light skin. Why, you could pass the paper bag test with no trouble at all."

"What is the paper bag test?"

"I'm not surprised you haven't heard of it, being a plantation girl, but it's very common here. If your skin is lighter than a brown paper bag, you are thought to have more white than colored in your family, and are, therefore, socially acceptable."

I must have had a strange look on my face because Lisette put her hand over mine. "Justine, are you all right?"

I nodded. "I'm sorry. I've never heard of this test before."

"Well, we don't have to go to the ball. Do you still want to?"

"Indeed, I do."

The two days preceding the ball passed slowly. We were in the middle of the term, our coursework had ceased to be interesting, and our classrooms were hot. Though piano was usually my favorite class, the studio that contained the school's two aging spinets was on the top floor, and I often felt I would pass out from the heat. Meanwhile, Lisette and I managed to concoct an unbearable anticipation. Over and over we told each other, "This is a most wonderfully clever idea." We had decided to keep the ball a secret from the other girls, a number of whom were not to be trusted. If Madame Broussard was to discover our deception there would be hell to pay.

On the afternoon of the big day, we were just leaving the classroom after solfeggio, Mlle. Dunnewold having released us early because of the heat, and I commented to Lisette, "I certainly hope the temperature is a bit cooler this evening or I shall simply melt."

"Hush up! Miss Big Ears is right behind you."

"Well," I said, in a voice loud enough for her to hear, "Miss Big Ears can sit on a tack for all I care."

"Miss Big Ears" was a girl whose father had been a cotton king. He no longer owned a plantation, but his daughter acted like she was the queen of our school. She tried to get in with the teachers by tattling on her classmates, but that just made her unpopular with students and teachers alike. At the time, I detested her, though looking back I realize she was just a sad and lonely girl.

Evening finally came, and who should be making the bed check rounds but Miss Big Ears, herself. No doubt one of the teachers had assigned it to her after hours of being fawned over. We were prepared, though, and she found us in our beds with our eyes closed and our lamp extinguished. She even went so far as to come into our room to be certain we hadn't substituted pillows for our sleeping selves. After she left we barred the door with a chair, dressed, and left by the window.

The ball was being held at the Odd Fellows Hall, near Lafayette Park, and by the time we arrived we were almost overcome by excitement.

"Oh, Lisette. This is going to be the best evening. I don't even care if we're found out. I'm so happy."

"Agreed, chere. This may be our most wonderfully clever idea, ever."

In one corner of the hall were four or five negro musicians playing jazz music, and a number of people were dancing to it. I was kind of hoping there would be a cakewalk, but when I looked around it was obvious that none of the women had brought a cake. In fact, although the men all appeared to be society types, the women were a rougher-looking lot. I was certain that many of them were crib girls, and most were women of mixed blood, quadroons. As I learned later, this was an event for the well-to-do men of New Orleans to find mistresses. A good number of these men were married, but that didn't seem to matter, and they were willing to spend large sums of money to find and keep their consorts. Of course, I had no idea that this was the purpose of the event; I was intoxicated by the elegant gowns, handsome men, and glittering chandeliers. The flowing champagne helped to blur my vision as well, and in this state I accidentally splashed a few drops from my glass onto Lisette's dress. I dabbed it with my hand kerchief as I apologized.

"Oh! I am so sorry, Lisette."

"Leave it," she said, pushing my hand away. She pointed to a group of men across the room. "Isn't that your young vegetable merchant?"

Peter stood talking with a number of men who were of similar appearance. All of them had dark hair, shiny with some sort of pomade, and they all wore oddly colored frock coats, maroon or dark green. Many of the men sported mustaches. Their conversation was obviously serious, with much violent gesturing. Peter appeared to be arguing with the other men. Sensing my shyness, Lisette pushed me in his direction.

"As much as I detest these foreigners, I know you won't be happy until you've spoken with him," she said. "Now, go on over there. And remember what I've taught you."

Her push unbalanced me, and I pitched forward, almost falling. My glass went flying and shattered on the hardwood floor. To make matters worse, the sound of the breaking glass coincided with the silence at the end of whatever song was being played. I swear, every eye in the Odd Fellows Hall was on me as I stumbled across the floor. I was mortified, but my humiliation had the desired effect. Peter saw me and left his companions immediately.

"Miss Justine," he said, taking my hand, "you must teach me this new dance step. No doubt it's from one of the northern cities. So graceful."

I was flattered that he remembered my name, but I wasn't about to let him get away with his teasing. "Why, if it isn't the gentleman from the opera. Forgive me for not remembering your name, but I've met so many people since then. I hope I'm not taking you away from some important deliberation."

"Not at all. I was just explaining to my friends the little-known fact that the most beautiful women in New Orleans are those whose names begin with the letter 'J'. Whether this is coincidence or not, I do not know."

Without my realizing it he had steered me onto the dance floor, and we were now whirling around the room with the other couples, my shattered glass, forgotten.

"Tell me, Peter. Are you a vegetable merchant?"

"Ah, cara mia. You remember my name after all. No, I help run a small game at Mr. Anderson's place, the Astoria Club."

"So, you're a gambler."

"Only where you are concerned. I deal faro for Mr. Anderson and, as the tailleur, I never take a risk." He turned us toward the door, and we stepped out onto the cast iron balcony. "But I will risk my heart for you, bella donna."

Peter was always spouting such nonsense, but I was young and impressionable and completely taken in. It was dark on the balcony as there was no moon that night, and the gas street lamp was on the other side of the building. We strolled past a number of other couples to a deserted corner, and Peter turned toward me and put his hand under my chin. "You've something on your cheek, cara mia. Look up."

I did as he asked, and he leaned down and kissed me. It was my first kiss, and I shall always remember it as the sweetest and the gentlest kiss I've ever known.

SEVENTEEN

Standing at the back of the Baton Rouge chapel in a black suit and tie, Wayne held his chauffeur's cap with both hands. "I'm really sorry about Mrs. Duchamp," he said.

Duchamp looked up from the spot on the carpet he'd been staring at. "Thank you, Wayne." He patted the big man's shoulder. It would serve no purpose to tell him exactly how Barbara had died. "I appreciate your concern in this time of mourning." He nodded toward the front of the room where his wife's relatives were gathered around her casket. "You'd think they were the only ones who'd suffered a loss." He shook his head. "I've got things to do. Come on, let's get out of here." He walked up to the casket, feeling the glares of his in-laws, and leaned in to kiss his wife on the forehead. He decided the mortician had done a remarkable job, considering. "Sleep well," he said, adding a little sob for effect. Then he turned on his heel and walked out to the Lincoln with Wayne in tow.

Out on the 10, heading toward New Orleans, Duchamp reached up and tapped his chauffeur on the shoulder. "Did you get that sliding panel fixed like I asked you?"

"It's all taken care of. I've got a good mechanic. The guy's a Buddhist. Thinks if he cheats a customer he'll wind up as a cockaroach in his next life."

"Good. Put the panel up. I'm calling Reverend Bob, and I'd like a little privacy."

The glass panel slid into place. As it did Duchamp heard Wayne swear, "Bob's an asshole. I don't see why you need to..."

It would take months to see any money from his wife's estate. He had an appointment with Samson Edwards in a few days, and he needed to be able to show him some good faith money. Until ownership of the house and boat were transferred to his name there was nothing he could use as collateral for a loan. Plus, he was certain his wife's family would contest the will. He was, temporarily, back at square one. His niece's forty million dollar painting was looking mighty good again.

Wayne's search of the girl's dorm room at Tulane had been a bust. Whatever paperwork there was giving Madeleine ownership of the painting hadn't been there. That likely meant it had been taken by the roommate's father, the scientist. What Wayne *had* done right was find the roommate's name and home address when he was searching her belongings. Subsequently, verifying her father's name and address had been easy. Someone needed to pay Mr. McKinney a visit.

Duchamp took out a cell phone he had purchased from a meth addict in back of the projects over on Tremé Street. It was, no doubt, stolen so couldn't be traced back to him. After using it he'd wipe it down and throw it in the trash. He dialed the number of an acquaintance in Illinois, one of his cellmates from the short stint he'd done up at Angola, the same place he had met Wayne. There had been four of them together in that stinking hole; Duchamp, Wayne, an embezzler named Joe Pasternak who everyone called The Mozo, and Bob Brysk. Reverend Bob, they had called him, and that name almost kept them from meeting. The guards had a hard time believing "Reverend" Bob would convert to Islam.

The four men were housed in different sections of the prison, Wayne and Reverend Bob in one camp and Duchamp and Pasternak, the two non-violent offenders, in another camp. But they had all heard about Eid al-Fitr, the feast at the end of Ramadan. Muslim inmates who chose to observe the month-long fast of Ramadan were allowed to take part in the enormous feast that closed out the holiday. During the fasting period, inmates skipped lunch but ate breakfast early and dinner late. They also were given time off from their work details for prayer and spiritual reflection, but the feast was the big attraction as the main course consisted of lots of meat, presumably from animals sacrificed specifically for the holiday. In order to participate in Eid al-Fitr the four men announced their conversion to Islam shortly before the beginning of Ramadan. The prison officials weren't fooled, but couldn't deny them their religious prerogative. They met at a long feast table, stuffing themselves, and only pausing to exchange a few words between courses.

Wayne might have been the most physically intimidating member of their little pack, but it was Reverend Bob who settled all their arguments with the other inmates. He wasn't afraid of The Dixie Mafia or any of the other prison gangs. In retrospect, Duchamp thought it likely that Reverend Bob had created as many problems for them as he had solved. Duchamp only spent six months in the state penitentiary. By the time Wayne got out Duchamp had married and was clawing his way up the social ladder of New Orleans society. As the other members of his prison coterie were released they contacted Duchamp. Fortunately, Wayne was the only one who elected to stay in Louisiana. Taking Wayne on as a bodyguard had been a risk, but it seemed to be paying off. Now, he needed help from Reverend Bob.

After his release from prison Reverend Bob founded a storefront church in southern Illinois. Duchamp had visited once while on a business trip. The Reverend had a shooting range in the basement of the church, and Duchamp had watched him empty the standard seventeen round clip of a Ruger SR9 in eight seconds—standing, then kneeling, then prone—looking, appropriately, like the praying mantis he resembled. There had been two perfect groupings on the target, one in the head and one in the heart.

The judge who sentenced him may have hoped Reverend Bob would learn something in prison, but during his time at Angola the only thing he learned was how to hate. It was a lesson he learned well. His only comfort in prison had been his Bible, in particular the Old Testament and the stories of the prophets. Elijah was his favorite, and he read and reread the chapters in which Elijah asked God to rain fire down from the heavens onto his enemies.

He was sent up for a convenience store robbery gone horribly wrong. He had been overconfident and had gotten close enough for the clerk to grab his gun hand. The gun had gone off and the bullet had struck a seven-year-old girl, killing her instantly. He was initially charged with felony murder, which could have gotten him strapped down to the lethal injection table, but since they never found the gun the charge was reduced to manslaughter and robbery. He served fifteen out of a thirty-year sentence. The other guests of the state, rapists, thieves and murderers, either shunned him or abused him. In the pecking order of prison life a child killer was only incrementally better than a child molester. Duchamp could barely stomach him and was relieved when Reverend Bob moved North on his release.

Duchamp settled back into the padded leather upholstery, which was always just a little too sticky for the Louisiana climate, and listened for a familiar voice on the other end of the line. When it came he said, "Reverend Bob, I've got a rush job for you up in Chicago."

EIGHTEEN

Hendrix jumped up on the couch and put his head on McKinney's leg, looking up at him with a look of solicitation. McKinney fished a piece of cheese out of the sandwich he was eating and gave it to the dog. He had been on hold for twenty minutes and sat with his shoulder holding the phone to his ear while he ate lunch and leafed through a monograph titled "Molecular Vibration in IR and Raman Spectroscopy." Mac Walters had given him the number of one of the conservation specialists at Northwestern University, a woman with a lilting French accent named Chantal. McKinney had been in the process of convincing her to loan him a portable Raman spectrometer to analyze the ink on "The City in the Sea" when she put him on hold to take another call. He didn't really have to analyze the ink at this point. He knew from his analysis of the paper that the document wasn't written prior to 1845, but he wanted to give his client a complete report. Besides, he was curious to see what kind of ink the forger had used. Examining it under the microscope he had thought it just looked like India ink, carbon suspended in a binder. The manuscript, back in its protective case, sat in front of McKinney on the coffee table. He scratched the dog behind the ear. "I hope she hasn't forgotten us." Hendrix closed his eyes and pressed his head into McKinney's hand.

There was a knock on the front door, and Hendrix barked. McKinney put down the journal and the sandwich and gestured for the dog to stay. *Must be Mrs. Vladic*, he thought. *The downstairs' door didn't buzz and everyone else should be at work.* He shifted the phone to his left ear, opened the door, and was surprised to see a tall thin man in a dark suit. The man had on a clerical collar.

"Mr. McKinney?"

"That's me. How can I..."

A gun appeared in the man's hand. He drew it so swiftly and with such economy of motion that McKinney barely registered the movement.

"Back up," the man said.

McKinney took a step back and raised his hands.

"Put your hands down. Who told you to raise your hands? I didn't tell you to raise your hands." The man spoke quickly, nervously. He motioned to the couch. "Sit."

McKinney walked around to the couch and sat next to Hendrix. The dog looked at the tall man and growled. "Listen," McKinney started, "I..."

"You and me don't have anything to talk about. Keep that dog quiet and pay attention. You have something I want. Tell me where it is, and we don't have any trouble."

McKinney inadvertently glanced at the case holding the Poe manuscript on the coffee table.

"In there, huh? Okay, thanks." The man picked up the case with his free hand. He kept his gun pointed at McKinney. "Phones?"

"McKinney handed him the cell phone. The man noticed it was on and held it to his ear. "Mr. McKinney will have to call you back," he said and slipped the phone into his jacket pocket. "Land line?"

McKinney pointed to the kitchen. The man went to the kitchen where a wireless phone and base station sat on the counter. He tore the cord out of the wall and put the phone in his pocket with McKinney's cell phone. The door to the back porch was in the kitchen, and the man noticed it. He opened the door and looked out and down the three flights to the back yard. McKinney got up off the couch and followed him into the kitchen.

"Come on, don't take the box. I've got a couple hundred dollars cash here, and you're absolutely welcome to it. That box isn't mine, but it's my responsibility. Please? Take the cash instead, and I'll forget I ever saw you."

"That's right," the man said, thinking about it, "you saw me." He set the box down by his feet and fingered the white collar at his throat. He pulled the collar off and stuffed it in his pocket. Then he raised the gun, aiming at McKinney's head.

McKinney took a quick diagonal step out of the path of the gun but toward the man, hoping to close the distance between them. The gun followed him, and then quickly swung back. McKinney heard a growl and caught a flash of black out of the corner of his eye as Hendrix darted past him, and suddenly the kitchen was filled with noise. Hendrix dropped at the thin man's feet. The man was aiming at the dog, preparing to fire again, when McKinney leaped forward, pressing the man's gun hand toward the floor with one hand while palming him in the jaw with the other. The man staggered back, out of the open door and onto the porch. The gun went off, but the bullet missed, tearing into the wood floor inches from the dog's head. The man grunted and steadied himself with a hand on the porch railing. He was bringing the gun back to aim when McKinney rushed him, landing a front kick to his chest and sending him over the railing. McKinney looked down into the yard. The man was stretched out next to a picnic table, his head resting on the concrete patio, his legs across a bench.

McKinney ran back inside to the big poodle. Hendrix's eyes were shut and there was a small pool of blood under his stomach, but McKinney could see the rise and fall of his chest. The dog was still alive. He rolled Hendrix further onto his side to find the wound. There was a hole in his abdomen and another in his back. The bullet had passed clear through. McKinney grabbed two hand towels and a bandage roll from the hall closet and bound the wounds as tightly as he could. He cradled the dog in his arms, picked him up and went out the back door, kicking the manuscript box back into the apartment as he ran. He glanced at the man's body as he hurried down the steps. It hadn't moved.

Later, all he would be able to remember about the drive to the veterinary hospital was that his vision was blurred by his tears and that he was begging the dog not to die. "I love you," he said, over and over.

NINETEEN

In the months that followed the festivities at the Odd Fellows Hall, I was the happiest I had ever been. Peter and I were inseparable. His work at the Astoria Club suffered as a result, and so did his standing with Mr. Tom Anderson. I neglected my schoolwork, relying on Lisette to let me copy hers. She still didn't approve of Peter, but at least she didn't refer to him as a dago, an insult I heard often as we strolled the streets of the quarter. To his credit, Peter never responded with violence. In fact, the only time I saw him respond at all was when a young tough had the nerve to spit at us, his sputum landing on the sleeve of my coat. Peter grabbed the youngster by the scruff of his neck and dragged him into a doorway. He whispered something to the lad, who blanched and, wrenching himself free, ran off down the street.

When I think of those happy times, the day that most often comes to mind is our last day together. It was a crisp Sunday in March, and I had managed to separate myself from the group of girls returning from chapel after services. Lisette covered for me, as usual. I met Peter in Congo Square, and we walked a bit, my hand in his. There was a vendor selling cala cakes, and knowing my fondness for them, Peter bought one, and we shared it as we ambled along. To this day the taste of sweet fried rice transports me back there. We ended our walk at Peter's room.

The room was cold, and in order to take the chill off, Peter went down the hall to borrow some coal for his brazier. I had been there before, but this time found myself fascinated by all the accoutrements of young masculinity. His dresser was a massive oak, much too big for the room, and on it sat a mirror and a set of matched, tortoise shell hair brushes. I picked up one of the brushes and imagined Peter running it through his thick black hair. A tray held some coins and matches, and there was an assortment of ties and collars laid out like weapons in his haberdashery arsenal. After he returned, and the small fire had warmed the room a bit, we undressed and crawled into the small iron bed. The sheets were heavy and stiff with starch, and at first, I shivered, as much from shyness as from the cold, but neither shyness nor cold lasted. Peter was so much taller than I that, as he moved on top of me, I feared being crushed beneath his weight, but he was surprisingly light. Holding himself above me with his arms against the thin mattress, and looking into my eyes, he whispered something gentle in his singsong language. Of course, I didn't know the words, but I understood their meaning.

⁂

The Saturday after our liaison all New Orleans went insane. A month earlier, the chief of police, a man named Hennessey, had been murdered, and with his dying breath he accused the Italians who controlled the dockworkers. In truth, there had been a small war brewing between two groups of Italian immigrants for control of the docks. Chief Hennessey seemed to favor one group over the other. Several Italians were arrested and tried for the murder, but the jury failed to convict any of them. As a result, thousands of New Orleanians took up arms, stormed the jail, and murdered the acquitted men. But that wasn't enough for the mob. It moved from the jail through the city like a wild beast, ferreting out Italians and beating or lynching them. And one of the accused men had the same name as my Peter.

I was upstairs in the piano room, practicing my lessons, when I heard about the riot. I'll never forget the look of horror on Lisette's face when she burst into the room to tell me.

"They are killing the Italians," she shouted.

My hands froze, suspended above the keys. "Who?"

"The city. My God, the city has gone mad."

She went to the window and opened the storm shutters, and then I heard it—the sound of the mob, not as individual voices, but as one angry scream. I raced down the stairs and into the streets, where I fought my way through the crowds to the Astoria Club, hoping that Peter was dealing faro that day. The place was deserted, the front door boarded up, and I dove back into that sea of killers, mostly men but some women, too, all carrying clubs and guns and ropes already tied into nooses. Peter's apartment was empty. The door had been taken from the hinges and the room ransacked. The mattress had been pulled onto the floor and Peter's clothing, torn from his closet, heaped on the mattress. One hairbrush remained on his dresser, and I took it with, clutching it to my bosom as I wandered the streets, not knowing where to search but hoping that chance would help me find him. On the crowded sidewalks I was bumped and jostled, and when the crowds thinned out I was confronted by angry, glaring faces—men who bent low to search my features for a trace of Italian blood.

It was well after midnight when I finally found my poor Peter. They had beaten him and stabbed him and hung him from a lamppost. His coat and vest were gone. One foot was bare. His handsome face was frozen in a rictus of fear, but his beautiful hair was hardly mussed. I sat on the ground under the lamp, too numb to cry, until morning when Madame Broussard and one of the teachers found me and brought me back to the school.

TWENTY

Duchamp drove over to the 10 and up to Metairie. He didn't usually drop in on Didi in the middle of the day, but this was an emergency. He was frustrated. Not sexually, but in a way he couldn't explain and that he was sure only Didi could make right. That was, he realized, the motivation behind most of the things he did. He lived with a persistent feeling that he was being cheated out of something that he deserved and a need to make it right.

A little boy in a pair of blue jean overalls answered the door. His arms were as thin as sticks and his skin was the color of cocoa. He grinned when he saw Duchamp.

"Hi, Uncle Ray. Whadja bring me?"

Duchamp lifted the boy up and spun him around. "Tyler, my friend, I have just the thing for a fine fellow like you." He reached into his jacket's side pocket and pulled out a small model glider. "If you put the wings on this thing the right way it'll do loop de loops." He put the boy down. "Where's your mother?"

"She's with a customer." He pointed. Flute music and the scent of patchouli drifted out from behind the closed kitchen door. Tyler held out the unassembled glider. "Show me!"

Twenty minutes later Didi emerged from the kitchen and led a heavy-set woman to the front door. As the woman left she handed Didi several bills, which disappeared into the pocket of her white floor-length caftan. Didi closed the door behind the woman and turned to Duchamp. "Raymond. What a nice surprise. What brings you out our way before dark?"

The little boy waved the glider over his head. "Watch this, Mom!" He threw the glider toward a bookshelf. Before hitting the shelf it looped up, over, and landed on the carpet. A big white cat lying nearby opened its eyes just long enough to sniff disdainfully.

"That's great, sweetie."

Duchamp whistled. "I take it Madame Morreau is back in business. You look gorgeous in that getup, and you know I love it when you wear your hair down."

Didi walked slowly toward the couch to give Duchamp the full effect, but he hopped up and met her half way, taking her in his arms and kissing her. She pushed him back and smiled. "Slow down, Raymond. You know bedtime around here isn't until seven o'clock."

Tyler picked up the glider. "I know you're talking about me!" he said.

Duchamp hung his sport coat on the back of a chair and, taking Didi by the elbow, led her out to the kitchen. He sniffed the air, noticing that the incense sticks were sitting upright in a Spider-man drinking glass. A deck of tarot cards was spread across the table. "So this is where the magic happens. Didi, I'm really upset about this Dauphin Pharma deal." He scooped up the tarot cards and began shuffling them. "Mind you, I'm not saying I believe in all this hoodoo, but can you give me any idea what my next move should be?"

Didi opened the refrigerator and took out two bottles of Abita Stout. Twenty minutes later Tyler came skipping into the kitchen carrying Duchamp's .38 caliber Chief's Special revolver.

"Look what I found in your jacket, Uncle Ray. Is it real?"

Didi blanched. "Tyler! Put that down!"

Duchamp held out his hand. "Give me that. What are you doing going through my pockets? Didn't your mother teach you right from wrong?"

"Well, hell," she said. "Don't yell at him, Raymond. You're really not the person to explain the difference between right and wrong."

Duchamp grabbed the little gun and stuck it in his trouser pocket. "I know the difference, and when I do wrong it's not a mistake. It's a choice."

TWENTY-ONE

"You have to go back to school. Don't you have finals next week?" McKinney put his hand on his daughter's shoulder. He had picked her up at the airport that morning and now they were sitting in the waiting room of the Wrigleyville Veterinary Clinic.

"The week after next, but it wouldn't make any difference if they were next week. I'm not going back until I know Hendrix is going to be okay." She plucked a tissue from the little box on the end table and dabbed at her eyes. "Don't take this the wrong way, but I really miss Mom right now."

"I miss her, too. She was always good in a crisis."

"And she really loved Hendrix. She would want to be here with us."

"Yes, she would. She was crazy about that dog." McKinney struggled for a way to comfort his daughter, to help her prepare for the possibility that Hendrix might not make it. "She was crazy about you, too. You know, your mother's the one who insisted we name you Angelina."

"After her Italian grandmother, right?"

"That was the official story for the relatives. The real reason was very different."

"Different how?"

"When we found out your mother was pregnant we started compiling a list of names. We put it up on the refrigerator with a magnet. There were names for both boys and girls. Your mother wanted to be surprised, so she always asked the ultrasound operator not to divulge your sex."

"I was a girl, right?"

"Ha! Yes, you were a girl. Anyway, we had this big list,

and it kept changing. We'd add new names that we liked and remove the ones we agreed wouldn't work."

"Like what, for example."

McKinney thought for a moment. "Like Kelly."

"What's wrong with Kelly?"

"Nothing, per se, but we went to a party once, and the people who gave the party had a big, green parrot named Kelly that could talk but only knew swear words. On the way home from the party your mother proclaimed, 'I am not naming our child after some foulmouthed bird.'"

"So the list got pared down to what, Angelina and some boy's name?"

"As I recall, the winning names were Carl for a boy and Lilliana for a girl."

"Lilliana? That sucks."

"Well, you were almost Lilliana McKinney, but your mother wouldn't give them a name until she'd had a good look at you. They let her hold you right after you were born. She studied your face for a long time, then said, 'She is no Lilliana. This is the face of someone who was born to help people.' She made me get right down next to her and look at you. She said, 'See. This is the face of a compassionate person.'"

"Did you think that, too?"

"You mother thought she could read personality in someone's face. I'm a scientist. I read people's personalities through their actions. Anyway, I asked her what she wanted to name you if you weren't a Lilliana. She said, 'This is Angelina, my little angel.' I said, 'That's not a name; that's a job description.' But she insisted. You had to be Angelina."

"Stop, you'll make me start crying again."

"Do you remember Darcy Kohler from your sixth grade class and that boy in junior high school, the paraplegic, what's-his-name?"

"Ryan?"

"Yeah, Ryan. Both of those kid's were being picked on by the other kids at school. You stuck up for them. In fact, you were the only one who did. I remember your mother and I had to go to your high school several times because you kept getting into fights with the boys who were bullying that Ryan kid. The principle was ranting about how you were unladylike and a troublemaker. He threatened to suspend you if you didn't apologize to whichever kid it was you gave the black eye. Your mother was very cool. She just looked at him and said, 'Angelina did the right thing. She's not apologizing for doing the right thing.' Then she got up and walked out of his office."

"I don't get what this has to do with wishing Mom was here."

"You're majoring in social work at Tulane. You're going to make a career out of helping people. Your mother knew you the minute you were born because that's the kind of person she was, too, someone who cared and was willing to stand up for her beliefs. If there's such a thing as a gene that codes for compassion, you inherited it from your mother. I know it sounds corny, but part of her will always be with you."

She blew her nose. "Dammit, Dad."

"I'm sorry, but you need to hear these things. We may be in for a rough patch. Money's tight, and I don't know if they're going to charge me for killing the guy who shot Hendrix."

"But that was self-defense!"

"Yes, but even if I'm not charged there could be a civil suit from the guy's family. The lawyer's fees alone would put us in a spot. And, we probably won't know for a couple of days whether or not Hendrix will pull through. I just want you to remember how much you're loved—by me and your mom."

"Thanks." She stuffed her tissue in her pocket. "We've been sitting out here for a long time. Let's go back to the Critical Care Section and see how Hendrix is doing."

McKinney drained his coffee and tossed out the empty cup. He took his daughter by the hand, and they walked down the hallway and through the big green doors.

TWENTY-TWO

I passed the next two months in a fog. My studies suffered, and I became withdrawn. Lisette was the only one I had any real communication with. Madame Broussard told my parents about my absence during the riots, of course, and how she had found me sitting under the lamppost, but without knowing the full story they were all at a loss to explain my behavior at the time or my subsequent malaise.

One morning, while dressing for class, I experienced a horrible nausea. Initially I attributed this to sickness or an underdone piece of fish, but as the nausea was recurring, and in a few days led to vomiting, I began to worry. One morning, after losing my breakfast, Lisette came back from the dining hall before I could empty the commode.

"You know what this is, don't you?"

"I simply have a springtime ailment, I'm sure, Lisette. There's no reason to be concerned."

She shook her head. "You really don't know, do you? My cousin experienced the same thing. Justine, you are with child."

At first I didn't believe it. Being pregnant seemed such a remote possibility. After a few more days of sickness, however, I had to admit to Lisette that she was probably right.

"What am I going to do? Sooner or later people will notice. I'll be asked to leave the school. My parents will be shamed."

"I have an idea," she said. "It's not a wondrously clever idea. In fact, it is rather an idea of last resort, but it's evident that you cannot have this child."

"I don't know. Except for his hair brush, it's all I have

of Peter."

"I don't deny it, and as your first love, he will always be the most special, but there will be others. What man, though, will want a woman with a bastard child? Don't throw away your chance for happiness."

"But how can I not? Even if I knew of an abortionist, I wouldn't go to her. They are dangerous. Many girls have died from their treatments."

"We will see Madame Laveau."

"The voodooist?"

"Yes. Perhaps she can give you a regulating medicine."

❦

Contrary to the tales you may have heard, Marie Laveau did not live in the swamp. She lived close to Congo Square on Rue St. Ann. Lisette tried to act like seeing the queen of the voodoo was the most natural thing, but I could tell she was nervous. I was frightened near out of my wits.

From the outside, Madame Laveau's house appeared no different than any of its neighbors, but as soon as we crossed the threshold we were in a different world. I have to say that the overriding impression was that she liked skulls. There were skulls everywhere. Human skulls sat on tables and bookshelves. Animal skulls hung from the walls. I recognized many of the smaller skulls—cats, for instance, but there were other skulls, too, from creatures I couldn't identify. Lisette guessed that the skulls with tusks came from the wild pigs that live in the swamp. And the house was filled with cats. There were plenty of black cats on hand, but there were also Tabbies and Siamese and some cats that defied classification. And the smell, my god! There were sensors emitting plumes of sweet incense on every table, but they couldn't mask the stink of those cats.

We were shown into a curtained parlor by a boy with a turban on his head. Seated on a horsehair sofa was one of the most beautiful black women I had ever seen. When I say black, what I mean is that her soft, evenly-toned skin was the color of sugar as it's caramelizing in the pan, right before it burns. My beautiful mother's skin was that same color. I, on the other hand, favor my father, who is descended from the French. Madame Laveau wore her hair up and wrapped in a scarf. Her long, white linen dress covered her legs, but I could see that she was barefoot. She appeared to be about forty years of age, but rumor said she was at least twice that. She smoked a pipe as we talked, that added its scent to the heavy air, and several times that afternoon I felt I was choking.

We were not invited to sit and stood in front of her as she looked from Lisette to me and back. Finally, she pointed at me and said, "You are the sick one. Sick in the body. Sick in the heart. Tell me."

I told her everything. I told her about Peter and about the mob and about the baby growing inside me. I wept as I spoke, but she just sat and listened, smoking her pipe and staring with her big, dark eyes.

"I will give you a potion," she said. "But it is a potion that works through you. It reads your heart. If you are not strong enough to care for this baby, if you do not want this baby..." She slapped her hand on her thigh. "No baby. But if your heart says otherwise..." She raised her hand with the palm to the ceiling. "Only the Loa can tell."

I took Madame Laveau's potion every day without fail. After a week or so the morning sickness stopped, but I continued to get bigger, and as the months went on, I let out the waist in all of my clothing. Finally I took to wearing an unbelted blouse over my skirt. Even this peasant clothing couldn't hide my girth. I skipped classes by feigning illness and avoided contact with everyone but Lisette. She would often bring food to our room, allowing me to avoid the dining room.

After my first month at school I had made it a point to avoid my cousin, Paulette, in order to keep my late night excursions a secret. Nevertheless, we had remained friendly and had seen one another going to and from classes. Paulette noticed my absence and came to check on me one Saturday evening after meals. She arrived at the door to our room just as Lisette was bringing my dinner and entered before I could jump into bed.

"Petite amie," she said. "What has happened to you?"

I looked at myself in the mirror for the first time in weeks. My hair was unwashed and hung down, limp and unbrushed. I wore my oversized blouse, and it too was unwashed. Even with the blouse one could see that I was pregnant. I panicked then, for I knew my cousin. I grabbed her hand and held her there. "Please Paulette, if you love me, don't tell father. I couldn't bear it."

She looked me up and down and shook her head. "You are in trouble, and you are my family. It is my duty to help you." She patted my hand and left the room. The next morning Madame Broussard paid me a visit, and on Wednesday my father arrived, having been fetched in a wagon by Lemuel, the school's handyman.

Father didn't scold me, but I could see that he was heartbroken. He refused to look at me and only spoke enough to tell me to pack my things, for Madame Broussard had decided to expel me, and we would be returning to the plantation that night. I'm certain the ride home was as painful for my father as it was for me. We made the trip in silence.

TWENTY-THREE

It was a busy day for Raymond Duchamp. He had phone calls to make and appointments to keep. An investigator from his insurance company was dropping in at mid-morning to interview him about his wife's death, and in the afternoon he was driving to Samson Edwards' private club in Algiers. He was more concerned about that meeting than the morning interview. He started the day with a phone call to Joe Pasternak, the embezzler turned investment counselor he'd called The Mozo during his short stint up at Angola. Pasternak had come to him for a loan after graduating from the Louisiana State Prison system, and Duchamp had obliged him. At the time he reasoned that he might make use of a businessman who owed him a favor, especially one who had a penchant for larceny. It was about time to call in his marker. He phoned Pasternak's office in New York's SoHo district and left a message with the receptionist. "When Joe comes in, tell him a friend called about some gris-gris."

The insurance investigator didn't show up until after eleven, and Duchamp realized he would have to get rid of him by noon to make it to his appointment with Edwards. He spoke quickly and dropped several hints about having another meeting, but the man, a rather plump fellow named Runyon, was in no hurry to leave.

"I don't imagine we'll have any real trouble with this policy, Mr. Duchamp, but it may take a little time. We have to make sure all our Ts are crossed and all our Is are dotted whenever someone dies under suspicious circumstances."

"Suspicious circumstances?"

"Yes, if they haven't been ill or under a doctor's care."

"Ah."

"I wouldn't worry too much. We'll get the old ball rolling. Now, how about another cup of coffee?"

Runyon sat in Duchamp's leather club chair for almost an hour, sipping his coffee, asking the same questions the police had asked, and looking around like he'd never seen the inside of a house before. Duchamp finally had to take the coffee cup from his hand and explain that he would be late for his other appointment if he didn't leave right away.

"Thanks for understanding," he said, pushing Runyon out the front door.

⤺

Edwards had reserved a private room for their meeting. It held two comfortable chairs, a well-stocked bar, and a five-foot tall humidor. He mixed a pitcher of whiskey sours, his specialty, and gestured to the humidor. "Help yourself. I believe there's a box of Cohibas in there somewhere."

Duchamp picked out a cigar and settled into a chair. He was about to bite off the end when he noticed the little cigar cutter on the table next to him. He picked it up, remembering he had read somewhere that only novices bite the ends off. Edwards handed him a drink, sat down, and began fiddling with his own cigar. It was obvious he was going to make his guest initiate the conversation. Duchamp tried to sound calm, but as soon as he opened his mouth he knew it wasn't working.

"Well sir, the deadline for inclusion in the Dauphin Pharmaceuticals project is coming up pretty soon, is it not?"

"Relax, Mr. Duchamp. Try your drink. I'm proud of this particular concoction. I was given the recipe by that TV chef, you know. The one who has the restaurant here. Anyway, I'll let you in on the secret. A really good whiskey sour uses only wood-aged Canadian whisky, and confectioner's sugar instead of syrup. Oh, and no egg. The whisky is smooth, so the egg isn't needed."

Duchamp tried his drink. "Very tasty. Delightful. Thank you for the recipe."

"Don't mention it. Now, yes; the deadline is next Friday. Can we count you as a member of our little association?"

"Absolutely. You absolutely can. I'm very excited about this project. I asked for this meeting, however, to inform you that I will need a little more time to raise the initial investment monies. Not long. A month at most."

Edwards finished lighting his cigar, leaned back, and ejected a plume of smoke toward the vaulted ceiling. "See, that's a problem without a solution. We currently have a surplus of investors, most of whom have already deposited their funds. I may turn one or two away as it is. Letting you ignore the deadline wouldn't be fair to them. Besides, if you're having trouble with your finances…"

"It's not that. My finances are fine. It's just that things are kind of up in the air right now, what with the estate and… Well, I didn't want to mention this because I don't want to sound like I'm…" He looked down at the carpet between his feet. "Mr. Edwards, my wife just died. She was killed in a tragic boating accident."

"I'm sorry, Duchamp. I didn't know."

"I was there, Mr. Edwards. She drowned. There was nothing I could do but…" He set his cigar in the ashtray and covered his eyes with his hands. When he looked up he said, "My finances are fine, really. It's just that the estate is a mess, but I'm taking a proactive, results-oriented approach to this thing."

They sat there in silence for a minute. Edwards took a mouthful of his drink and held it for a moment before swallowing. He sighed. "I have, for many years, lived by a very strict set of rules, Duchamp, and they have served me well. I am about to break one of those rules, and I hope I won't regret it. Because I consider myself to be a gentleman, and because you're in the midst of an emotionally challenging situation, I will loan you two hundred thousand dollars. I will then accept the two hundred thousand as a down payment on your initial investment. The entire five hundred thousand will be due two months from today, plus something small. Oh, let's say four percent on the two hundred thousand—five hundred and eight thousand total."

Duchamp gritted his teeth. The mercenary bastard. He forced a smile and took his hands away from his face. "Eminently fair. You are too kind. I thank you, Mr. Edwards, and I assure you that I won't let you down. The Dauphin project will get my complete attention."

TWENTY-FOUR

"His breathing seems awfully shallow." Angelina sat in a chair next to Hendrix and stroked his head. The dog was still in a coma. His fur was matted, and there were shaved patches where IVs had been inserted.

McKinney gestured to the bags suspended from hooks at the head of the palette. "His slow breathing is partly due to the medication. They've got him sedated so he doesn't wake up and tear out these tubes."

"I wish I didn't have to go back to school."

"I know honey. I'll keep you informed of any changes." He looked at his watch. "Your flight leaves in a few hours. I'm glad you flew up, but you've got to get back to your studies."

"Yeah, my studies." She bent down and kissed the dog's forehead. "I get why my major requires classes in math, but statistics? Yuk. And my psychology class? The professor doesn't lecture from the text. All she can talk about is her groundbreaking research and how the scientific community hasn't recognized her genius, yet. The whole class is struggling."

"Sounds like you're getting good practice in the art of recognizing phonies, and there are plenty of them out there. You don't have to tolerate that, you know. Holler a little bit. Put up an argument." McKinney looked around the room. They were surrounded by cages filled with sick animals. Some, like Hendrix, were hooked up to IVs; most were sleeping. On the far wall was a glass-doored cabinet filled with medicine bottles. Next to it were several small desks for the veterinarians and technicians. Only one technician sat at her desk; the rest were out in the reception area.

"Psychology class, eh? Let's try a little experiment in

observation. Take a look around this room," McKinney said, "and tell me what you see."

"Why?"

"Humor me."

Angelina took a quick head count. "In the cages are four large dogs, two small dogs, a litter of puppies, three, I think, but I don't see the mother in their cage. Across the room are three cats in separate cages—smaller cages, and, for some reason, there's a cage with a squirrel in it right next to a cage with some kind of hawk. It's a good thing the squirrel's asleep, or he'd be freaking out."

McKinney tilted his head toward the technician. "And her? Watch her for a minute. What can you tell me about her?"

"Well, she's blond, though given the color of her roots I'd say it's a dye job. She looks like she's in her mid-twenties. She's about average height and weight."

"What do you mean by average? There is no average."

"Okay. She appears to be about five foot four and under a hundred and twenty pounds. She's wearing the same scrubs and clogs as the rest of the staff, so I can't tell anything about her by her clothing."

"Look again."

Angelina squinted. "She's wearing a brightly-colored beaded necklace and a large button or pin. I can't read it from here."

"It says 'Birthday Girl.'"

"Ah. That explains the Mylar balloons on her desk."

"Good. Now, just watch her for a few minutes. See if you can observe her actions without drawing any conclusions about their meaning."

Angelina gave McKinney an annoyed look but did as

she was asked. She watched the young woman shift back and forth in her chair a few times until one of the puppies barked. The woman got up and walked slowly to the cage, peered in, and then walked up and down the row of dog cages, checking on her patients. On the other side of the room one of the cats started whining. The technician didn't look at the cat but walked back and sat down at her desk again, resting her chin in her hands. Angelina reported all this activity and added, "I don't think she likes cats."

"Maybe not," McKinney said, "but we don't have enough information to arrive at a conclusion about that."

"Well, she seems unhappy or bored or something. You'd think she'd be in a better mood since it's her birthday."

"Some people don't like birthdays. I agree that she appears unhappy. It might have something to do with her birthday, or it might be due to something wholly unrelated. The point of this exercise..."

"Yes, please! What is the point?"

"The point is that, in addition to whatever courses your program requires, one skill you should try hard to cultivate is the ability to quietly observe your environment and your subjects. Observation of detail is crucial for a forensic scientist, and is no less important for a social scientist, which is what you are studying to be. To be an effective social worker you'll need to be an effective observer, to recognize and analyze patterns of behavior. And, interpreting behavior accurately will require you to put those behaviors in context. Context is everything. You know how good a toasted marshmallow tastes when you're sitting around a big campfire, and you've just pulled the gooey charred mess off your stick?"

Angelina nodded.

"Toasting a marshmallow over a gas flame while

standing in front of the kitchen stove just isn't the same. The flavor of the marshmallow might actually be better, but it still won't taste as good. Context is everything. This type of observation and interpretation is something you can train yourself to do. Believe me, it'll come in handy."

The technician started to get up from her chair again when the phone on her desk rang. She sat back down to answer it, and as she spoke, she became more animated. McKinney couldn't hear what she was saying, but he thought her tone sounded upbeat. He walked over to the technician's desk as she hung up the phone. "Happy birthday. Is today the big day?"

"Yep. The big two nine. One more year until old age sets in." She looked at McKinney's thinning hair. "Oops. Sorry mister, I didn't mean..."

"No problem. So, are you celebrating tonight?"

"Yep. That was my boyfriend who just called. He's taking me to dinner and a show right after work. It was a surprise. Good thing I keep a change of clothing here. I won't have time to go home, first."

"Well, have a wonderful evening."

"Thanks."

McKinney started back to where Angelina was watching him with an amused look on her face. She called from across the room, "Are you a cat-person or dog-person?"

The technician looked confused for a second, then, realizing what Angelina was asking said, "Dog-person, of course. Cats are just bad attitudes with fur."

McKinney winked at Angelina. "You got lucky," he whispered. "Come on. It's time to go to the airport."

She turned to Hendrix, kissed the unconscious animal, then slipped her arm around her father's waist as they left the veterinary hospital. "Can we stop for a hotdog on the way,

Dad?"

"Tofu dog."

Angelina sighed. "Whatever."

∽

McKinney finally found time to continue his examination of the Poe poem. He had checked it for damage after the robbery attempt, but he was still nervous about touching the document. He borrowed a small Raman spectroscope from the document conservation department at Northwestern University and went back to the lab at the Walters Institute. While he was setting up and calibrating the instrument, Mac Walters came into the lab. He wore another of the colorful Hawaiian shirts from his collection and looked more like Ernest Hemingway than a distinguished scientist.

"McKinney, what are you working on now?"

"Hey, Mac. Just an age determination of an old document. How are you?"

"Dandy. My lower back is in constant pain and my allergies are acting up, but business is good. In fact, I might have a couple of cases I can throw your way. You have any experience with food or makeup?"

"Makeup?"

"You know, lipstick and things like that."

"Not directly, but the procedures are pretty much the same. SEM for inorganics and micro-chemical or GCMS for organics. Unless, like this old document, the samples can't be consumed. What are the cases?"

"Civil law suits. Someone eats something or slaps on some makeup and gets sick. We examine the evidence to see if it contains something it shouldn't—an allergen, a heavy metal. We've got a backlog of these cases, now. You can take your pick."

"Thanks, Mac. Say, what do you know about paper?"

They suited up and went into the clean room. Mac examined the manuscript's fibers under the microscope, then McKinney switched on the ultraviolet light.

"How old is this paper supposed to be?"

"About a hundred and seventy years."

"Well, it's not. The whole thing lights up, especially the little lines where the paper was creased or folded."

McKinney said, "I noticed that, too. I think the forger soaked a sheet of modern stationary in tea to stain it, then crumpled it and baked it in an oven to make it brittle."

"Sure, every inexperienced forger's trick to age a document. He should have just purchased some antique stationary that was made in that time period. How much is it selling for?"

"Four hundred thousand dollars.

Walters whistled. "You might have just saved the buyer a lot of money."

"I doubt it would've emptied his wallet."

"Who's the buyer?"

"Logan Bradley."

"I just saw an article about him in Forbes. He's not doing as well as people think. His last two video games flopped. His company lost a bundle of money, and its stock plummeted. I'm surprised he has the money to spend on an extravagance like antique poetry."

McKinney was surprised. "I hope he can afford to pay me."

TWENTY-FIVE

In the weeks leading to Christmas all of our conversations were strained. Mother was supportive when we were alone together, but with father in the room she acquiesced to his wishes and remained silent. I spent much of my time in the old slaves' quarters, reminiscing with Betina and waiting for the baby to arrive. In past years Betina and Millicent had been part of our celebrations, but this year, because I had chosen to spend my time with them, they were excluded from the festivities. I felt as low as a skunk when I told them, at Father's insistence, they would not be allowed to join us at the Christmas table this year.

I hoped the baby would arrive on Christmas day, perhaps as a symbol that God was welcoming my child into the world, but luck was against me again, and the boy was born several days before. Mathieu Peter Boisseau was born on December the twenty-second in the year eighteen ninety-one. Even naming my baby Mathieu, my father's given name, couldn't soften his heart. He saw it as a trick and refused even to be in the same room with the child, for fear he would grow to love him. Christmas was a dismal affair with my father refusing to speak and my mother whimpering and dabbing at her eyes. Only Millicent was in spirit, singing as she worked in the kitchen on the meal. She and Betina ate in the butler's pantry while Mother and Father and I ate in the dining room. Mathieu stayed in his bassinette with Millicent gently rocking him while she ate. No one spoke a word during that meal. It was so quiet that I could hear whenever Mathieu became restless, and I often got up from the table to check on him.

The silent treatment from my father continued until

New Year's Day when I finally confronted him. He was sitting on the front porch, with a heavy blanket about his shoulders, smoking his pipe. There was a chill in the air, so I threw on a wrap and sat on the top step, at his feet.

"This cannot continue, Father. True, I made a mistake, but that mistake has given you a beautiful grandson. Will you deny him the pleasure of knowing his grandpapa?"

He refused to answer and pretended that his pipe needed relighting.

"And what of me?" I asked. Am I not still your jeune ange?"

"Ange?" He spat the word back at me. Au paradis les anges pleurent. You have fallen from their graces."

"Cher Papa…"

He stood and repeated, "Ange!" Then threw his pipe from him, turned, and stalked into the house. I retrieved the pipe from the yard, intending to give it to him, but that was the last time we spoke. He avoided me after that, refusing even to take his meals with us. I kept his pipe and occasionally take it out and look at it. It still seems strange that he should be so long gone when I can see the marks of his strong teeth on the pipestem.

I couldn't stand living so close to my father's disappointment. As soon as little Mathieu was old enough to travel I asked Bettina to take us to New Orleans. I had had communication from Lisette, who claimed to have another of her wonderfully clever ideas. Several of the girls at Madame Broussard's agreed to keep us in their rooms. Mathieu and I would move from room to room, staying with Lisette or one of the other girls. In the evenings, during bed check, we would hide in the chapel. The altar had a false back which afforded us just enough room to curl up inside until everyone was asleep. Then one of the girl's would fetch us, and we would spend the night in her room. Of course, we didn't take into consideration that babies must cry. It was Mlle. Dunnewold who first discovered us. I was sitting cross-legged on the floor, resting against the dark mahogany of the altar, with my baby suckling at my breast. We were waiting for bed check to finish, and I could still hear the sounds of the girls as they ran up and down the halls, going to their rooms. I was perfectly content to sit there in the dark. The altar was smooth against my back, and the air held the comforting scent of the altar candles. My legs, however, were cramped, and when I shifted my position Mathieu gave a little cry. Mlle. Dunnewold must have suspected we were in the chapel because she was suddenly there, staring down at us and shaking her head.

"You don't belong here," she said.

I begged her to keep my secret, and I believe that she did, for we remained unmolested that night.

The following evening Mathieu would not be comforted. We were in Lisette's room, and Madame Broussard burst in, followed by one of the teachers.

"You," she screamed, "are no longer a student of this academy! You and your bastard are not wanted here. You set a poor example for my students."

I could see that Lisette was agitated. Her fists were clenched, and she glared at Madame Broussard. I tried to silence her, but she wouldn't be quiet.

"You pomposity. You are the one setting a poor example. Your lack of charity shows your true character!"

As you can imagine, Madame Broussard was only spurred to action by this outburst. Mathieu and I were put out on the street, though old Lemuel did leave us with a basket of supplies. Lisette's father was contacted, and it's my understanding that he enrolled her in a school over in Alabama.

TWENTY-SIX

Duchamp didn't trust Brysk. It was over a week since they had spoken, and he was getting anxious. Edwards had only given him two months to raise the five hundred and eight thousand dollar buy in, and he was nowhere near it. He had combed the house, looking for anything of value, and, other than some jewelry and a small coin collection, he had come up empty. He bought another stolen cell phone and called Reverend Bob's number. What he got instead was the secretary at Brysk's church, who informed him that the good Reverend had been called home by his maker. *Unacceptable*, he thought. *What the hell is Brysk doing, getting himself killed when he's supposed to be taking care of business? If you want something done right...*

He tossed the throwaway phone in the waste basket and switched on the intercom. "Wayne? You in the kitchen, again?"

Wayne's voice came back sounding muffled and far away. "I'm baking us a batch of cookies for desert tonight, double chocolate."

Duchamp strode out to the kitchen and found Wayne covered with flour and surrounded by broken eggshells and boxes of ingredients. He had a large mixing bowl under his arm and was pounding away with a wooden spoon at a lump of dough the size of a football. "I don't know about this recipe," Wayne said, "this cookie dough is hard as a rock."

Duchamp dipped his hand in the bowl and pulled out a small hunk of dough to sample. "Tastes like crap. Don't worry about it; just get a bag packed. We're driving up to Chicago in the morning."

"What's the deal?"

"I need that painting, and I'm betting the ownership papers are at the roommate's father's place. We're going up north to get them, so when you're through cleaning up out here pack your gear and service the car. I want to get an early start." He plucked the keys to the BMW off the hook. "I'm going to Didi's. I'll see you in the morning."

Wayne looked crushed. "But, what about dinner? I've got a cassoulet in the oven."

"Bag and freeze whatever you don't eat." He shook his head and went out to the garage. "Some bodyguard," he mumbled.

❦

He was walking up the steps to Didi's condo when his non-throwaway cell phone rang. He didn't recognize the number, so he let it go to voicemail, then played it back. The caller's voice startled him. "Mister Duchamp? Runyon here. You know, from the insurance company. We need to talk again. I'll be in your neck of the woods tomorrow afternoon. Does two o'clock suit you?"

Duchamp was glad he hadn't picked up. Now he could leave town without having to fabricate an excuse not to meet with the man. He pulled out his keys and let himself into Didi's condo. Except for the cat, which looked even fatter than it had the last time he saw it, the place was empty. He went to the kitchen to get something to drink and saw a note stuck to a bottle of rye whiskey sitting in the middle of the kitchen table. *Fix yourself a drink and relax, Raymond. We're at the playground trying to expend a little of this child's energy. Honest to God, he is driving me C-R-A-Z-Y. Back soon. Kiss kiss.*

Duchamp crumpled the note, ignored the whisky, and

pulled a bottle of Abita out of the refrigerator. He shooed the cat off the sofa and sat down, oblivious to the white fur that now clung to his Berluti cardigan. He was glad to have a little time to himself to think. He might yet have to kill off a few more of the Dauphin Pharma investors, but that alone wouldn't get him in the consortium; he needed money. According to the prospectus he had been given at Samson Edwards' lunch meeting, he would only have a year after the buy in to raise the rest of his investment capital—five million dollars. It was possible that his wife's will might be settled by that time, possible but not probable. It was just as improbable that the insurance money would come through in time to pay off the buy in. No, he needed the painting. He would have to go to Chicago and get the inheritance papers from that scientist fellow, one way or another.

He had just settled back to read the copy of yesterday's Times-Picayune he had picked up from in front of a door down the hall when Didi burst in with Tyler in tow. They both carried shopping bags and wore big, animated grins.

"Oh Raymond, wait 'till you see the cool matching shirts we bought. They're so bright; you should probably put on your sunglasses." She set down her purse and reached into the shopping bag. "Prepare to be amazed."

"I thought you were at the playground."

"We were. I stopped to shop on the way home."

Tyler pulled a t-shirt out of his bag. "Hullo, Uncle Ray. Check this out."

"Hello yourself." He turned to Didi. "Why isn't he in school?"

"Teachers' conference. He went a half day." She pulled her shirt out of the bag and held it up for him to see. She and Tyler both had tie-dyed shirts that read, "Dare To Be

Awesome."

"Huh. 'Dare To Be Nerds.' I guess it could be worse. You could have both gotten those shirts that say, 'I'm With Stupid.'"

Didi dropped her shirt back in the bag. "What crawled up your butt? We had a really fun afternoon and don't need you ruining it with your nasty remarks."

"I'm sorry. I'm just in a sour mood. The shirts look nice."

Didi marched through to the kitchen, and Tyler sat on the floor next to the couch.

"I know what'll cheer you up, Uncle Ray—a joke. I learned a whole bunch of new ones from this kid in my class. His name is Brandon."

Duchamp leaned back on the couch, aware that he was trapped. "Go ahead. Tell me a joke."

"What's six inches long, is gross and slimy and has three eyes and big, sharp teeth?"

"I don't know. What?"

Tyler giggled. "I don't know either, but it's sitting on your neck!"

Didi called from the kitchen. "That's just your Uncle Raymond's head, dear."

Duchamp ignored the jibe. "Tyler, my fine fellow, you'll have to excuse me for a little bit. Your mother and I have some grownup talking to do." He pushed himself up from the couch and went out to the kitchen. "Didi, I need your advice."

Didi finished pouring a glass of iced tea and put the pitcher back into the refrigerator. "You mean you need my gift."

"Whatever you want to call it."

"Well, that's nice to hear you say, Raymond. I thought

you were a skeptic. You know, making fun and all."

"So sign me up. I'm a believer."

She sat down at the kitchen table and gestured toward a chair. "Tell me all about it."

Raymond sat. "Don't we need the tarot cards?"

"I don't think so. You and I have a spiritual connection. I'll be able to read you without them."

"I need to raise the buy in money quickly, and I'm convinced my best chance is to get my hands on that Turner painting. The documentation and ownership papers are in Chicago. Wayne and I are driving up tomorrow to get them. What's our chance of being successful?"

"Woo. That's a tall order, Raymond. Close your eyes and give me your hands." She reached out and took his hands, pressing her palms into his. She closed her eyes, too. They sat that way for several minutes. Finally she opened her eyes and released him. "This feels like a risky venture. I get a sense of danger, but I can't tell who it's associated with. I think you're right about the painting being your way to get the money we need, but keep Wayne close to you. I think there's going to be some trouble."

"But will we succeed?"

"I feel that your chances are better than not, but I can give you something that will improve your chances."

"What's that?"

"A charm."

"What kind of a charm?"

Didi smiled. "A voodoo charm. Stay put. I have to get my kit out of my closet."

Raymond waited a minute, then got up and followed her into the bedroom. As he passed through the living room he noticed Tyler, asleep on the couch. The boy had curled himself around the cat.

Didi was standing on tiptoe in the walk-in closet, wrestling a suitcase from the top shelf. Duchamp came up behind her and took the case. He set it on the floor and bent to kiss the back of her neck. She leaned back into him, so he slid his arms around her waist. They stayed that way for a minute until Raymond moved his hands up to her breasts.

"Hold your horses, Raymond. We'll get to that as soon as Tyler is asleep."

"He is. He's napping on the couch. Out like a light."

Didi went to the bedroom door and peeked out. "Tuckered him out." She gently closed the bedroom door and, taking Raymond by the hand, led him back into the big closet, closing the sliding door behind them.

"The closet?" he asked.

"In case Tyler wakes up," she said and slid her hand down the front of his pants.

TWENTY-SEVEN

McKinney drove straight to Nina's from the lab. He had brought a blazer along, but under it he still wore the same black t-shirt and jeans he had started the day in. He thought she would tell him to wait downstairs when he buzzed her at the front door, but she surprised him, and in a voice sounding tinny and far away through the speaker, invited him upstairs. She was waiting for him on the landing and took his hand to lead him into the apartment, leaning up awkwardly to kiss him first.

Nina's apartment wasn't anything like he had imagined. Everything was orderly, but there were large stacks of papers on every surface. Law books were pyramided on the desk in her living room, and the dining room table was covered with case files and court briefs, stacked high but all oriented in the same direction, their edges neatly aligned. In stark contrast were a number of colorful prints on the walls, abstract expressionist works by Pollack, Hoffman, and de Kooning. McKinney imagined they were part of the effort to reprogram her mind.

Nina said, "Promise me we won't talk about work tonight, Sean. I've had a truly bizarre week."

"Okay, but now I'm intrigued. What happened?"

"I was in the middle of a murder trial, a drive-by shooting, and I really believe my client is innocent. He has a verified alibi. It looked like we were about to wrap things up today when the prosecution asked to call one more witness, a young woman who was at the crime scene. She was obviously nervous; she started shaking as soon as she took the stand. She had only been asked to state her name when she blurted out that her testimony had been coerced by the police and that my client's family had threatened her. Then she vomited all over the witness stand and passed out. They had to call the paramedics to take her out and put her in an ambulance."

"Wow!"

"Yeah. The judge declared a mistrial. I don't know if the State's Attorney will charge my client again." Nina gestured to an overstuffed chair, the only uncluttered seating in the room. "I have to put on some different shoes and grab a sweater. I'll be right with you."

On the wood floor next to the chair were several coffee cup stains and a number of paperback novels. McKinney imagined this was her spot, her messy little lifeboat on the ocean of her orderly life. He sat. She disappeared into the bedroom. McKinney sniffed his shirt and wished he'd gone home to change, first. He'd have to wear his jacket all evening. He picked up one of the paperback books—Kerouac. *Can't get any messier than that*, he thought. She came out minutes later with a light cotton sweater, low-heeled shoes and an indigo-colored silk dress that contrasted nicely with her blond hair.

They had reservations at a little tapas restaurant. Finding parking in the city wasn't easy, and Nina's apartment was close to the Red Line, so they took the El south to Lincoln Park. They arrived just as the hostess was giving their table away. Instead, they ate at the bar, facing one another on the high stools and sharing small plates of grilled fish and sharp Spanish cheeses. McKinney quickly backed up one gin and tonic with another. Nina no longer peered out from behind her hair but looked at him directly, giving him the full effect of her green eyes. He found himself acutely aware of their proximity, and as the evening progressed he felt more and more a part of her gravitational field, as though if she moved he'd be pulled along with her. He told her about being worried that Angelina was so far away from home and about the attempted robbery and how afraid he was that Hendrix might not survive and how terrible he felt that he'd killed a man, even though the man had shot his dog.

"I guess I never gave this much thought, but one of my goals was to get through life without killing another human being. I've been lucky. I didn't grow up in a war-torn country, and even now I live where the worst violence is usually a robbery or a domestic. Most of the gang killings take place on the south or west side."

"It sounds like he didn't leave you much choice, Sean."

"Yeah. And that's why I'm so angry. I know this sounds crazy; I mean, he's the one who's dead, but I'm mad at him for making me kill him. He put me in a position where I had to react the way I did. I feel like that asshole took a piece of my soul. By killing him, I am diminished."

"Diminished how?"

McKinney paused, taking a sip of his drink while he collected his thoughts. "I'm not entirely sure I believe in a human soul, but if we do have souls they're undeveloped when we're born. Babies, children—they're the very definition of selfishness. They are at the center of their own small worlds. People like Gandhi, King, and Mother Teresa had well-developed souls; they viewed the world from the perspective of we, not me. If we have souls, they grow as we grow. They are the repositories for our learned moral conscience, our ability to empathize with the rest of life on this planet. Am I a good person? Am I a moral person? The act of killing instilled an element of doubt. It took something away from me."

She put her hand over his. " I meet people every day who are incapable of asking themselves those questions. Maybe being able to ask is enough."

"That would be nice, but I don't think it's that simple." He realized the dark turn their conversation had taken and noticed the bartender and the four people at the table in front of the bar listening in—eavesdropping. He winked at her and raised his voice a little. "So, Gladys, I know you're still a little self-conscious about it, but I think your eyebrow transplants came out fine. They look very natural."

Nina looked at him quizzically for a moment then grinned. "I'll tell ya, Charlie, it was a painful operation, but they seem to be healing nicely."

"Didn't you tell me your original eyebrows were burned off in a fire?"

"No. They were blown off in an explosion. You remember when I had that accident in the kitchen? A pot of beans blew up and took my brows right off. Garbanzos, as I recall."

He reached out and stroked one of her eyebrows with his thumb. "Well, they look and feel like the real thing. Didn't you tell me they were made entirely of hair from the hind leg of a dog?"

"That's right, a cocker spaniel."

"There's just one little problem with them, Gladys. Nothing important, mind you. Just something I noticed on the way here."

"What's that?"

The bartender had taken a step closer, and a couple at another table stopped talking and were openly staring at them. McKinney could feel himself starting to laugh. He wasn't sure he could get the punch line out. He paused a second and took a deep breath. "Every time we walk past a fire hydrant, you look surprised."

After they left the restaurant, they decided to walk a bit. They strolled north, along the edge of the park, the gorgeous old mansions and brownstones to their left and the park with the lake beyond to their right. McKinney noticed the way their shadows contracted and stretched on the sidewalk as they walked in and out of the circles of light cast by the streetlights. He walked with his hands in his pockets. "Thank you for recommending me for this freelance assignment," he said, "but I'm afraid your friend isn't going to be happy with my results."

"Oh, no. The poem is a fake?"

"I'm afraid so. Not even a very skillful one, at that. The paper it was written on is too modern. It wouldn't have been available during Poe's lifetime."

"Why do you say it's not a skillful fake?"

"The paper was stained with tea and then subjected to heat to make it appear old, but it fluoresces, which shows that it's been treated with chemicals to make it appear whiter. The forger could have simply purchased some hundred and seventy-year-old writing paper from an antique dealer. He was lazy."

"Logan will be disappointed, but at least you saved him a bundle of money." She hooked her arm through his. "I can't remember when I've enjoyed myself this much, Sean. I don't date often. I'm kind of shy, you know, because of the OCD thing, and I don't have many friends. My work keeps me pretty busy."

"I'm glad. I mean I'm glad you're having a good time. This is a rare treat for me, too. You're easy to talk to, which is helpful because I tend to talk a lot. My daughter says I'm loquacious. I gave her a thesaurus when she was in the sixth grade. I just hope I didn't scare you off by telling you all my horror stories."

"No. I understand why you feel bad about killing that man. Life is precious. I once found a dying pigeon in the middle of the street. It had been hit by a car. I picked it up, put it under a tree and sat with it, talking in a soothing tone of voice, until it died. Can you imagine? A pigeon, and I was sad for it the whole rest of the day."

McKinney said, "You're a woman after my own heart."

She pulled him closer. "Could be."

They cut through the park to the bike path so they could see the lake while they walked. The sun was down, but the moon was up, and McKinney watched the ripple of its reflection on the water. The reflection appeared to follow them as they walked. Nina put on her sweater and took McKinney's hand in hers. He noted that there was strength behind the softness of her hand. He gave her hand a gentle squeeze, and she squeezed back, and then a sort of sexual energy passed between them. McKinney had known on that first night he kissed her that, sooner or later, they would wind up in bed together. Some part of him knew her now, or rather, anticipated her—the feel of the soft hairs at the base of her spine, the taste of salt just above her collarbone, the warmth of her exhalation on his ear. He sensed these things about her. He wanted to know them.

They walked without speaking for a bit. A cool breeze blew in off the lake, and a light shower fell on them from a sky that had been clear moments before. Nina pulled herself into the crook of his arm, and they hurried back, ducking into a short tunnel. The air in the tunnel was dense and mildewy. The moon had passed behind a cloud, but they could see the glow of the streetlights at the other end of the tunnel. They kissed for a while, and her fragrance, a blend of all the smells that defined her, filled his senses. She took one of his hands from her waist and put it on her breast. He felt her nipple, firm under his palm and, with his other hand, pulled her tight against him. The sound of footsteps along the walk robbed them of the moment. Almost in a whisper, Nina said, "I know this takes away some of the spontaneity, but would you...I mean, if you'd like to...can you spend the night?"

McKinney raised her hand to his lips and kissed her knuckles. "You're sure?"

She nodded. "Let's walk back to the El."

"The hell with the El," he said, leading her out of the tunnel, "Let's take a cab."

Nina's bathroom was as neat and orderly as McKinney had imagined it would be, maybe more so. The towels were expertly folded. There were cubbyholes for all the tubes and bottles and brushes. Nothing was out of place, and the shine from the scrubbed porcelain was almost blinding. He had slipped out of bed while Nina slept, hoping to use the bathroom and clean up without waking her, but as he was splashing water on his face he heard the sounds of breakfast being prepared. He pulled on his pants, sniffed his shirt, and strolled, barefoot, out to the kitchen.

Nina stood at the counter, dressed in a silk robe decorated with bright blue butterflies, and holding an oversized mug. "Good morning," she said. "I have scrambled eggs and toast made, if that's okay. Oh, and fresh coffee in the pot." She gestured toward the table. "Will you stay for breakfast? I mean, I don't want to presume..."

"Good morning, yourself. Of course, I'll stay. Thanks."

"I didn't know what your schedule was. If you had—

have—somewhere to be. You were already up when I woke."

"No. I'm free 'till noon or so." He poured a cup of coffee and took a sip.

"How's the coffee?"

"Not bad."

She spooned eggs onto plates and sat across from him at the table. "Are you hung over?"

"Nope. I feel fine. How about you?"

"I also am fine. I mean..." She looked down at her plate, letting her hair fall forward to half-hide her face. "I'm sorry, Sean. It's been a long time since I've had breakfast with anyone. You weren't in bed when I woke up. I thought maybe you'd left."

"I didn't want to wake you. Before I went into the bathroom I was enjoying watching you sleep. You sleep curled up with your arm across your knees, almost like a cat. It's very cute, and that's not a word I use lightly."

"Well, I don't want you to feel like you're obligated to stick around if you have somewhere else to be or have something else you'd rather do." She turned the handle of her coffee mug parallel to the edge of the table, then clasped her hands and put them on her lap. "I might be feeling the teensiest bit..."

"Uncomfortable?" he offered.

She nodded, not looking up from her plate. "Yes, I'm sorry."

"Lady, you're really going to have to stop apologizing. Life is filled with little missteps and blunders. If you spend your time worrying about all that minutiae you'll miss the important stuff." McKinney picked up his cup, walked to the sink, and poured the coffee down the drain. He filled the cup with water, sipped it, swished it around and spat it out. "Like this," he said. He bent down and kissed her. It was a long kiss, as passionate as any from the night before. She pushed herself up from the table, one hand grasping the back of his neck, helping her keep contact with his lips. McKinney loosened the sash around her waist, and the robe fell away, leaving the butterflies in the kitchen with the uneaten breakfast, as they walked to the bedroom.

TWENTY-EIGHT

After I was *asked* to leave Madame Broussard's I spent a week on the streets of New Orleans. On two occasions Lemuel tracked me down to give me food and blankets. He never said, but I believe that he brought them at the behest of Mlle. Dunnewold. Mathieu and I slept in the park on most evenings. I had found a spot in a thicket where we wouldn't be seen. After sundown I put Mathieu on my stomach and wrapped us both in a blanket. My fear was that I would turn over in my sleep and crush him, but I never did, and my courageux bébeé generally slept through the night.

During the day I sought employment. As you can imagine, no one was interested in hiring a woman carrying a baby, and as the week wore on, I looked more and more disheveled. I'm afraid I didn't smell too good, either, as Mathieu had long since run out of clean diapers, and we were making do with scraps and rags. On our seventh day of living on the streets I finally ran out of food. I was both hungry and frightened, for my milk had become thin, and little Mathieu was crying whenever he was awake. My hunt for work took us past one of the Italian fruit markets, and I thought perhaps one of the grocers might have known Peter and would give me work or at least a little food. The only person in the market was a shriveled old woman wearing a long black dress and a black headscarf. I must have looked like a beggar because as soon as she saw me she began waving me away and screeching something unintelligible in Italian. I had never stolen before, but I was desperate, and I snatched up a handful of carrots and several red apples and bolted for the door. The hag ran after me, screaming, and just as I made the sidewalk a muscular man in an apron arrived. He grabbed me and held me there while the old woman, his mother I believe, fetched the police. Mathieu and I spent the night in the parish jail on Royal Street, and honestly, it was a relief after our nights in the park. The next day I appeared in the docket at the court of Judge Guy Dreaux. I remember his name because I had heard some of the girls at Madame Broussard's speak of him. He had a reputation as a harsh jurist, sending scofflaws to prison for relatively minor infractions. When it was my turn to stand before the judge and plead my case I was struck dumb.

"Young lady, you have been accused of theft and vagrancy. Do you understand these charges?"

I sobbed a little and nodded my head.

"Where do you live?" he asked. "Who are your people?"

Again, I couldn't speak.

"These are serious charges. If you are found guilty, your child will be taken from you and put in a government facility. Do you understand? Can't you speak up and give some account of yourself?"

The thought of losing Mathieu gave me my tongue, and I told the old judge everything. "My husband was cruelly murdered, and I have been disowned by my family. A week ago my Mistress turned me out into the streets. My child and I have no home. I have sought work in vain and am reduced to begging. Please sir, don't take my son from me. He is all that I have of good in this world."

Judge Dreaux looked at me and shook his head. "You are, yourself, but a child. Children birthing children—this saddens me. I am placing you both in the care of the nuns at The House of the Good Shepard. It is a reformatory, but the nuns are compassionate. They will let you keep your baby and

---

will teach you how to be a mother. Perhaps you will learn a trade." He turned to the officer of the court. "Fetch the matron for this girl." Then he looked at me with, what I believe were, tears in his eyes and said, "I wish you well, girl."

✐

The head of The House of the Good Shepard was wrinkled old Sister Constance, and like her name, she was solid and inflexible. She gave me to Sister Berenice. When I say she gave me to her I mean that each nun at The House of the Good Shepard was responsible for several girls. Sister Berenice had two other girls besides me. When I first met her I almost laughed. She was short and squat and had big bug eyes that peered out from behind her wimple. She looked like a marmoset. To her credit, Sister Berenice really tried to help me. She had a sunny disposition, and often sang little songs as she walked the halls, checking on her wayward charges. Perhaps she would have been able to get through to me at some other time, but I was still too traumatized by my recent losses to pay her much attention.

The nuns put me to work in the laundry, a long room filled with steaming washtubs, ironing boards, and folding tables. It was almost unbearably hot, and I'm sure I would have succumbed had it not been for the open windows on both sides of the room, which gave some relief. I, of course, resented washing and sewing linens for the hotels and sporting houses in the Vieux Carré, thinking it beneath me. It is truly amazing what short memories we humans have. It was only days since I was living in the streets and begging for my supper, yet I somehow felt life owed me more than to work as a laundress.

All of Sister Berenice's girls were about the same age, but there were many younger than us at the House and several older. One of her girls worked in the kitchen, but the other worked with me in the laundry. Her name was Caitlin, but everyone called her Catey. She wasn't particularly masculine in appearance, but she was tough. Fights between the girls were common, and it was certain that if there was a commotion, Catey was in the middle of it. In fact, Catey once saved my life.

One of the older girls, Betty, was charged with picking up and delivering the laundry to the various establishments that used our services. I had gotten a late start that day because Mathieu was a little colicky, and I was reluctant to trust his care to the nun who watched the nursery. Consequently, I was late getting the sheets pressed. While I was struggling to press and fold the several dozen sheets I had been given, Betty came up behind me and slapped the back of my head.

"Hey, Princess, get your ass moving. I've got places to be."

Foolishly, I tried to explain myself to her, but I hadn't spoken more than a few words when she slapped me again, this time across my face. I was stunned.

"That's not necessary," I said. "I'm hurrying as fast as I can."

This time I saw the slap coming and grabbed her hand before she could hit me. That only made her madder. She threw me to the floor, pulled the sheet I had been ironing over my head, and started kicking me with all her strength. One kick caught me in the forehead, and I almost passed out. They told me later that she had grabbed the flat iron and was about to use it as a bludgeon when Catey grabbed her by the hair, dragged her into a storage closet and locked the door. The girl remained there the rest of the day. As she was unable to deliver the laundry I had to deliver it myself.

There were only a half dozen deliveries to be made

that day, but the farthest was way over on Customhouse Street, which I believe they now call Iberville Street. This was a sporting house owned by a madam named Lulu White. I had been pulling my little laundry cart all afternoon and was tired and probably looked a fright. I still wore the enormous blouse I had bought to hide my pregnancy, only now it looked like I was modeling a small tent. Lulu herself answered the door, and for the longest time we stood and stared at one another. I imagine she was as horrified by my appearance as I was mesmerized by hers. She was a chocolate-skinned woman, no taller than I, though quite a bit heavier, and she wore an enormous red wig. Her fingers were covered with rings and her arms with bracelets. She wore no less than a dozen necklaces, one of which held a lorgnette, which she raised to her eyes as she examined me.

"You're late," she drawled. "Bring the sheets in and wait. One of the girls will bring you the dirties to be washed."

She stood aside and held the door while I staggered in with my load of sheets. One of the crib girls grabbed me and made me walk with her from room to room, leaving the clean linens and collecting the soiled. As I left the house with my new burden, Miss Lulu stopped me.

"Girl, are you a virgin?"

I didn't know how to respond. I suppose I still felt the shame of my father's recriminations. I almost said that I was, but to do so would have been to deny both Mathieu and Peter. Finally, I shook my head.

"Well, that's all right. I'll tell you what. When you get tired of washing men's desires off our sheets you come see me. I'm certain we can find something better for you to do."

We girls all slept in one large dormitory room on cots lined up in two rows. Each girl had a small table and a washbasin next to her cot, and I kept my few possessions on my table and under my cot. That night, after I got Mathieu to sleep, I snuck over to Catey's cot to tell her about Lulu White.

"I used to make deliveries there," she said, "and Miss Lulu made the same pitch to me. She's always looking for new whores, and her clients will pay a hefty price for a virgin. I worked for her a couple times, but Sister Berenice keeps us pretty busy here. There aren't a lot of opportunities to sneak off."

"You mean you were a crib girl?"

"Not exactly. Miss Lulu's crib girls all live there. I guess you'd say I was a part-time whore."

"But you went with men for money?"

Catey laughed. "I sure as hell didn't do it for fun."

I was stunned. I knew, of course, that the men all went to those women for "relief," but I couldn't imagine actually doing it myself. When I was with Peter it was an act of passion, a way to express the love I felt for him. Anything else just seemed wrong. I'm certain that had I not had the responsibility of providing for my son I would never have considered it. "Did the men pay you well?" I asked.

"They paid Lulu, and she paid me. I don't know what her cut was, but I bet it was more than fifty percent. I didn't bring any of it back here. One of these little bitches would've swiped it the instant my back was turned. I took enough to treat myself to a nice dinner and a few drinks and left the rest with Miss Lulu. She says I have an account with her. Any money I earn in the future goes into the account, and I can have my money whenever I want. As soon as I've done my time here I'm going to use that money to go north."

I tiptoed back to my cot and slid in beside Mathieu. He whimpered a little but didn't wake, and as we lay there I could just make out the curve of his cheek and his tiny nose by the moonlight drifting through the shutters. He was beautiful and helpless. He hadn't asked to be brought into this world, and he certainly hadn't asked to be fatherless and in the care of an indigent girl who couldn't even care for herself. The things I learned from the instructors at Madame Broussard's, grammar, piano, solfeggio, were not marketable skills. I was much more likely to be able to support my child using the skills I had learned from Lisette. The pout, the hair flip, the hooded eyes, these were techniques I could exploit. I needed to talk to Lulu White.

TWENTY-NINE

Wayne held a small screw jack against the doorframe opposite the lock. He wedged a short length of two by four between the jack and the other side of the frame. Four quick turns of the jack bowed the doorframe out enough to allow the door to swing inward on its hinges. He pushed the door open and knocked the two by four out of the way. It clattered to the floor.

Duchamp fingered the black cat bone in his pocket, looked around the empty hallway, and peered over the railing to the floor below. "Keep it quiet."

Wayne started to enter but, as an afterthought, stopped to wipe his feet on the mat. "Let's hurry up. Man, going through other people's things gives me the creeps."

"The creeps?"

"Yeah. Who knows what kind of weird shit this guy's into?"

"He's a scientist. What kind of 'weird shit' do you think he's into?"

"I don't know. He's probably got cages of drug-addicted monkeys or jars filled with brains or something."

"Well, if he's got jars of brains in here we'll pick a nice one out for you."

They stepped into the apartment, eased the door closed and pulled on their gloves. Duchamp pointed to the bedroom. "You start in there. I'll check the living room and the kitchen. And don't miss anything."

Duchamp watched Wayne shuffle off, then crossed to the bookcase and opened the fold-down desk. The interior was piled high with papers, and he had just started to shuffle through them when he heard Wayne call from the bedroom.

"I don't have to go through this guy's underwear drawer, do I?"

"You need to look anywhere he might have hidden some papers. We don't know what size they are or what they look like, so I would say, yes, look in his damn underwear drawer."

It took Duchamp half an hour to go through all the papers in the desk and flip through the books on the bookshelves. He found nothing but science journals, receipts, and unpaid bills. In his frustration he swept the stack of papers onto the floor. He shouted, "Any luck in there?"

Wayne came out of the kitchen eating a sandwich. "Nothing. I even kicked through the pile of dirty clothes on the closet floor. This guy is a P-I-G pig. And there's hardly any food in his fridge. This is just peanut butter and banana." He looked at Duchamp's reddening face and held out the sandwich. "Want me to make you one?"

"We're supposed to be searching, not helping ourselves to his pantry."

"I know. I searched the bedroom, bathroom, and kitchen. Unless he's got some great hidey-hole, those papers aren't here. Heck. Most of what's in the kitchen is microscopes and test tubes and stuff."

Duchamp kicked some papers out of his way and stalked out to the kitchen. He read all the notes attached to the refrigerator and opened all the drawers and cabinets. He opened boxes of crackers and cereal and dumped the contents in the sink.

"Let me know if you find a prize, Boss."

"Funny. Go have a look in the living room, will you? See if there's anything I missed."

A minute later he heard Wayne call out. "Uh oh. You're not going to like this."

Duchamp went back out and looked at Wayne's outstretched hand. "What is it?"

"A key for a safe deposit box. You can tell by the letters and numbers engraved on the side. This guy has a box in some bank. That's probably where those papers are, stashed away with his passport and his grandfather's pocket watch."

"And we don't know which bank."

"Even if we did, we couldn't get in without a picture I.D."

Duchamp cleared all the magazines and books off the coffee table with his foot. Then, he took the key and positioned it prominently in the center of table. He wanted McKinney to see it there. He knew what he had to do now.

"All right, Wayne, finish your sandwich and pack up. We're through here." He walked to the door and took one last look around the living room. They'd drive back to New Orleans that night, and when he got back he'd start planning the next move. He was going to kidnap the scientist's daughter.

THIRTY

McKinney took the stairs up to his apartment two at a time. The simple idea that someone he liked, liked him back was enough to elevate his mood. It was raining and his hair had gotten soaked during the short walk from his car. He wiped the rain off his forehead and had a momentary flash of memory, recalling how he felt when, as a gangly fifteen year-old, he had mustered the courage to ask Nancy Gilmer to the movies. He had phoned her on a dare from a friend's house, and after she said "yes" he had walked home in the pouring rain, happily oblivious to the soaking torrent. Still buoyant from his time with Nina it was this same euphoria that he felt now, and immediately lost, when he stepped into his apartment and realized someone had broken in.

He had come up the back steps and in through the kitchen door, and the first thing he noticed was the jumble of boxes and their contents that had been dumped in the sink. He backed out onto the porch, out of the line of fire if the intruder was still inside but still able to see most of the kitchen through the window. He took out his cell phone and whispered his address to the 911 operator, then hurried back down the stairs and positioned himself in the gangway alongside the apartment building so he could see anyone leaving by either the front or back door.

Mrs. Vladic was in the back yard, working in the garden, and shuffled over to chat with McKinney. The old Russian woman had on her gardening smock and a Cubs hat.

"Everything okay, McKinney?"

"Someone broke into my apartment. I'm just waiting for the police. They're probably gone, but you might want to wait here with me, instead of going back inside."

"No problem. You've been watching spring training?" She tapped the bill of her cap. "We've got a good pitching staff this year. You know, it's all about the pitching."

"So you've told me." He pointed back toward the garden. "Isn't it a little early to be planting?"

"Just preparing the soil. Got to have good soil."

A patrol car pulled into the alley, and McKinney excused himself and walked out to meet them. Mrs. Vladic called after him, "Try not to leave any more dead bodies in the yard. Okay, McKinney?"

The officers only stayed long enough to have a look around and write up a report. McKinney's quick inventory indicated that nothing was missing from the apartment, and he immediately thought of the poem, the Edgar Allen Poe forgery that he had locked in a desk drawer at the Walters Research Institute. What else would a burglar be looking for, a burglar who had ignored a laptop computer and a flatscreen TV? Granted, they were a few years old, but wasn't the poem what the previous burglar had come for? McKinney moved from room to room, surveying the damage and trying not to jump to conclusions. Like the children's game, he looked for anything that didn't belong. Even in the mess there were patterns of order, chaotic patterns. He looked for things that looked out of place. He made the circuit several times. The first round revealed his safe deposit box key sitting in the middle of the coffee table in the living room. It seemed unlikely that it had been tossed there haphazardly rather than placed there deliberately, but he kept that possibility open and moved on. The front door was the obvious point of entry. He used his phone to photograph the tool-mark impressions on the doorframe. They didn't look like scratches from a crowbar or jimmy, but he was certain they belonged to whatever the burglar had used to open his door. Both the lock on the doorknob and the deadbolt were still locked; they hadn't been picked. The impression in the wood was deep, as though a lot of force had been applied, and one of the straight edges was interrupted by an obvious flaw, a crack near one end. This was a nice individual characteristic that would help identify the instrument that had left the impression, if it could be found. In the kitchen he found a banana peel and a knife in the sink among all the cereal and crackers, the knife covered with brown streaks that smelled like peanut butter. He carefully placed those in small paper bags. He took the peanut butter jar from the refrigerator and bagged that, too. There was always the possibility that DNA or fingerprint evidence could be obtained from them. He still had a few friends at the crime lab.

When he was finished taking photographs, McKinney propped a kitchen chair under the front door knob to keep the door closed, cleaned the mess off the couch and sat down. The impromptu inventory of his apartment had revealed an excess of crap. Sure, there were his old blues and jazz albums, photos of Angelina and her mother, a few pieces of art that he liked, but everything else was junk. The kind of junk the onslaught of advertising he encountered every day told him would lead to a happy fulfilled life. Had he turned into a mindless consumer without realizing it? Emptied of daughter and dog, and invaded by strangers, his apartment felt foreign and unwelcoming, like someone else lived there. Someone McKinney wasn't sure he liked.

ꝏ

Despite the mess in his apartment or, rather, because of it, McKinney felt the need to get out. He went to tai chi class to clear his mind and work up a sweat. That he hadn't been to class in several weeks made no difference to Master Kuo, who always greeted him like they had seen each other the day before.

"Ah McKinney, you're just in time." The small man waved a hand at the group of people who were just starting a short Yang-style form as a warm up.

McKinney took a spot at the back of the room and went through the graceful, flowing moves with the class. Afterward, they paired off to practice the controlled sparring exercise called pushing hands. Not really a combat exercise, pushing hands helps develop awareness of slight changes in an opponents energy and posture. It's an essential component in learning to use tai chi for self-defense and one of the unique characteristics of tai chi that McKinney liked best. It requires, as Master Kuo would say, a kind of unfocused focus. As he moved back and forth with his partner, McKinney tried to relax, to think only of the almost nonexistent physical connection between their arms, feeling for slight changes in pressure and direction. McKinney had trained with this student before. In previous sessions the man had been stiff and self-conscious, and McKinney had little trouble throwing him. Now though, as they moved across the floor, he was having a hard time reading the other man's energy. He took a second to wonder if the man had improved that much since they last trained together, and in that instant he stiffened, almost imperceptibly, but enough. The man sensed an opening, and sent McKinney stumbling into the wall behind him, the man's fa jin, explosive energy, driving the breath from McKinney's lungs.

Master Kuo clapped his hands and laughed. "So, the mighty have fallen. See McKinney, that's what happens when you don't practice."

After a little stretching the class settled on the floor for the ten minutes of meditation Master Kuo required at the end of each class. "You cannot learn to control your body if you can't control your mind."

McKinney allowed his breathing and his heart rate to slow and began the mental exercise of circulating his chi or internal energy. Soon though, his thoughts drifted to Nina. Sex was dangerous territory for him. He had never subscribed to the Playboy credo of sex without consequence. As a young man he had engaged in a couple of one-night stands that left him feeling uncomfortably guilty. Not in the Biblical sense, he had always thought religion went about trying to influence behavior in the wrong way, threatening punishment rather than emphasizing personal responsibility. Instead, he felt like he had let those women, and himself, down somehow. Oh, he understood that they were no more interested in a relationship than he was, and he was old enough to know that people, especially young people with raging hormones, liked to pretend that lust was love, but wasn't sex more than just rubbing one another's bits in the hope of releasing some endorphins? Wasn't it supposed to be a way to communicate emotion? Shouldn't sex, at the very least, be a way of saying, you are important to me? It should strengthen both partners and diminish no one. He liked Nina. Wasn't that enough?

He thought about his wife, Catherine. She would have accused him of overthinking. Mister Science Guy, always analyzing. She would have told him to stop worrying, go with the flow. *That's what tai chi is all about.* He brought his awareness back to his surroundings and noticed the room was quiet. He opened his eyes. All the other students were gone. Master Kuo stood by the door. His street shoes were on, and he was holding his jacket.

"I hate to disturb you," he said, "but class is over. Let's

go next door. I'll buy you a beer."

THIRTY-ONE

I decided I would like the job of delivering the freshly laundered sheets and, with Catey's help, began a campaign to secure the position. We began by telling Sister Berenice about Betty's attack on me in the laundry. Then I explained that I would probably be a faster delivery girl than a laundress. Sister Berenice seemed not to care about the speed or quality of our work, so this approach had no affect on her, whatsoever. Finally, my dear Catey decided to shortcut the process and eliminate the competition. One evening at dinner she picked up her plate and tableware and moved to the seat across from Betty. The other girls knew something was about to happen, and all conversation ceased. Betty looked up from her plate, her fork poised in front of her open mouth, just as Catey flipped a spoonful of buttered grits into her face.

She wiped her face with her sleeve and snarled, "You're dead."

Catey managed to get the next spoonful into her eye. "S'matter? Don't like grits?"

Betty cleaned the mess out of her eye and looked down the long table to where Sister Claudine sat. "As soon as we're alone, bitch."

Sister Claudine was a novice and, though it was her job to keep an eye on us at meals, she always asked one of the other nuns for guidance. Catey turned to the girl sitting next to her—one of the younger girls. "You have a stomachache. Start moaning."

The girl looked like she couldn't believe Catey had spoken to her. "I feel all right, Catey."

Catey put her face an inch from the girl's and repeated

through clenched teeth, "You have a stomachache. Start moaning." The girl gave a little whimper, and Catey raised her hand. "Sister Claudine. Sick girl here!"

Sister Claudine scurried across the room and bent over the girl. "My, my, my; what have we here?"

The girl was terrified, but she did as she'd been told and moaned. Sister Claudine hustled her out of the room. "Let's go find Sister Rose, dear. She'll have a look at you."

As soon as they were out of the room Betty hurled herself across the table, hoping to get the jump on Catey, but Catey was ready for her. She pushed back from the table and, as Betty came flying toward her, grabbed the front of the enraged girl's shift and pulled down while stepping to one side. The effect was that Betty dropped face first onto the chair in which Catey had been seated. All the girls heard the crunch of her nose breaking. It was, I must say, horrific. She lay, unconscious on the floor, until one of the girls ran to get the Sisters.

✑

Lulu White was a smart woman. She spent her time with me, during those first visits, just showing me around the place and introducing me to her girls. I delivered clean laundry to her house three days a week, and on each of those days I hurried to finish my other deliveries so I would have sufficient time at Miss Lulu's. One day, after I'd been delivering her laundry for about a month, she said, "Well girl, are you about ready to give it a try. You've been coming around, bending my ear and drinking my tea, for a good long while, but I know it's the money to be made at Miss Lulu's that interests you."

It's true that I was scared. I had heard stories from some of the crib girls of men who were crazy, or violent, or who wanted them to engage in acts that were disgusting and degrading. Again, Miss Lulu showed her common sense. She had waited for the day that old Judge Hopkins was there.

Judge Hopkins wasn't a judge; he was a banker, now retired. His first name was Judge. He was a gentleman of the old South whose wife died right before he left the bank. He had been coming to Miss Lulu's once a month since then for companionship. He demanded little more than a sympathetic ear and some hand manipulation. His visits rarely took more than thirty minutes. Judge Hopkins was probably my easiest client, and one whom I remember fondly. I called him Monsieur Judge, and he referred to me as Déchue. Miss Lulu impressed upon me the importance of using a false name so that crazy or love-struck clients wouldn't be able to find me. I chose Déchue, I suppose, as a sort of penance, a reminder of my father's disappointment.

That first foray into the world of prostitution would have been a disaster had it not been for Monsieur Judge. I rushed through all my other deliveries so that I could arrive early at Miss Lulu's. I determined that between arriving early and staying a little late, I had a solid two hours. As soon as I walked in the door Miss Lulu turned me over to one of her more experienced girls, an unusually blonde woman who was not happy about having to take me under her wing.

"Chantal, take this pauper upstairs, and see what you can make of her. She has an appointment with Judge Hopkins in a half hour."

Chantal grabbed me by my upper arm with a grip that left bruises and pushed me ahead of her, down the hall and up the staircase, to a room with a small stove, a wash basin and a long rack of the gaudiest clothing I had ever seen. She poured some water from a kettle on the stove into the washbasin.

"Strip and wash." She handed me a towel and jar of foul-smelling brown liquid. "When you've washed, rub some of this between your legs."

"What is it?"

"If you've got insects, it will kill them. If he's got insects it will discourage them."

Judge Hopkins was a sweet old man, and I must confess that had it not been for the sex, such as it was, I would have viewed him as a second father. From that first day he expressed an interest in my welfare and often slipped me a little extra money, admonishing me to, "Keep this hid from Lulu, or you'll never see a sou of it."

❧

As time went on I worked for Miss Lulu with more regularity. I had decided to build up an escape fund so that Mathieu and I could move north. I never spent any of the money I made at Lulu White's. Instead, I established an account with her, the same way Catey had. There was a little spending money from the gifts Monsieur Judge gave me, but I mostly used it to buy things for Mathieu that the nuns didn't supply. They kept us in food and were a constant source of clean diapers, but he was growing and needed new clothing and the occasional toy. Had I been smarter I would have realized that bringing any purchase to the House would cause suspicion. Sister Berenice would have been willing to look the other way, but Betty still had it out for me, and she made a big show of it, waving Mathieu's little doll and rattle in the Sister's face and demanding to know how I could afford such "extravagances." Sister Berenice didn't indulge her but later took me aside to question me. She handed me the toys.

"I'm afraid I have to ask, Justine; where did you get the money to buy these things?"

I knew I couldn't tell her the truth, but I'm afraid I wasn't quick enough to give her a clever answer. I looked down at the floor and tried to look contrite. "I stole them, Sister." I believe she knew that was a lie, but she just clucked her tongue and handed me the toys.

The next time I went out to deliver laundered linens I noticed one of the girls from the House of the Good Shepard walking on the other side of the street. I gave her a wave and didn't think much of it, but later that afternoon I noticed her again, standing across from the St. Louis Hotel where I was to drop off a bundle of towels. I began to notice a girl from the House every time I went out. It wasn't always the same girl, but they always had the same air of casualness, as though they had nowhere to be and just happened to be standing or walking along my route. I knew I couldn't spend any time at Miss Lulu's with one of those snoops hanging about, so I decided not to entertain any customers until my shadows had been recalled. This might have worked had I not missed seeing the girl who was following me on my last delivery day. It was Betty, of course, and she was much cleverer than the others. She had memorized my route and timed her arrival at each stop so that she got there after I had gone in to make my delivery. She knew I was inside because I always left my little delivery cart parked by the entrance. Miss Lulu had informed me the day before that Monsieur Judge would be there and looking forward to seeing me after so long an absence. I searched up and down the street before going in and, seeing no girl from the house, decided to spend time with my favorite customer. That night all hell broke loose.

Despite having a quiet voice that sounded like a child gargling marbles, Sister Constance shouted, "You have shamed yourself and The House of the Good Shepard, and you have shamed me. You were seen entering a house of consignation on Customhouse Street from which you did not emerge for two hours. You have money in your pocket, which you could not have had when you left this morning to make your rounds. This is behavior of a most onerous nature and must be dealt with accordingly."

Sister Berenice held me, lightly, by the arm while Sister Constance's bony hand shook the money she had taken from my pocket in my face. I was too panicked to think of a plausible lie, so I just stood there, dumbly nodding my head. Sister Berenice tried to intervene on my behalf, but it was a half-hearted attempt.

"Now Sister, we don't know for certain..."

"She is one of your charges, Sister Berenice, and if you can't manage them any better than this..." She shook her head. "I'm reluctant to make any decisions in the heat of anger, but this is not your only troublesome girl. It may be time for a reassignment. As for you." She turned her attention back to me. "You are a mother; are you not? We may not be able to prevent you from destroying your own life, but we will not permit you to destroy your child's life, as well. I believe I have just the solution for this little problem."

Sister Berenice tried to comfort me as she escorted me back to the dormitory.

"Don't fret. I'll have a word with Sister Constance. I'm sure she'll be more sympathetic once she's had some time to calm down."

I thanked her for her help and went to the nursery to fetch Mathieu. I gave him his supper and went to bed. I was in no mood to face the other girls at dinner that night.

A few days later I was at my post, ironing the linens that I was to deliver that afternoon, when Catey came up behind me and tugged at the back of my apron.

"You'd best come with me," she whispered. She took

my hand and led me down to the nursery. Just short of the doorway she pulled me aside. "Peek around the doorframe, but don't let them see you."

I did as she said and saw my Mathieu being cradled in the arms of a well-dressed woman wearing an enormous feathered hat. A large man in a frock coat stood next to her and made cooing noises while he lightly pinched Mathieu's cheek. I was stunned. I didn't know what to do. Catey took me by the arm, again, and led me back down the hall.

"What are they doing?" I asked. "Why is that woman holding my baby?"

"The Sisters mean to give him away. Them or some other couple will adopt him."

"They can't do that. He's my child. Why would they want to do that?"

"Sister Constance says you're not fit to raise him. She wants to give him to these aristos because the woman is barren."

"What about me? Don't I have a say?"

"Sure, you've a say. The same say as the rest of us. You can stay here and take it or cast your ballot with your feet. Take your baby and run as far away from here as you can."

That night I wrapped our meager belongings in a blanket, tied the blanket across my back and tiptoed down the hallway to the front door. Mathieu and I were off to Lulu White's.

THIRTY-TWO

Duchamp couldn't get enough of Wayne's tuna salad. Adding the chopped anchovy sautéed in olive oil had been a stroke of genius. The guy was turning out to be a pretty good cook. He had instructed Wayne not to answer the phone without checking the caller I.D. first. He didn't know what Runyon wanted to talk to him about, and he didn't want to find out. Now though, the caller I.D. was showing him the number of Joe Pasternak. He picked up. The voice on the other end said, "Tee Ray, my man!"

"Please, don't use that name, Joe. I can't imagine you'd like me to call you The Mozo. It's not the sort of name one associates with a well-respected investment counselor and a pillar of the community."

"Point taken, Raymond. I was just feeling a little nostalgic. Life inside may have been boring, but it was infinitely less complicated than my life is now. I have some news that should uncomplicate things for both of us, though."

"Such as?"

"I've found a buyer for your painting."

"How much?"

"You know that a stolen painting only brings a fraction of its value, right?"

"Yes, yes. How much?"

"The cheap bastard started at two million, but I remembered your instructions not to settle for less than ten. We're splitting this, right? Fifty-fifty?"

"Sixty-forty is what we agreed." He was getting angry, now, but careful to control his tone said, "How much?"

"Eleven. I showed him all the auction records for

Turners over the last fifteen years. Bring me the painting, and I'll take care of the rest. I've already got one of my guys working on a new set of documents to establish provenance for my buyer. Eleven mill, Tee Ray!"

⁕

Duchamp waited in the Lincoln while Wayne and the meth head went to the girl's dorm. Wayne had argued against the plan all morning, not because he didn't want to kidnap the girl but because he didn't want to involve the meth head.

"People like that can't be trusted. He'll get spooked and run off or get whatever that thing is where they start to sweat and shake when they're coming down off their high. Then I'll be left trying to deal with the girl and his bullshit, too. I hate these damn meth heads. Where the hell did you find this guy?"

"He used to be a shrimper, then he started using crystal and lost his boat. Now he lives over in the projects. He does little jobs for me once in awhile. He got us a whole box of burner phones."

"Well, why can't you come up there with us? You handle the guy."

"I've told you. A kidnapping takes three people, two to handle the girl and one to act as lookout and wait with the car. I can't trust the speed freak to wait with the car, and you're stronger than me. You'll have an easier time handling her. Take your cell phone. Call me right before you go into the room, and keep the line open. I'll be able to hear what you're doing, and if anything goes wrong, I'll come up to help."

The speed freak's name was Mark and, despite his neatly ironed pants and clean shirt, he smelled like a plate of coleslaw that had been left out in the sun too long. He was as tall as Wayne, but probably weighed fifty pounds less. Duchamp had promised him a bonus if he showed up straight. The man had made an effort. He was alert and ready to do whatever he was told and, though he was sweating profusely, he didn't have the shakes. Duchamp listened as Wayne jimmied the back door open and directed his assistant into the building and up the back steps. He heard the knock on the door to his niece's room, a short scuffle, and then Wayne's voice asking for advice.

"Man, both girls are here. I thought you said your niece would be in class."

"I thought she was. Well, they've seen you, now. You'll have to take them both.

"There're not going to come quietly. The other one doesn't seem to be afraid of the gun, and she's arguing with the meth head."

"Well, keep her quiet."

Wayne turned to Mark and said, "Hey, Stinky, keep her quiet. Put your hand over her mouth. If she bites you, you can slug her."

"Don't hurt them, Wayne. Use the plastic straps to cuff them. Gag them if they won't be quiet."

"Oh shit."

"What?"

"The fucking guy slugged her. I don't think she's out, but she looks woozy. What should we do? I don't want to carry her. She might wake up and start squirming."

"Try walking them down the back steps. I'll meet you at the back door and help you take them to the car. Can you walk her?"

"I guess if I hold on to her, but I can't walk her and hold the gun on the other one at the same time. I'm not giving my gun to a meth head, so don't even ask."

"Okay. Have Mark walk her. Check the hallway and

the staircase before you bring them out of the room."

They put the girls in the backseat of the car with Mark, who sat glaring at Angelina and sucking his hand where she bit it. She was sprawled out on the leather seat with her eyes closed and her head on Madeleine's shoulder.

"I shoulda knocked this bitch clean out is what I shoulda done."

"Shut up, Mark." Duchamp didn't turn around, but he knew Madeleine had recognized him. Well, that was the way the skein was unwinding. He'd just have to work with it. Surely, the scientist would swap the ownership papers for his daughter. He couldn't take her to his house, though. That would really be foolish. He couldn't let the speed freak get away either. No telling who he'd run his mouth to. Besides, he might still be useful. He'd drive the lot of them out to his father's old fish camp near Slidell. He had spent plenty of time there as a kid and knew all the different channels that he could use as escape routes out of there, provided the old jon boat was still in the boathouse. He'd stop and pick up a little outboard motor and a jerry can of gas on the way. First, they had to swing by Didi's. He got out his cell phone. Her voice on the other end answered, "Psychic hot line."

"Then why didn't you know it was me?"

"Raymond. Darlin', I was just thinking about you."

"And I was just thinking about you. Call your mother and ask her if she'll look after Tyler for a few days. Things are happening, and I need your help."

THIRTY-THREE

McKinney went with Nina to return the forgery of "The City in the Sea" manuscript to her friend, Logan Bradley. He had imagined the millionaire living in an ornate stone mansion up in Winnetka or Kenilworth and was disappointed to learn that he lived in a Lincoln Park condo. It was a very nice condo, of course, but didn't have the gravitas called for by an original Poe manuscript, forged or not. Even stranger was the condo's décor. The wide foyer was lined with vintage video games, arcade versions of Pac-Man and Space Invaders. The living room was filled with cocktail table versions of these same games, including the granddaddy of them all, Pong.

They were let in by a uniformed butler and seated at a Frogger table next to a window overlooking the zoo and Lake Michigan beyond. Opposite them was a fireplace over which hung a number of plaques—awards from the video game industry. McKinney thought it odd that the fireplace was lit and noticed that the screen was open. It had been a chilly spring, but today was in the upper sixties. Perhaps it was to provide atmosphere. It was a real wood-burning fireplace, popping sparks onto the carpet and scenting the condo with the smell of burning pine. The butler brought them each a glass of sparkling water. He set the glasses on coasters he pulled from a pocket then disappeared down a hallway that McKinney imagined went to the kitchen.

McKinney whispered to Nina, "Where do you suppose he keeps his rare books and manuscripts?"

She whispered back, "He probably has a room especially for them. I think he owns this whole floor. Why are we whispering?"

"I don't know. Except for the crackling fire and the beeping of the games it's very quiet in here. It feels like a video game museum."

Logan Bradley came in holding a phone to his ear. In his other hand was a half-full bottle of beer. He was wearing, what looked to McKinney like, jeans, sneakers, and a plain white t-shirt. He put his hand over the mouthpiece, said, "Be right back," and went out. Nina pointed a finger at her open mouth and made a gagging noise.

McKinney asked, "What?"

"He's wearing a four hundred dollar Calvin Klein t-shirt. I'll bet his pants cost five. And those beat up sneakers? Thom Brownes. Probably go for seven hundred or more."

"So he's wearing clothing that looks normal, that should have cost less than a hundred dollars, but it cost sixteen hundred dollars? Why would he do that?" He wasn't whispering now. "Why would anyone do that?"

"Shh. Keep your voice down. I hoped he'd outgrown that kind of hubris. When we were in college there were all these rich kids who thought they could impress people by buying expensive crap. It was like they were saying, 'I've got so much money I can just throw it away.' None of us middle-class kids were impressed. We just thought it was sad that someone would pay seven hundred dollars for shoes, especially since there are so many people in the world who don't even own a pair of shoes."

Logan Bradley came back into the room. He said, "Sorry 'bout that, Ni-Ni." bent to kiss Nina on the cheek and shook McKinney's hand. "Nina told me what you found. So, the damn poem's a fake, eh? May I see your report?"

McKinney handed him the folder containing his notes and watched as the man flipped through them, laid the folder on the Pong table and set his beer bottle on top of it.

"That asshole."

"Who?" Nina asked. "Who's the owner?"

"My tennis partner, Ian Jamison. We've been playing together for over five years. I never would have believed old Ian would try to screw me, but there it is." He pointed at the folder. "In black and white."

"I'm sorry," Nina said.

McKinney held out the box containing the fraudulent poem, and Bradley took it.

"This is the worthless piece of shit, eh? Oh Jamison, you are in for it now, you bastard." He opened the box, removed the poem, and hurled the box across the room. He shouted, "Lousy son of a..." and tore the paper in half.

Nina rose up in her seat and said, "Logan, no!" but Bradley tore the paper again, marched to the fireplace, and laid the pieces onto the top log. The edges of the paper curled. The paper smoked for a few seconds, then burst into flame.

"Didn't you need to return that? What's your tennis partner going to say?"

"Fuck him. He'll be lucky if I don't sue him. I should sic the cops on him or something." He turned to McKinney. "I've got your report if he tries to get back at me for destroying his forgery, but I may have to have my attorneys depose you. Don't worry, you'll be paid for your time."

"And the analysis?" McKinney asked.

"Of course. Send me a bill." He looked at Nina. "Ni-Ni, I'm pretty upset. I hope you'll excuse me." He turned abruptly and left the room. The butler appeared almost immediately and showed them to the door.

It was close to rush hour, so McKinney and Nina had

to stand as they rode the bus back North, up Clark Street. They both gripped the overhead rail and stood face to face, occasionally being jostled into each other or into one of the other standing commuters.

"That was quite a performance," McKinney said.

"Yeah. Wait. What do you mean?"

"Burning the poem. That was staged for our benefit."

"What makes you think that?"

"We were shown to a room with a fire burning in the fireplace. Logan Bradley was in some other room when we arrived. The butler brought coasters in for our drinks. They use coasters in that room, but Logan had to set his beer bottle on top of my report because there was no coaster for him. He had been in another room, so why the fire?"

"Maybe they lit the fireplace just for us."

"Maybe. Why didn't they close the fireplace screen? Sparks were popping out and singeing the carpet. Then, despite his show of anger, throwing the box and tearing up the poem, he carefully laid the paper on the fire instead of crumpling it up and tossing it in. He knew he was going to burn the poem and didn't want to be talked out of it."

The bus hit a pothole and they were tossed together, Nina's forehead smacking McKinney on the chin.

She leaned up and kissed his chin. "Why would he stage that?"

"I don't know, but I think he did. I think there's something about this transaction that he's not telling you."

"Well, I'm going to ask him." She kissed him again, on the mouth this time. "Are we going to your place?"

"It's still a wreck. I haven't straightened it up, yet."

"Okay, my place it is."

THIRTY-FOUR

I only spent a few weeks at Lulu White's. The other girls, who had been rather cool to me before, were crazy about Mathieu with the result that I now had a houseful of new friends. There was never any problem finding someone to watch the child while I was with a customer. Lulu, on the other hand, was not fond of children. She made a grand production of leaving the room whenever I came in with him, claiming that the "smell of babies" gave her headaches.

My new friends began to share their stories with me while they played with, and fawned over, Mathieu. Most of those stories were about their customers—the fat drunk, the soldier who cried like a baby, the deformed preacher. The stories that disturbed me most, though, were the ones about Lulu White's miserliness. Several of the girls had asked her for an accounting of their finances and been shown a set of books that reflected less than half their earnings. I had no intention of working as a whore for the rest of my days. I needed to know that my savings were secure so I could make a life for myself and my son, but whenever I asked Lulu how much was in my account she'd chuckle and say, "If the men like you well enough, you'll be rich while you're young enough to enjoy it."

I left Lulu White's because of Monsieur Judge. Rather, I should say Monsieur Judge helped me to leave Lulu White's. One hot afternoon Mathieu just wouldn't be comforted by any of the girls. There were times only his mother would do, consequently I left Monsieur Judge waiting while I rocked the child to sleep. When I explained what I had been doing he asked to see the boy. I fetched Mathieu from the little crib we had devised for him. Upon seeing my son, Monsieur Judge immediately broke into tears.

"You are a mother," he cried.

"Well, of course. You knew that. We've talked of it often."

"But I never thought..." He reached for Mathieu, and I handed him over, cautioning silence as the boy still slept. Monsieur Judge cradled him in his arms. "He is a beautiful child. As beautiful as his mother."

"You exaggerate, Monsieur, but I thank you."

He kissed Mathieu on his forehead and handed him back to me. There were tears on the old fellow's cheeks, and he produced an enormous kerchief from inside his coat to wipe them. He sat down on the only chair in the room, a large cane chair that practically enveloped his small frame, and motioned for me to sit across from him on the bed, which I did. His shoulders were hunched and he took on an air of sadness.

"I'm afraid we are very near the end of our time together," he said.

I didn't understand his meaning at first and looked at the clock on the bedside table. He continued, "I mean that I will not come to see you again. I wish there was some way to make you understand what our time together has meant to me. You have managed to bring some joy and a touch of lost youth into the life of a lonely old man."

I started to speak, but he waved his hand to silence me.

"I understand that ours was a transaction, a service rendered for coin, but I've been with others in your profession, and you are the only one who seemed truly glad of our visits. We have talked and laughed together, and I never once sensed that you were dishonest with me. I had thought it merely a skill you had learned, but now I understand that it is your gift." He sighed. "I see now that you are indeed a mother, and that is how I must think of you."

"But what does that have to do with us? If you enjoy my company, why can we not continue as before?" I started to panic. Monsieur Judge was the only customer I was truly glad to see.

"This might simply be the lunacy of an old man; I'll admit I have not kept up with modern schools of thought, but it seems to me that, as a mother, you have accepted a higher calling. My recollection of my own dear mother is of her angelic countenance, smiling down on me. I could never do or say anything to tarnish that sweet woman's memory. I must accord you the same respect."

"But we could just talk." I felt myself on the verge of tears. "I won't even charge you much, only Lulu White's percentage."

He rested his hand on my knee. "We'll speak again, tomorrow. I will be here at the noon hour. You must be ready for me at that time, and you must have your child with you."

I started to ask him why he wanted Mathieu there, but he simply hushed me and left the room, still dabbing at his eyes as he went.

∽

I did as I was asked, and the next day Mathieu and I were both present. The boy was awake this time, and when Monsieur Judge held out his index finger Mathieu grabbed it with his tiny hand. As before, I sat on the bed, and Monsieur judge occupied the chair.

"I have been aware for some time that you are supposed to be a ward of the Sisters at the House of the Good Shepard and that you are hiding here in violation of the law."

I gripped the iron bed frame so tightly that my fingers

ached. How had he discovered this, and what did he intend to do? My breathing grew heavy, but I kept silent.

"I tell you this because I know you cannot freely roam the streets of New Orleans. Your options outside Lulu White's are limited. Lulu White is also aware of this and would likely use it to her advantage. Should you decide to leave her employ you would have to move from the city, and that would require money. No matter how long you work here, Lulu White will never give you enough money to leave. She will ply you with excuses."

"I'm sure you're right. I do want to leave some day, but for now I believe Mathieu and I are safe here."

He locked his eyes to mine and spoke slowly, drawing out each word. "You are not. Perhaps you are out of the Good Sisters' reach here, but there is a price that all women who remain in your profession must pay. As dear as you are to me, I was selfish enough that I would have let you pay that price, but I see now that your child would pay as well."

"To what do you refer? What price?"

"Your own view of your worth. You would only know men for whom you are an item to be purchased. You would think us incapable of giving you love and unwilling to give you respect. You would learn to hate us, and your son, who would then view the world with a jaundiced eye, would adopt this hatred as well. You must leave this profession, and you must leave this city."

"But you have, yourself, pointed out the flaw in this logic. I have no money. This is what I must do to survive. And why do you tell me these things when you are about to abandon me? You tell me this is our last meeting, and you implore me to leave." I picked up his hand. "Why won't you continue our relations, such as they are. If I am dear to you then you know how much I need a friend, for I have none."

He took his hand back, reached into the pocket of his jacket and withdrew a large envelope. "I am your friend, as you will see. You have told me that the child's father was killed in the anti-Italian riots. The boy is, for all purposes, Italian. In this envelope is a ticket for passage on a ship to Venice, Italy as well as a thousand dollars to establish yourself when you get there. The ship leaves tonight. Tell me that you will go, and the envelope is yours."

"But Monsieur, this is my home. How can I leave New Orleans?"

"I chose Venice because it is very much like New Orleans, or so I've heard. However, do not delude yourself, New Orleans is no longer your home. One way or another, it is your prison."

THIRTY-FIVE

The only way in to the fish camp from the pavement was a rutted road that wound through the mangroves and was half submerged during the rainy season. Duchamp wasn't sure the Lincoln would make it. The car didn't have a lot of ground clearance, so when he drove in the ruts the undercarriage scraped along, uprooting weeds and making him even more nervous than he was already. Despite having spent a good part of his youth at this camp, he was still creeped out by the Spanish moss hanging from the trees. His father had teased that it was witch's hair. It gave the dilapidated cabin an eerie look. The car had a full load, Duchamp and Wayne in the front with Didi between them and Angelina, Madeleine and Mark in the back. Wayne sat turned in the passenger seat so he could keep an eye on the two college girls, but he didn't seem to be paying much attention to them, gazing out the window as they drove and occasionally glancing at the little .38 Chief's Special in his hand as though he wasn't sure why he was holding it.

Duchamp stopped the car in sight of the cabin and made them all get out and walk. The road was muddy for the last quarter mile, and he didn't want to chance the bullet-proof car getting stuck, especially if they had to leave in a hurry. They sank up to their ankles in the mud, and Mark spit on the car as it lumbered past. "This is some motherfuckin' bullshit is what this is."

The cabin at the fish camp was right on the Old Pearl River, hidden in the bayous out past Slidell. The jon boat was in the boathouse, suspended above the water on a pulley system. There was a small concrete pad on high ground behind the cabin, and Duchamp worked the car back and forth until it sat on the pad facing the rutted track. He told Mark and Wayne to take the girls into the cabin and went to the boathouse to lower the old aluminum boat into the water and install the new outboard motor. He wanted the option to run by land or water if the need should arise. He also wanted to be warned if anyone approached the cabin. He opened the Lincoln's trunk and took out a roll of twine and a box of empty bottles and cans he had brought for that purpose. He walked back up the road and stretched a length of twine across the road at, what he estimated to be, bumper height, fastening it to trees on either side. Then, he strung the bottles and cans between two trees closer to the cabin and connected the two strands with more twine. A car driving toward the cabin would catch the string and raise a racket—the same alarm system he and his brother had rigged as kids. He opened the trunk again and took out two guns, a 9mm Glock in a holster that he clipped to his belt and a pump action Remington shotgun. He lifted out a large box of supplies and a cooler of food and drinking water. He put the shotgun back in the trunk, closed the trunk lid, and went around to the front of the cabin. The dilapidated structure sat up on concrete flood blocks for the times when the river breached its banks.

The two college girls sat at the edge of one of the wooden bunks. Their hands, still strapped at the wrists, were in their laps, and they were careful not to touch the filthy mattress. Madeleine hung her head. The five bunks, the chairs, the dinette table; everything was covered with a thin brown film. The cabin hadn't been used in years and moisture had combined with dust to coat the furniture. There was mold in the sink, though that didn't matter to Duchamp since there was no running water. In fact, the state of the cabin didn't bother him at all. They wouldn't be staying long, a few days at most.

What did bother him was Wayne. The big guy had been acting skittish since they grabbed the girls. Duchamp needed to be able to count on him. He set the cooler on the floor and the box on the table and lifted out a bag of groceries. He pointed to the bag.

"I've got everything you asked for, Wayne. There's about four hundred dollars worth of food here. Not exactly gourmet chow, but dinner's your department. I'm sure it'll be delicious."

Wayne nodded, still looking distracted.

Mark said, "When do we eat, Big Guy? I'm runnin' on empty here."

Wayne didn't answer.

Didi pulled a roll of paper towels from the box and used one to clean off a chair. She set the Spider-man backpack she had borrowed from Tyler on the chair and looked at the girls. "Well, I'll tell you the first thing we ought to do. We ought to get our little captives here to clean this place up. It's disgusting and probably unhealthy. We certainly don't need to catch some kind of fungal infection or get a lung ailment from mold spores. Why don't you untie their hands, Raymond, so we can put them to work? Believe me, they are not going to run off and risk being ripped apart by gators like a couple of wild pigs." She looked at the girls. "Are you darlings?"

The girls shook their heads, and Duchamp pulled a small folding knife from his pocket and cut their restraints. Didi handed the paper towels and a bottle of disinfectant to Angelina, then she unzipped her backpack, took out a dried sage smudge stick, and lit it. Pungent smoke curled up from the sage as she walked around the little cabin, giving it a good psychic cleansing. "I knew this would come in handy."

THIRTY-SIX

McKinney got home a little after nine. He came in the back door, through the kitchen. He still hadn't fixed the lock on his front door, which was jammed shut.

Things hadn't gone well at Nina's. The absence of the abstract expressionist paintings from her living room should have been a clue. They had made love, and afterward, she pushed McKinney out of bed. "Go wait in the kitchen," she said. "I have to make the bed." He waited in the kitchen for a half hour. Finally, he heard the sound of a vacuum cleaner and went looking. He found her sitting on the bedroom floor, naked and crying, the bed made, their clothes folded, and the vacuum cleaner standing in the middle of the room making a terrible growling noise. He switched it off and sat next to her on the floor. He tried to put an arm around her shoulders, but she pushed him away. "Go home, Sean. I'm not normal." She pointed at the crisp hospital corners on the neatly made bed. "This is my normal." She refused to be comforted, so he had come home.

He bent to take a bottle of Negra Modello out of the refrigerator, and when he straightened up he noticed the light on his answering machine blinking.

The first message was from Beth, "Sean, there's a Live For Today meeting next Tuesday night at seven. We'd love to see you there."

Maybe he was reading meaning into her message that wasn't there, but it sounded like it wasn't so much "we" but Beth who wanted to see him at the meeting.

The second message was a woman's voice, too, only huskier and with a little drawl. She spoke slowly. "Mister

McKinney. You have some documents we would very much like to have. They are the ownership papers to a valuable painting. It's titled Massacre on the Zong and was painted by an artist named Turner. Those documents are among the papers you were asked to examine by your daughter's roommate, Madeleine Duchamp. We have invited Madeleine and your daughter to stay with us for a while." Her voice sounded playful now, confident. "They would both appreciate it if you would bring us those papers. We will phone you again in a little while to give you directions. You see our place is a little bit off the beaten path."

After the answering machine clicked off, McKinney used his cell phone to call Harve Duchamp.

THIRTY-SEVEN

The less I tell you of our voyage to Venice the better. It seemed interminable, and I was seasick often. Mathieu didn't fare any better.

Venice was a city of contrasts. The first thing I noticed was the fairytale beauty of the canals and the little boats that traversed them. The boats were painted in bright colours and the oarsmen, gondoliers they are called, were colourfully dressed as well. The whole city seemed to swell and recede with the tide. The people, too, moved with this rhythm as they went about their daily tasks. A great many of them were merchants, with the rest being tradesmen of some sort. Riding in one of the boats along the Grand Canal or crossing one of the hundreds of bridges always presented a delightful spectacle that was tainted by the stench that rose from those waters. While the streets of New Orleans could stink of discarded food and horse manure, Venice stank of the sewerage that was released into the sea.

Upon arrival, I took Mathieu to one of the smaller Catholic Churches on the island, the Chiesa di San Salvador near the Rialto bridge. Saint Mark's cathedral was too imposing a structure, and I surmised that the priests would be too busy to help a foreign woman who spoke little Italian. The Chiesa di San Salvador was indeed the correct choice. It was a hot day and a long walk from the boat landing along the narrow twisting streets, and by the time we reached the church I was exhausted and Mathieu was more than a little fussy. I had bundled our few belongings into a blanket which I carried slung across my back. I knew I was in the right place, though, because when I entered the church I was greeted by the most beautiful painting of the angel Gabriel telling the Holy Virgin of The Lord's plan for her. At any other time I might have thought the look of surprise on her face comical, but at that moment I felt that she and I had much in common for, if The Lord gives our lives direction, I couldn't fathom His purpose in bringing me to Venice any more than Mary had understood the message of the seraphim.

I was standing admiring this magnificent artwork and wiping the perspiration from my face when one of the priests, Father Beniamino, approached me. I was distressed by my poor attempt to speak his language, and in frustration, I lapsed into French. As a happy accident, we had that language in common. There was, in fact, a community of French expatriates to whom the Father introduced me. It was a small community, Catholic but secular in nature. In the months to come we would spend many happy evenings in the Piazza San Marco, drinking sweet vermouth and sharing stories of our homelands. A married couple, Lucien and Inès invited me to stay with them. Lucien's mother lived with them in their small palazzo on the Rio de la Tana, and she took charge of Mathieu as well as Lucien and Inès' daughter.

One warm evening, as we strolled along the Riva degli Schiavoni to our favorite restaurant in Piazza San Marco, a young man wearing an open-collared boater's shirt and a red kerchief tied around his neck approached us. My first thought was that he wished to sell us a ride in his gondola or that he was one of the many beggars who frequented the Venetian Piazze. His hair was matted and dirty; his face was beard-stubbled, and his manner toward Lucien was rough. The man ran up to us, slapped Lucien on the back, kissed both Inès' hand and mine, and shouted, "Bonsoir, frère Lucien et ses petites poupées. Quand est-ce que nous mangeons?" He was Lucien's brother, Alain Duchamp, and, yes, he was your grandfather, and a more disreputable looking character I had never seen. His appearance, he assured us, was the result of some sort of rowing contest, but I wasn't convinced.

The four of us crowded around a small table that the waiter had covered with a variety of breads and cheeses. He was about to mix us a round of the Austrian drink, Spritzer, when Alain pulled the young man aside, pushed a pile of coins into his hands, and whispered something to him. The waiter trotted off to a little shop across the square and returned with a bottle of absinthe and a small dish of sugar cubes. "We did not rid ourselves of the Habsburgs to continue drinking their soda water," Alain said and handed us each a sugar cube and a glass and gave us our instructions. "There are several ways to partake of this nectar," he said. "You can balance the sugar on a slotted spoon and pour cold water over it into the absinthe, giving it a cloudy appearance, or you can use my technique." He poured the absinthe into his glass, then held a sugar cube between his front teeth and drank, allowing the liquid to flow over the sugar.

I poured a little of the liquor into my glass and sipped it. It's initial astringent flavour repulsed me, and I almost spit it back into the glass, but I didn't want to appear foolish, so I swallowed quickly and smiled. The aftertaste was of licorice or anise and was not entirely unpleasant. My tablemates were all busy preparing their own concoctions, so I thought my discomfort had gone unnoticed. Alain, however, must have seen my grimace. He patted me on the back.

"Well done, mademoiselle. I take it this is your first meeting with the green fairy?"

"We have an establishment in New Orleans called The Absinthe Room, but, yes, I've never tasted it before."

"Allow me to suggest that you use the sugar next time.

It improves the flavour."

I placed the sugar cube precariously between my teeth and took another sip. The sweetness made it easier to tolerate the foul stuff. Alain was pleased.

"Génial! In the words of France's second greatest poet, Baudelaire, one must intoxicate oneself unceasingly. You are off to a fine beginning."

"You say Baudelaire was France's second greatest poet; who is the first?"

Alain stood and, with a flourish of his hand, bowed from the waist. "I am pleased to recite for you this evening, if you wish. By the third absinthe my words will flow more freely than this delectable concoction."

Lucien tugged at the hem of Alain's shirt. "Brother, please. Sit down. Must you always...?"

Alain sat. "Indeed, brother, I must." He suddenly became quite serious. "Life is meant for living. What good can there be to merely pass through it like sleepwalkers, our bodies animate but our hearts asleep? It will be as if we never existed to begin with. I need to assure myself that I am here."

"Of that," I said, feeling bold, "there is no doubt."

He looked at me for a moment then threw his head back in a full-throated laugh. "Oh, we shall have to keep you. Brother, you have unearthed a gem." He turned in his chair then and began to survey the piazza. It was just dusk, and the light glittering off the water painted the paving stones with oranges and purples. There were swallows overhead, soaring through the air to dine on whatever insects hadn't been blown out to sea by the evening breeze. Children's feet slapped the pavement, and the balconies were crowded with people. A small band played off in a far corner, but the tuba was the only instrument whose sound carried to us. The fashionably dressed characters who flooded into the piazza seemed to step in time to its pulse. Alain pointed to an elderly couple coming from the imposing structure of Saint Mark's Cathedral. The woman was stooped and tightly gripped the man's arm. He shuffled along slowly, scanning the ground in front of them by turning his head from side to side. As they approached I could see that the old fellow was compensating for an eye that was clouded over. Still, they were smartly dressed, and the woman smiled up at him as they walked.

"An ode to the old."

I put my hand on Alain's arm. "Quiet," I said. "They'll hear you."

He lowered his voice and continued. "When I was a young man, I saw with a young man's eyes. I desired the world, but no matter how quickly I pursued, it was always just beyond my reach. I lived in the someday. Now, I am an old man, and I see with an old man's eyes, and you are my world and, I am here with you in the now."

I looked at this sweaty, smelly, drunken man, perhaps not France's greatest poet, but not bad. "Génial!" I said. I saluted Alain's poem with another sip of the wretched licorice potion, but before I could speak again my attention was drawn to the old man's coat as he and his wife continued across the square. It was a white frock coat, similar to those worn by Louisiana planters. From the back, the man reminded me of my father. I hadn't thought of him in quite a while, my attention having been occupied by concern for my son. I was inundated by a wave of sadness and left the table. I found a dark corner under one of the balconies where I could stand by myself and cry. I spent several minutes there, sniffling and missing my family and feeling ashamed of my tears. I was a woman of the world, after all, with a son to raise in a strange country. I couldn't afford the weakness of regret or maudlin sentiment. I no longer owned a hand kerchief and was wiping my nose on my sleeve when Alain appeared beside me in the dark. He held out a rag, which I used to blow my nose.

"I didn't mean to upset you."

He really was an egotist. "It wasn't your poem. The old gentleman reminded me of my father."

"Your father is dead?"

"We are estranged." I wiped my eyes. "It's nothing." I held out his kerchief and noticed that it was the one that had been about his neck. He put his hands behind his back.

"You may keep it," he said.

THIRTY-EIGHT

"You left him a message?!"

Didi looked hurt. "Don't yell at me, Raymond. I'll call him back. I just wanted to give him something to think about."

Wayne had taken Didi out in the boat, running it upriver until they could see Highway 10 and get a weak cell phone signal. It seemed that one of the flaws in Raymond's plan was the lack of cell phone reception at the cabin. Didi had called the scientist, left a message on his machine, then dropped the burner phone over the side. It was a good thing they had brought a whole box of phones.

Duchamp said, "It just seems like a bad idea to me, is all." He worked to sound calm. "I'm trying to keep control of the situation. I don't want this guy having any advance knowledge."

They were outside the cabin, sitting on empty fuel drums down by the water. There was a crisp breeze keeping off the mosquitoes, and it was hot as hell in the cabin. Duchamp had screwed big eye bolts to the bunks and cuffed the girls to them. Let them sweat. He needed to know where they were.

Didi put her hand on his arm. "Darlin', you worry too much. I'm going in to check on the girls."

He watched Didi walk up the steps to the cabin, rolling her hips as she walked, teasing him, even though there was no place for them to be alone, except maybe the Lincoln parked out back. As she went in, Wayne came out, and Duchamp called him over. He dug in his pants pocket and came up with a handcuff key. "Wayne, take this and unlock our guests. Bring 'em down here." He handed Wayne the key. "And ask Didi and Mark to come out, too. I want to have a little chat with everyone."

Wayne shrugged and went back inside, emerging a few minutes later leading everyone down to the river. Didi held the two girls by the arms. Mark lagged behind, a peanut butter sandwich in one hand and a joint in the other. Duchamp waited until they were all at the river's edge, then stood and faced the group, knowing what he wanted to say but debating the best way to get his point across. He decided to start with a little joke. "You're all probably wondering why I've called you here today." No one cracked a smile. "All right, let's square the circle. We are partners in an enterprise that is going to make us a lot of money." He looked at Angelina and Madeleine. "Except for you girls, of course. This is a risky venture, but I've planned it thoroughly. However, it's going to take cooperation from each of you, and when I say cooperation I mean do as you're told. No complaining. No backtalk." He looked at Didi. "And no improvising."

Mark raised the hand holding the sandwich. "Be that as it may, bitch, you still ain't told me what my cut of the fuckin' pie is. We're out here in the swamp gettin' all bit up by bugs and shit. I'm takin' the same risk as y'all and figure I oughta be in for an equal share." Wayne rolled his eyes and laughed. Mark pointed the sandwich at him. "And I'm sick of Shitting Bull here and his fucked up remarks. I'm guessin' your maw didn't teach her papoose any motherfuckin' manners."

Wayne slapped the sandwich out of Mark's hand and lifted him off the ground by the front of his shirt. Duchamp snapped, "Enough!" Wayne shook the meth head once and set him back on the ground. Mark picked up his sandwich, pealed the two slices of bread apart, and proceeded to lick the peanut butter off.

Duchamp said, "See, this is what I'm talking about. This kind of bickering is counterproductive."

Mark said, "Well, I ain't too happy about the sleeping arrangements, neither. You got six people and five bunks, and I ain't sleepin' in that car again. With the windows up it's like an oven, but if I put 'em down, the skeeters…" Wayne slapped him on the back of his head, and he shut up.

∽

Duchamp was letting Didi pilot the boat now, showing her how to steer, the boat turning the opposite way you moved the tiller. They traveled downriver to the Chef Menteur highway bridge. "Just keep the bank on your left," he said, "and it'll take you directly here. Keep to the right on your way back." He pointed to one of the channels on the other side of the river. "Don't get mixed up and head up one of those traînasse, or you'll wind up back in the bayous. It's a maze in there. You'd likely run out of gas before you found your way out. Then you'd just be dinner for some gator."

There was a little gravel boat landing with highway access next to the bridge, and Duchamp told Didi, "Throttle down and pull it in slow." The slanted prow of the boat scraped into shore, and Duchamp hopped out and walked up to the roadway. He listened for traffic before stepping up onto the bridge and looked up and down the highway to make sure no cars were approaching. Then he pulled a roll of wire and a large red kerchief from his pocket and tied the kerchief to one of the bridge's steel girders.

He took the tiller on the way back to the fish camp, sitting Didi on the center seat and pointing out obstacles for her to avoid the next time she took the boat out. "Anytime you see ripples on the surface it's probably a rock, a log, or an animal, and you don't want to run up on any of 'em."

"And why am I the lucky gal who gets to pick up the papers? Why can't you send Wayne or go yourself? What if the police are waiting for me?"

"The police aren't going to be waiting for you. This guy knows what'll happen to his daughter if he calls the police. You be sure to remind him when you call to give him his instructions. He won't risk it."

Didi turned and looked Duchamp in the eye. "You wouldn't really hurt those girls, would you?"

"Of course not," he said, but he glanced away, unable to hold her gaze.

"Stop the boat," she said.

"Why?"

"Stop the boat, Raymond, right now, or I won't make the call or go to the rendezvous. I want to read you."

"Don't be ridiculous," he said, but he put the motor in neutral, letting the boat slow down and then drift while the engine idled.

Didi swung her legs around to sit facing Duchamp. She held her hands out, palms up. "Come on, Raymond." Duchamp placed his hands on hers and closed his eyes. They sat that way, nose to nose, for several minutes while the little skiff moved slowly with the current. Clouds rolled by overhead, but didn't obscure the sun. The day was heating up. Beads of sweat rolled down their backs. Finally, Didi dropped his hands and sighed. She sat back on her seat and looked at Duchamp. "Well, someone's going to die, Raymond. I can't tell who, but I'll tell you right now, if you harm those girls we're through."

∞

Duchamp sat on a box on the cabin's front porch and cleaned his Glock. He didn't need to clean the gun, but it gave him something to do, a way not to look obvious while he eavesdropped on Wayne's conversation with Madeleine's roommate, Angelina. Wrapping his fingers over the top of the gun, he nudged the slide back, pushed down both sides of the slide lock and removed the slide. He pushed the recoil spring and guide rod up and removed the barrel.

He had noticed the girl observing them in the cabin while they ate dinner. Wayne had used an old washtub he'd found to rig a fire pit out back on the car pad. He'd boiled some potatoes and ears of corn then thrown in the crawfish he and Mark had dug out of the muck under the riverbank. Everyone agreed it was delicious. While the others jabbered away in between bites of corn, Duchamp had watched the girls. Madeleine ate with her head lowered, avoiding eye contact with any of the kidnappers, but Angelina was watching them, scrutinizing them and listening to their conversation. She even tried to join in, hesitantly asking Wayne what the secret to his tasty cooking was. Wayne smiled modestly and told her he had thrown in a bag of Zatarain's Crab Boil seasoning.

The girl's attitude over dinner had been disconcerting. She was studying them. Now she and Madeleine were sitting on the steps, and Wayne was sitting next to her, swapping recipes. "You guys get a lot of fresh figs down here," Angelina said. "My mother used to slice them and serve them in heavy cream for desert. It's a really simple thing to do, but people think it's sophisticated, and they're sooo good."

Duchamp screwed a bore brush onto a cleaning rod and worked it back and forth through the barrel, then wiped all the metal parts with a clean rag, oiled the slide rails, trigger bar, and barrel lug and reassembled the weapon. He leaned forward, trying to hear what the girl was saying, now.

"If what you really want is to be a chef, why not just go to cooking school? Why are you hanging out with these guys?"

She pointed at Mark, who was down by the river trying to make a hammock by tying a blanket to some rusted pipes attached to the boat house.

Wayne thought for a second. "You make it sound easy, but believe me, there's more to it. Tuition is high, and I don't really have a job. I mean, I do okay as a bodyguard, but I doubt I'd qualify for a student loan. Convicted felons don't usually have high credit scores."

"So, you're going to raise your tuition money by kidnapping people?"

He ignored the question. "Besides, bodyguarding is a full-time gig, so finding the time to go to classes would be tough."

"You'd find the time. Maybe you need to get a different job. Work as a waiter for a while. If you got in at a high-end New Orleans restaurant, you'd make great tips. I can tell. You've got good people skills. Anyway, I don't know about Maddie's family, but my dad hasn't got any money. There's no way he can afford any kind of ransom. I had to take out a bunch of loans to go to Tulane. I'll probably be paying them off for the next thirty years. Unless..." Angelina stopped talking and looked down between her feet at the rotting wooden step. No one spoke for several minutes. Wayne looked at her, waiting for her to finish her thought. Angelina let out a little sob, and Wayne looked away, knowing what she was thinking, knowing she was frightened.

Duchamp tapped in a full clip, racked the slide, pointed his gun off the side of the porch, and pulled the trigger. The noise startled a flock of birds that took off screeching over the marsh. Didi stuck her head out of the cabin door to see what was happening, and Mark came trudging up from the boathouse. He said, "What's with the gunfire, bitch? You see a water moccasin or somethin'?"

Duchamp stood up. "I'm tired of listening to the Ladies' Recipe Exchange Club. Madeleine, you and your friend take care of your outhouse duties, then go cuff yourselves to your bunks. I'll be along in a bit to check your cuffs. Wayne, go down and top off the gas tank on the outboard motor. I want that boat ready to run."

THIRTY-NINE

McKinney took a shuttle from Louis Armstrong International Airport to the car rental agency. He had been home when the woman called him back, and her instructions had been very specific. "Get the papers from your safe deposit box first thing in the morning. Go immediately to the airport and fly to New Orleans." (She suggested he book a flight that evening. He did.) "Rent a car and check into a hotel. Tell me your cell phone number." (He told her.) "Make sure your cell phone is charged and is getting a strong signal at the hotel. If it is not getting a strong signal, move to a different room. If you contact the police or anyone else the girls will die. We will call you tomorrow afternoon with further instructions."

Worry and fear kept him from sleep. All the horrible possibilities of what might be happening to his daughter filled his mind so that, after a few hours, he was almost paralyzed by panic. Panic was followed by guilt and recrimination. *I'm her father*, he thought. *I'm responsible for her safety.* By morning he had settled his mind, knowing that the only way to get his daughter back was to focus on the problem dispassionately. He had to apply the same kind of scientific objectivity to solving this problem that he brought to his work. If he allowed emotion to interfere with reason...

He called Harve Duchamp as he was driving out of the car rental lot, certain he wasn't being followed, and told him to come to the Holiday Inn out on Causeway Boulevard in Metairie. He decided not to go back to The Chimes. He wanted to be close to Highway 10 so he wouldn't have to mess with traffic in town. He also didn't know how much the kidnappers knew about him and didn't want to risk having them observe his movements.

He had phoned Harve from the bank that morning, being careful in case the kidnappers had planted a listening device in his apartment or his car. Harve had driven into New Orleans immediately after their conversation, so it didn't take him long to get to McKinney's hotel. McKinney had barely settled in when he heard the knock on his door. Harve came in, followed by a short heavy-set man dressed in a lightweight brown suit.

"McKinney, this is Mister Runyon. I believe I mentioned him to you, though not by name. He's the investigator my friend at the Justice Department recommended. Flew down from San Francisco to help out."

McKinney held out his hand and Runyon shook it. "Mister McKinney. I understand you're the one who found the diary in Sylvie's apartment. I'm usually more thorough. I'm a little embarrassed that I missed that."

"Don't be. It was hidden pretty well." McKinney gestured to the two straight-backed chairs in the room and sat on the end of the bed. "You're not the one who ripped that place apart, are you? It was really trashed."

"No. I think it's safe to say it was the kidnappers, probably looking for the papers you brought with you. I went back and interviewed the neighbor you mentioned. All she was able to add was that Sylvie enjoyed smoking pot and partying on the weekends. When I confronted her with the coded diary entries she admitted to supplying Sylvie with marijuana. This pot business was all pretty smalltime. I don't think the neighbor's connected to Sylvie's disappearance."

Harve Duchamp held out his hand. "Can I see those papers, McKinney?" He leafed through the ownership papers, pausing to study the photograph of the Turner painting,

Massacre on the Zong. "That's what I thought. He's insane."

McKinney asked, "Who?"

"My brother, Raymond. I suspected him when you said the kidnappers were after a painting. The man's crazy. Sure, Mawmaw Boisseau had a copy of this painting hanging in her dining room, but it was just a photograph or a print. She lost the original during the Second World War." He nodded at Runyon. "Mister Runyon here has been poking around in Raymond's affairs, pretending to be from the insurance, trying to get some sense of what he was up to."

Runyon said, "I lost track of him a few days ago. He and that big chauffeur of his gave me the slip. Harve insists we keep the police out of this, and I'm inclined to agree. These characters don't have any idea what they're doing. One of them might panic and shoot somebody."

"Mister Runyon also refuses to let me carry a gun. As I've told him, that won't matter. If Raymond's hurt Madeline or Sylvie, I'll kill him with my hands." Harve Duchamp's voice was choked with emotion, and he stopped talking for a moment. Then he cleared his throat and continued. "I'm sorry you and your daughter got mixed up in this, McKinney. It's my family's business. My brother has always been unstable, but this..." He shook his head. "I wouldn't have involved you for the world."

"We'll get them back, Harve." McKinney turned to Runyon. "It was a woman who contacted me. She's supposed to call me on my cell and tell me where to go to make the exchange."

"What we'll do," Runyon said, "is get a room here in this hotel, up a floor if there's one available. We'll keep out of sight, just in case, but when she tells you where the meet up is, we'll follow you."

Harve said, "We might not have to follow him."

"What do you mean?"

"I think I know where they're keeping the girls. Let me tell you about my brother."

FORTY

A lain didn't live in the family palazzo with his brother. He maintained his own apartment in a building occupied by members of the Venetian art community. A number of excellent painters and printmakers lived there. I imagine that several of their names would be familiar to you, but the artist with whom Alain visited most often was the Englishman who lived across the hall from him, Walter Sickert. There was a bar on the ground floor of their apartment building, and the two of them could often be found there in the evening, holding court and inventing cocktails. Walter's French was quite good, and to my delight, he was teaching Alain English.

Lucien and Inès had been extraordinarily kind to Mathieu and me. In addition to giving us lodging Inès gave me clothing that, she claimed, she no longer wanted. The funds Monsieur Judge had given me were being quickly depleted, however, and I needed to find a source of income to keep Mathieu fed. There were, of course, prostitutes in Venice, but I was determined to change the course of my life. Monsieur Judge was right; my responsibilities demanded that I use my brain and not my body. I was also afraid that Alain would not be interested in an expatriate whore, and I was very interested in him.

One evening, at the bar, I mentioned my job search to Alain, and he offered, what appeared to be, an ideal solution. Walter and his artist friends were in the habit of hiring locals to pose as models for their paintings. If I could find a costume that made me look like a Venetian girl I could hire out as an artist's model.

"The only drawback," Alain said, "is that Walter and

---

the others generally hire prostitutes to pose."

"Do they expect other services?"

"On occasion. Does this bother you?"

"Of course it does," I said. "I am not a street-walker."

"A street-walker in a city where the streets are water. That's a fine jest." He grinned. "And it gives me an idea. Walter is the only one who knows who you are. If you can learn a few words of Italian, we can pass you off as a Venetian prostitute." He pushed my hair up to the top of my head in the local fashion. "We shall call you Giuseppina."

I held my hair in place, looked at my image in the mirror over the bar and laughed. Starting my new life by pretending to be a prostitute seemed quite ironic. We informed Walter of our plan that evening, and he and Alain invented a cocktail in my honor. The Giuseppina is simply sweet vermouth with a splash of Napoleon brandy. It is rather potent, and there were a number of evenings that Alain had to help me home after I had partaken of my namesake.

Our plan, however, worked perfectly, and it wasn't long before I was earning a decent wage as an artist's model. The work was simple, mostly sitting on the steps in front of a church or pretending to sew lace table coverings. Alain proved to be an ingenious manager, and for several months he convinced artists to hire Mathieu and me as a sort of Venetian Madonna and child. We were usually posed with the sea in the background, and in the late afternoon light Mathieu's little face did take on an angelic glow. Walter paid me to model on several occasions with the added benefit that, when he tired of painting or sketching, we would fetch Alain and make a tour of the galleries.

Most of Walter's paintings were sent to Parisian galleries, for people on the continent couldn't get enough of the "authentic Venice," but there were a number of other artists whose works were on display there. We spent hours passing from gallery to gallery. I learned more about art in my first week as an associate of those two gentlemen than I had in all of my schooling. I enjoyed all of the paintings I saw, especially those by artists for whom I had posed, but there was one artist in particular whose work had an emotional impact on me. Joseph Mallard William Turner had visited and painted Venice when it was part of the Austrian empire, but a number of his canvasses still hung in Venetian galleries. His paintings were alive with colour, and even those that were seascapes seemed to vibrate with movement. To the untrained eye his work seemed sloppy, as though he had made his brushstrokes in a haphazard fashion, but Alain argued that his work was actually quite meticulous and that he meant the viewer to get only an impression of the objects in the paintings, as though one had seen and then quickly looked away. Walter himself used this technique, but while his paintings seemed static, Turner's were cataclysmic.

One afternoon, while I was mooning over a Turner painting, Alain came up behind me and kissed the top of my head. "Most women are frightened by Turner's raging seascapes," he said. "You are a special creature, my little Giuseppina."

I was in love with those paintings; I was in love with Venice, and I was in love with Alain. I looked at him over my shoulder, softened my eyes, and gave my hair a flip. I was about to respond with a flirtatious remark when I noticed the look on his face. It may have simply been my conscience, but that look seemed to ask, why is your impersonation of a whore so accurate? In that moment I had a clear picture of both the benefits and the liabilities of using my sex as an instrument of attraction. I wanted more than a flirtation with Alain, and I wanted him to view me, not as a bit of fluff but as a peer. Whether he was capable of thinking that way about a woman, I didn't know, but I vowed that I would do my best not to manipulate him. Love can only last if it's acquired fairly and given freely. "The power of these paintings is astonishing," I said. "I wish Turner was still with us so I could tell him how wonderful they are."

"He's been dead for a half century, but I'm sure he would have appreciated the compliment. There's one other gallery here in Venice that has a Turner canvas, and I think it will be of particular interest to you. Come; I'll show you." He took my hand and led me out of the gallery and into the narrow labyrinthine streets of the city.

FORTY-ONE

Duchamp saw Wayne and Didi talking together back by the Lincoln and knew it meant trouble. To his recollection, they had only met once before, not long after Wayne got out of prison and was pressuring Duchamp to hire him. They hadn't seemed to like each other back then, so this newfound chumminess had him worried. He walked back to the car pad and tried to join their conversation. "Y'all should come talk down by the river. The breeze keeps the mosquitoes off." He slapped the back of his neck, giving emphasis to his words. "Besides, I've got the girls cuffed together down there. It was too hot in the cabin. I don't like to leave Mark by himself with them. There's no telling what that idiot might do."

"I'll ring that fucker's neck if he molests those girls," Wayne said. "The way he looks at them….well, you know what he wants to do. Anyway, we don't really understand how we get the money from this painting, but when we do, what happens to the girls? They've seen us. Madeleine knows you."

Didi said, "You can't seriously think that either of us would condone killing those girls." She put her hand on Duchamp's arm. "Raymond, we are not murderers."

"I understand your concerns. There may be some difficult decisions to be made along the way, but don't forget, this score is going to make us millionaires. As for the mechanics of the transaction, it couldn't be simpler. My associate, Joe Pasternak, has a buyer for the painting and…"

Wayne interrupted, "The Mozo?"

"That's right. The Mozo has ownership transfer papers already drawn up. I have them right here." He patted the trunk lid on the Lincoln. "When we get the original ownership documents we send them along with the signed transfer papers to Pasternak. He handles locating the painting, collecting the money, and depositing it with my bank on Martinique."

"What makes you think your niece will sign the papers?"

"Loyalty. We hurt her friend until she signs."

Didi said, "I don't think we should hurt either of the girls, Raymond. I don't know how you think we're going to get out of this, but if we're caught we need the girls to say they weren't mistreated."

"I've gotta tell you, I'm getting cold feet here, Boss. Ever since you hired that meth head I've had the feeling that this whole deal was fucked up. Maybe we should just call it off. Take the girls back to New Orleans and tell them it was all a joke or something."

"I'm inclined to agree," Didi said.

"Nobody's calling anything off." Duchamp fished his keys out of his pocket and opened the Lincoln's trunk. "I'm putting a stake in the ground here." He took a black briefcase out of the trunk. "Come with me. I think it's time we did a little downsizing."

"Raymond!"

"It's just an expression, Didi. Come on."

They walked back down to the river where Angelina and Madeleine were sitting, handcuffed together, in the shade of a cypress tree. Mark sat on the dock, dangling his feet in the water. Duchamp wiped the sweat off his neck and dragged an empty fuel drum into the shade to sit facing the girls. He glanced behind him at Wayne and Didi waiting to see what he was going to do. He pulled some papers and a pen from his briefcase and set them in front of Madeleine.

"These are transfer papers for the painting you inherited

from Mawmaw Boisseau. I want you to sign them where it says owner. There are three places. I'll show you where to sign."

"I don't own that painting. I don't even know where the real painting is.
You heard father at Christmas; that was just a print hanging in Mawmaw's living room."

"Your father thinks he's smart. Well, you let me worry about finding the painting." He held out the pen. "Now sign these papers, and when your friend's father gets here tomorrow morning with the rest of the documentation we can all go home. I don't know about you girls, but I could surely use a nice cool shower. It's hot as hell out here, even in the shade."

Mark had been listening to the conversation from the dock. He shouted up at them, "Yeah. Y'all girls are startin' to smell ripe."

Madeleine shook her head. "I don't know why I should sign anything for you, Uncle Raymond. I don't know if you're aware, but what you've done, bringing us out here and all, is kidnapping. Plus, that one over there," She pointed at Mark. "punched Angelina. If you'd asked me I could have told you there wasn't any painting. All I inherited was an old secretary desk and the most uncomfortable chair you ever sat in. The seat is made of horsehair, and the hairs are stiff and stick right through your pants. You know, I hate to think what Pawpaw would say if he could see you now. I think he'd be ashamed of you."

"Are you referring to my father, Claude?"

"That's right. Pawpaw Claude."

Duchamp smiled. "Chere, did I ever tell you about the last time I saw my father? When he was in the hospital, dying?"

Madeleine shook her head.

"He was in the ICU. The old man was practically blind, but he was still sharp. I sat on the end of his bed and said, 'It's me, Raymond,' and reached out to take his gnarled old hand. He said, 'Raymond, where's your brother? I got something to tell him.' Well, I said he could tell me. I practically begged him to tell me, but he just kept asking for your father. An hour later your father came strolling in, and do you know what Claude wanted to tell him that was so goddamn important? He said, 'Hervé, I want you to know I'm proud of you.' So, I reckon you're right, he would be ashamed, but it doesn't make a damn bit of difference to me. Now, how about signing these papers?"

Madeleine didn't answer. Mark got up, wrung the water out of the bottom of his pants' legs, and walked over to stand in front of the girls. Angelina looked up at him, but Madeleine seemed mesmerized by the river water pooling at his feet. "You give me fifteen minutes alone with these girls, and they'll sign any shit you want 'em to. They'll be so fuckin' happy to sign your papers they'll sign 'em standin' on their heads and singin' God Bless America."

Angelina clenched her fists and started to stand, but Duchamp put a hand on her shoulder and pushed her back down. He studied the girls, trying to figure out if Mark's threat had worked. He glanced back at the worried looks on Wayne and Didi and knew the time had come to say goodbye to one of his little band.

"Madeleine," he said, "I don't go in for torture or sexual abuse or whatever Mark has in mind for you girls. I really want that painting, though. I'm very serious about this. What can I possibly do to impress upon you how serious I am?" He unholstered his gun and placed the barrel of the 9mm under Madeleine's chin, using it to lift her face, shifting her gaze from the puddle at Mark's feet to Duchamp's eyes. "I know," he said. "I have just the thing." He took the gun from under her chin, stood quickly, and shot Mark in the head. He looked down at the meth head's blood spattered across his shirt and asked, "Didi, do you have a t-shirt I can borrow?"

FORTY-TWO

McKinney was already showered and dressed when he got the call giving him his instructions. Before heading out to his rental car, he phoned Harve Duchamp.

"I know right where you're headed, McKinney, and I know a back way in. Mister Runyon and I are leaving right now."

"Better give me fifteen minutes," McKinney said. "In case they tracked me somehow and are watching the parking lot."

He drove east on 10 to the 90 and then out across Lake Saint Catherine to the swamps. Despite his concern for Angelina, he felt an odd calmness that he attributed to finally being able to take action. Flying to New Orleans and waiting at the hotel had made him anxious. Now he was moving. He was going to get his daughter. It was already muggy out, but he drove with the windows open, smelling the salt breeze that kept it from getting too hot and wishing he was making the drive under different circumstances. The old two-lane highway was surrounded by flatness, and McKinney could see almost to the horizon in all directions, the view only occasionally broken by little buildings set up on stilts. It wasn't barren, though. There was water everywhere he looked, and it was flush with the low green vegetation that was able to survive the brackish waters. Flocks of sea birds and an occasional heron attested to the abundance of fish that lived in the marshlands. After he passed the last of the businesses advertising swamp tours, he slowed down and looked out at the vast expanse of sky. The inland sky was clear, but out over the Gulf the blue was dotted with steel gray clouds, some pregnant with rain, some showering the waters below. It was a little like driving back through time, the wildness of nature giving him a sense of what the land had been like before humans smothered it with strip malls and housing developments.

He slowed even more when he crossed the bridges over the twisting Old Pearl River, the woman on the phone having told him to look for a red cloth tied to a girder and a pull-in leading down to a boat landing. He saw the cloth on the third bridge he crossed and pulled over to get out and look around. A voice from under the bridge said, "Get back in your car and drive across the bridge. Turn left at the pull-in and park."

He did as he was told, but after he parked, he slipped the car keys under the front seat. When he got out he saw a tall man with raven black hair waiting for him. The man wore a plaid shirt, open to the waist and with the sleeves cut off. He was built like a bodybuilder, a black-haired bronze giant. Just beyond, at the water's edge, was an aluminum boat with a woman sitting at the stern. The man walked toward him, gesturing with the revolver in his hand for McKinney to turn around. He did, and the man patted him down, looking for weapons. The whole scene felt surreal to McKinney, dreamlike, meeting this black-haired giant under a bridge in the backcountry.

"Okay. You can turn around."

McKinney turned to face the man, who shifted his gun to his left hand and held out his right. Instinctively, McKinney reached to shake the man's hand.

"The fuck are you doing, man? I'm not here to make your acquaintance. Give me the papers you brought."

McKinney shook his head, getting his focus back. "Where are the girls? We're supposed to have an exchange, right? The papers for the girls."

"The girls are safe. We'll release them when we know

we're in the clear. In case you've done something stupid, like calling the cops, they're our bargaining chip."

"No deal. You get the papers when I get the girls."

The big man turned and stormed back toward the boat. "Fuck! I knew this would happen. Fucking Tee Ray." He turned back, brandishing his gun, and approached McKinney. "I could just shoot you and take the papers, man. Put one between your eyes and leave you here for the nutria."

"The what?"

"Nutria. Swamp rats. Listen, don't fuck with me, man. Give me those papers. Now."

"Hey, I don't care about the papers or the painting. I'll be glad to give you the papers when I get the girls back. I didn't call the cops, but I did tell some people where I was going and when to expect me back. They'll call the local cops, the state cops, and the FBI if I don't show up on time with the girls, so we'd better get moving." He walked past the man with the gun and headed for the boat.

The woman in the boat stood up and shouted, "Wayne, what are you doing?"

"He won't give me the papers. He wants to see the girls."

The woman sighed. She sat back down, her shoulders slumped. "Of course."

They sat him on the middle seat with the big man in front, riding backwards, holding his gun on McKinney. The woman sat at the tiller. She started back, hugging the left bank, then remembered, *Don't get mixed up and head up one of those traînasse, or you'll wind up back in the bayous.* She steered the boat to the other side of the river, and they moved slowly through the water, the quiet only disturbed by the chugging of the outboard and an occasional squawk from a startled bird. The woman broke the silence. She tapped McKinney on the shoulder, and he turned to face her.

"Give me your cell phone."

McKinney pulled his phone from his pocket. His hands were shaking, almost uncontrollably. Fear and anger had spiked his adrenaline levels. He tried to control it; he didn't want them to see that he was afraid. She took the phone and dropped it overboard.

"GPS," she said. "Listen, I need to tell you something. The guy we're going to meet? He's crazy. He killed a man last night. The two of us," she pointed to Wayne, "don't have anything against you or your daughter or the other girl. We don't want to hurt anybody. I swear, Mister…"

"McKinney. My name is McKinney."

"Mister McKinney, we want everyone to get out of this safe and healthy, but the other guy…"

"Raymond Duchamp."

The woman stopped talking. Her eyes got big, and she bit her lip. "Well, hell. I guess you know all about it then, don't you?"

"Some of it." McKinney nodded at Wayne. "Duchamp's chauffeur?"

Wayne said, "Bodyguard."

"I heard you say Wayne's name, of course, but you I don't know. I understand Raymond Duchamp's wife is dead. I'm going to guess that you're his girlfriend."

"Okay, fine. Please, let us take you back to the highway. I know how you feel. I've got a little boy, myself. Wayne and I'll keep the girls safe, and once Raymond gets the papers we'll make him let them go. Honestly, we just want out of this, and giving Raymond what he wants is the safest way for all of us."

"I can't do it. I appreciate your good intentions, but you've got my daughter. I'm not going anywhere without her." He turned back around and studied the river, trying to memorize any prominent features or landmarks in case he had to bring the girls out by water.

The woman opened up the throttle, and the boat sped upriver. They made the rest of the trip in silence.

FORTY-THREE

It was late afternoon when we entered the Prandini Gallery, and the light was bad; most of the paintings had to rely on the fading sunlight for illumination. Alain led me past a series of religious icons and a few landscapes by local painters of dubious talent. What he was seeking hung in the back of the gallery, suspended near the ceiling, almost in shadow. It was a large canvas, and even in the gloom, I could tell that the scene was chaotic, a jumble of colours and images. I had to strain to make out detail.

"This is Massacre on the Zong by Turner. I thought it would be of particular interest to you, having grown up on a sugar cane plantation in one of the southern United States."

The image began to reveal itself to me as I studied it. There was a ship on a storm-torn sea, the waves around it breaking into whitecaps. Above the sea was a sky swirling with clouds, and in the sea, dozens of small objects floated in the water near the ship. "What relation has this ship to the old plantation days?"

"The ship is the Zong, a slave ship carrying men and women from Africa to the colonies. When the ship ran low on water, the captain and crew threw more than a hundred Africans into the ocean to drown. When the ship reached the Americas the owners demanded payment from their insurer for the murdered slaves. It was apparently a famous court case in its day." He pointed up at the painting. " See, in the water are the bodies of the drowning men and women."

I was horrified. I fled from the gallery, and with my vision obscured by tears, I nearly fell into a canal. I sat on the edge of that canal and sobbed. That men and women should be torn from their homes and robbed of their freedom so girls like me could wear fine dresses and attend expensive schools was a difficult pill to swallow, but this? This was a mass murder that had been committed in the name of that same economic engine. I remembered Betina, my truest childhood friend, and kindly Oncle Joseph who had suffered so at the hands of my grandfather. Having acquired some distance from plantation life, in both time and place, I was finally able to see the terrible injustice of it. I suddenly imagined myself as a crawfish. A crawfish never questions the mud because that is what it lives in and has known all its life. That's where it finds security. I was finally sticking my head out of the mud.

Alain came out of the gallery and sat down next to me with his back against a post. "I didn't realize you would be so affected by Turner's painting. I'm sorry if it upset you."

"You couldn't have known. I miss my family, but I am appalled at our involvement in such an inhuman enterprise. That painting brought out some intense emotions, but I'm grateful you showed it to me. It's a powerful painting, even without knowing the subject matter."

"When we marry I'll buy you another painting as a wedding gift, perhaps a different Turner."

I laughed. "Oh, no. If we marry, this is the painting I want. It will help me to remember that life is complicated. I love my dear parents, but they were a part of that cruel world."

Alain stood and, taking my hand, pulled me to my feet. "When we marry," he said.

FORTY-FOUR

McKinney knew the man was furious before the boat reached the dock. He could see him pacing back and forth, waving a gun in the air and shouting unintelligibly. He got out of the boat slowly, afraid a sudden move would get him killed, and watched. The man had blond hair, obviously dyed, brown and grey showing at the roots. He was wearing a t-shirt that was several sizes too small and proclaimed "Dare To Be Awesome." He pressed the barrel of the gun to McKinney's forehead and shouted, "What the fuck is he doing here, Wayne? Can't you do anything... Didi! What did I say about improvising?" He glared at McKinney. "That's it. I've had enough. Where are the papers? Didi? Please tell me you've got the papers. Give me the papers so I can kill this guy and get out of here."

Wayne was slipping lines from the dock over the fore and aft cleats on the little boat. Didi ran to Duchamp and put her hand on his arm, the one holding the gun to McKinney's head. "Please Raymond, calm down. Everything's going to be fine. Mister McKinney has the papers with him. He just wants to make sure the girls are all right."

Wayne finished tying up the boat. "I assured him no one would be hurt. We'll just make a straight swap, the girls for the papers."

"Oh, you assured him, did you?" Duchamp smacked McKinney in the head with the Glock. McKinney saw it coming and tried to ride it, turning in the direction of the blow. Even so, it knocked him down and opened a cut on his forehead. He stayed down, taking the opportunity to look around, assess his situation. He saw a small pool of something that might have been blood a few feet away, in front of a steel drum. The surface of the puddle had a partial skin on it, like pudding gets when it starts to coagulate, and there was a trail of droplets that led into some bushes. McKinney thought he saw the bottom of a shoe in the bushes. The girls were nowhere in sight, but he could see a cabin behind the man with the gun. The man had to be Raymond Duchamp. He could see vague similarities to Harve, bone structure, skin color, but Harve had a softness about him. This Duchamp was all flat planes and hard edges. He probably weighed as much as Harve, but Raymond's weight was muscle. Beyond the cabin McKinney thought he could see the hood of a car.

Duchamp was still yelling at Wayne and Didi, taking his eyes off McKinney. McKinney considered trying to jump him, but he was still frightened, his breathing heavy, and he wasn't sure what Wayne would do. He still hadn't seen the girls. He pressed his hand to his head and struggled to his feet, moaning, making a production of it, but keeping his eye on Duchamp.

"Okay tough guy, come and see your daughter." He shoved McKinney ahead of him and stuck the gun in his back, prodding him along with the barrel. They walked up to the cabin. Wayne and Didi followed behind. McKinney braced himself for the worst, but when they went inside he saw Angelina and Madeleine, alive, sitting on wooden beds, their wrists cuffed to large metal rings.

"Dad!"

He hurried to Angelina. She tried to stand, but the handcuffs pulled her back down. McKinney sat on the edge of the bunk and put his arms around his daughter, hugging her to his chest and kissing the top of her head. He started to speak when Duchamp shouted, "Where are my papers? You've seen your daughter, now give me my fucking papers."

McKinney kissed his daughter one more time, whispered, "Don't worry," and stood up. "The papers for the handcuff key."

"Fine." Duchamp fished his key ring out of his pocket, took a little key off the ring, tossed it to McKinney, and set the rest of the keys next to a black briefcase on the kitchen table.

McKinney looked at the cuff key and handed it to Angelina, He unbuckled his belt, pulled it off, and laid it across his palm, exposing a small zipper running the inside length of the belt. Controlling the trembling in his voice, trying to sound casual and put everyone at ease, he said, "I used this to carry money on a trip to Italy once. This belt held a lot of Euros." He unzipped the belt and slid out the four pages that comprised the ownership papers. They had been folded into a long narrow bundle. He handed them to Duchamp, who sat down and began unfolding and smoothing the papers out, one by one.

Didi picked up the key ring and moved toward the door. "I'll be right back," she said. Duchamp, examining the letters, barely acknowledged her.

McKinney reached into his pocket and pulled out the photograph of Massacre on the Zong. The edges were bent, but the image was still recognizable. He motioned for Angelina to unlock Madeleine's cuff, too and moved to the table to hand Duchamp the picture. "Here's a little something that was in with the papers. I thought you might like to have it, so I brought it along." This was, he knew, the crucial moment. They had the papers and would be ready to go. If Duchamp had killed Sylvie, he wouldn't have any second thoughts about killing the three of them. He focused his attention on Duchamp, hoping to get close enough to take his gun. He tried not to think about what Wayne and Didi would do.

Duchamp looked up from the table. "What's that?"

McKinney held out the picture. "An old photograph of the painting. It was clipped to those letters."

Wayne said, "We're all set, right? Let's get out of here and get those millions."

Duchamp snatched the photograph from McKinney's hand and said, "Back up." To Wayne he said, "We're just about finished here. Why don't you go out and start the car." He looked at the table. "I guess Didi has the keys."

The big man didn't move. McKinney took another step toward Duchamp, but before he could act Didi came back in holding a pump action shotgun.

"Raymond? Darlin? It's time for us to go." She leveled the shotgun and pointed it at Duchamp. "Let's just get in the Lincoln and drive and leave these people here. Wayne and I promised; no one else get's hurt."

"God damn it, Didi. You two are going to get me sent back to Angola." His hand dropped to the gun in his holster but stopped when Wayne pulled the Chief's Special out of his pocket.

"She's right, Boss. Things aren't working out like we'd planned, but we can still salvage this. We'll get the money from the painting and get out of the country. If we disable the boat, we'll be out of town before these three even get back to the highway."

"Oh, so now you and Didi are making the plans? You two have this all figured out, do you?"

Didi said, "Come on, Raymond. Don't be like that. Wayne's right. We can still come out of this okay."

Duchamp opened the briefcase, put the letters and photograph in on top of the signed release papers, and snapped the case closed. He picked up the case and looked at Madeleine. "Tell your daddy I said, 'a bientot.'" He was moving to the door with Wayne and Didi on his heels when they heard the jangling and clinking of cans and jars out behind the cabin.

McKinney followed Didi out the door and around the side of the cabin. He saw the Lincoln sitting on the car pad and another car coming toward them, just up the road. He called to Didi, "Don't go with them. I'll testify that you helped us."

Didi looked back but kept running. "I can't. I've got the car keys." She stopped long enough to hurl the shotgun into the swamp then ran on. She caught up to Duchamp as he started firing at the approaching car. She said, "Stop it, Raymond," and unlocked the doors. They piled in and Duchamp gunned it. The Lincoln threw up a shower of mud as it tore down the rutted road toward the other car.

McKinney looked back and saw Angelina and Madeleine coming around the side of the cabin. He waved them back. "Go down to the river, and wait. I'll meet you down there." To no one in particular he said, "This doesn't look good." He watched the Lincoln veer off the road, bouncing over the ruts as Duchamp tried to go around the other car. There was a clear path through the mangroves, and for a second McKinney thought the car was going to make it. Then the Lincoln's front wheels sank into the mud up to the chassis. The rear wheels spun furiously, fishtailing the car until they, too, sank into the mud. The driver's side door opened a few inches and stuck, blocked by the mud. The passenger door flew open, and the three kidnappers piled out and waded through the mud, making it back to the road just as the other car slid to a stop behind them. Duchamp snapped one more shot at the car and shouted, "Get to the boat!"

FORTY-FIVE

Alain and I were married at the church in which the Italians had killed an elephant. It is one of the many sad stories that Venice has to tell. One year at carnival time a circus was brought to the island. During the circus parade, one of the elephants panicked, killed its master and ran through the streets, finally running into a church where it was cornered by the army. They fired upon it many times, but its skin was too thick, so they brought up a canon. The first shot missed and lodged in the wall. It was still there on our wedding day, and we both touched it for luck. The second shot killed the poor beast. Its corpse was towed to the garbage heap on the Lido. This all happened many years before I came to Venice. I mention it only because, since my marriage to your grandfather, the happiest part of my long life, proceeded from so much tragedy, I have always thought it appropriate that our marriage should begin at the site of that tragically surreal incident. The icing on the cake, though, was the terrible flooding that took place that day. There had been a storm, and the water rose to cover the streets and flood the buildings. There was at least an inch of water on the floor of the little bar downstairs from Alain's apartment. It was feared the city would soon be under water.

Lucien took the part of best man, and Inès was my bridesmaid. Mathieu was just learning to walk, and we scandalized the attendees by having him stand between us, holding his hands to keep him from falling. He wore a little jacket that Inès stitched for him from a blanket. Your grandfather did buy me Turner's Massacre on the Zong for a wedding gift, much to Walter Sickert's consternation. You children, no doubt, have seen the large photograph of this painting on display in our Baton Rouge home when you came to dinner with your parents. The original hung in both Venetian and Parisian art museums for many years. I couldn't bear to part with it, but I felt that it had such historic significance that it needed to be shared with the world rather than spend its life hanging above my dining room table. The museum and I had an arrangement in which I loaned them the painting for an indeterminate period, meaning I suppose, that they would keep it until I decided to take it back. I never would have, but that choice was taken from me in World War Two when the Nazis invaded France. They stole many beautiful works of art, and my Turner was among them. It was never recovered and, for all I know, hangs in the library of some German art collector. I loved that painting for so many reasons.

We left Venice shortly after the wedding. Lucien and Inès were convinced the city was sinking. Your grandfather, Mathieu and I accompanied them back to France. Their family owned an estate just outside Paris. Alain's parents were a little cold to me at first. That was to be expected. They had not been invited to the wedding, and I was, after all, a creole. It was Mathieu who thawed them. He was a precocious child and enjoyed playing with his grand-père. We had our own small cottage on the estate and lived there happily for many years until I received word that my mother was ill.

Father had been dead for several years. Shortly after his death, mother paid some detectives to track me down. She came to France to visit us once; I believe it was when Mathieu was nine or ten years old. She visited with us for a month but refused to stay in France. When she got sick we moved to Louisiana so I could take care of her. Your grandfather bought our home in Baton Rouge, and that is where your father and aunt were born. We named your father after Alain's father,

Renard, and he was a sly fox as a boy. Your aunt we named after my own dear mother, Regine. As soon as all three children were old enough to go to school I returned to school myself, earned a certificate, and went to work at the hospital, where I had a long and fulfilling career. Now your grandfather and I are retired, and I am able to look back on a long life with few regrets. Had I not taken the path I did, I would not have arrived where I am today.

Well, I believe that's all I have to tell you. Now, it's time for you to go out into the world and write your own stories. Claude, you look after your sister. I'm certain you will both grow into strong, intelligent people; after all, you have Boisseau blood in you! Think of your old grand-mère once in a while, and remember that she loves you.

Justine Marie Boisseau Duchamp
March 3, 1953

FORTY-SIX

McKinney watched Didi wrestle the girls onto the boat, holding each tightly by the upper arm. Duchamp stood in the rear, behind Didi, and put his gun to Madeleine's head. He shouted, "Let's go, Wayne. Get that bowline off." and pressed the starter on the outboard motor, bringing it to life. Wayne had his back to the boat, moving toward it. He and Runyon were facing each other, their guns held low, but ready. Harve and McKinney stood on either side of Runyon.

Harve said, "Don't do this, Raymond. She's your niece for God's sake."

Duchamp smiled. "You don't get to tell me what to do. Not anymore."

Wayne looked over his shoulder, then turned and, instead of untying the rope, stepped aboard the boat. The big man slipped the Chief's Special in the waistband of his shorts, plucked Angelina out of Didi's grip and set her on the dock, making it look easy.

Duchamp yelled, "What the fuck are you doing?"

"The fuck are you doing, Tee Ray? We agreed not to hurt the girls. We talked about it. They stay here." He looked at Runyon. "Lower your gun, buddy. I'll get you the other one." Runyon didn't say anything, but he lowered his gun. Wayne turned back to reach for Madeleine, and Duchamp shot him.

Wayne tumbled backward onto the dock, and the little revolver slipped out of his shorts and skittered across the planks. Duchamp crawled forward, trying to keep his gun trained on Madeleine while heading for the bow to release the line. Angelina picked up Wayne's gun and screamed, "Jump, Maddie!" Madeleine wrenched her arm free and went over the side, into the water. Duchamp slipped the line off the boat's bow cleat and started moving back to the idling outboard motor, keeping an eye on Runyon.

McKinney saw Angelina point the revolver in her hands at Duchamp. Duchamp saw it, too and began to shift his aim from Runyon to Angelina. Harve Duchamp shouted, "Raymond, no!"

Then, time slowed for McKinney. He had an odd feeling of clarity. It was as though everyone was moving in slow motion. Small details vividly stood out. He saw Angelina closing one eye as she aimed the gun, the tip of her tongue protruding from between her lips in concentration. He saw Runyon raising his gun, drawing a bead on Duchamp. He saw Duchamp's eyes widen, registering Runyon, but his arm still moving in an arc, the gun coming about, fixing on Angelina.

She was about to fire when McKinney hit her. He rushed her and, lowering his center of gravity, pushing with both hands, turned the explosive energy of the tai chi technique into a smooth powerful shove. Angelina sailed off the side of the short dock and landed, butt first, in the shallow water. The Chief's Special plopped into the mud. A bullet zipped past McKinney's head and another grazed his leg, tearing his pants and slicing a red line across the top of his thigh. He didn't hear either shot, but he heard the three that followed and turned to see Runyon shoot Duchamp, placing three shots in the man's chest, the holes lined up vertically like little buttons on his "Dare To Be Awesome" t-shirt.

Sight went out of Duchamp's eyes, and he crumpled, falling against Didi's legs, then twisting and slipping head first into the water. He bobbed at the surface for a few seconds then slowly rolled onto his back and sank, his dyed-blond hair the last thing they saw before the water closed over him. Didi sat down on the little plank seat in the stern, looking dejected but not surprised. "Well, hell," she said.

Harve Duchamp was helping his daughter onto the dock, and Angelina was scrambling out of the water when Didi put the outboard in gear and twisted the throttle, gunning the boat away from the dock and down the river. Runyon lifted his gun, took aim, then lowered it without firing. Harve watched her speed off and said, "Uh oh. She went to the right." Runyon holstered his gun under his coat and looked at Wayne. He said, "This one's still alive," and bent down to examine the wound.

"Dad, are you crazy!" Angelina was covered with muck, her hair matted and her clothing soaked. "You made me bite my tongue!" She rubbed her tongue with her fingers. "What did you push me for? I had him." She sat down and pulled off her shoes and socks. "What if there had been an alligator in there or snakes? Poisonous snakes live here in the water, you know."

McKinney put his hands under her arms, lifted her to her feet, and hugged her. "You were going to shoot him."

She pulled her head back to look her father in the eye. "He was going to hurt my friend."

"And you wanted to protect her. I get it. That's another of the million reasons I love you, but taking a person's life?" He shook his head. "I killed a man recently. I had a reason to, but I'll always feel bad that I did it. I think about it all the time. That isn't something you should have to live with."

FORTY-SEVEN

Hendrix had only been home for two days, but he was already looking stronger. He was able to go for short walks and was eating everything put in front of him. He lay on the couch in his Wrigleyville apartment, his head on Angelina's lap, McKinney combing the mats out of his fur. He still had a bandage wrapped around his middle, but his tail was wagging.

Angelina said, "This is the best. I like New Orleans, but I love being home with my two guys."

McKinney said, "I concur. Why don't you transfer to the University of Illinois? You could live at home and see your 'two guys' whenever you want."

"Not happening, Dad. I'm home for the summer, but Maddie and I are getting an apartment together off-campus in the fall."

"You are? Don't you think you need to ask your father about that? Even if I give my permission, what makes you think we can afford it?"

Angelina stopped scratching Hendrix behind his ear and turned to face her father. Hendrix gave her a look then closed his eyes again. "All right, this is supposed to be a secret. Maddie wanted to tell you herself, so you've got to promise me that you'll act surprised and not let her know I told you. She said she was going to call you this weekend."

"What secret? What are you talking about?"

"You have to promise. Raise your right hand, and repeat after me. I..."

McKinney raised his hand. "I..."

"...do solemnly swear..."

"I'll be doing plenty of swearing if you don't tell me what you're talking about."

Angelina glared at him. "...do solemnly swear..."

"All right. I swear. I'll act surprised. Now, what's the secret?"

"Maddie's father is going to pay the rent on our apartment, and he's paying for my tuition and books next year."

"He doesn't need to do that. Maddie shouldn't have asked him."

"She didn't. It was his idea. He's really grateful for all your help."

"Well, that's nice of him, but I hardly did anything."

The front door intercom buzzed, and Angelina slid out from under Hendrix to answer it. She said, "Hello?" There was silence for a moment and then, "This is Nina Anderson. Is Sean home?" Angelina buzzed her in and opened the front door.

"I'll take Hendrix for a walk so you two lovebirds can make kissy-face." She plucked a leash off its hook next to the door.

"Okay. Don't go too far, though. He's still pretty weak."

Nina smiled at Angelina and patted Hendrix on the head as they passed one another in the doorway. Despite the warm weather, she wore a skirt and blazer, her work outfit. McKinney stood and motioned toward the couch.

"Have a seat. Can I get you something to drink?"

"No thanks, Sean. I can't stay." She held out an envelope. "I have money for you from Logan Bradley."

McKinney looked in the envelope.

Nina said, "It's cash. Two thousand dollars, and I had

to negotiate for that. I'm sorry it's not more."

"That's all right. I'm glad you stopped in. I've been trying to get in touch with you for a couple of days."

"I know. I've been ignoring my voice mail. I wasn't ready to talk to anyone, well, to you."

"Why not? We kind of left things in a weird place. I think we should talk about it."

"I can't, Sean. I can't go out with you, and I'm embarrassed to discuss it."

"You don't have to be embarrassed with me. Come on; sit down. We'll just talk."

Nina sat on the edge of the couch, her hands clenched in her lap, looking down at the floor. McKinney thought she looked ready to jump up and run out the door. He pulled up a chair and sat opposite her.

"So, why can't you go out with me?"

Nina took a deep breath and slowly looked up, like she was gathering her courage. "There's something you should know about me, about people like me, people with psychological problems. We want to have normal relationships, but worrying about our problems gets in the way. I'm so self-absorbed..." She glanced at her watch and then at the door. "I really like you, but when I think about you I don't think, 'What would make Sean happy?' or 'How is Sean feeling?' I think, 'What does Sean think of me?' See? It always comes back to me."

"You don't think other people think that way?"

"Not all the time. I spend so much time worrying about my OCD that it consumes my thoughts. 'Am I exhibiting OCD behavior now? Can people tell I'm exhibiting OCD behavior? How can I disguise my OCD behavior?' 'Why do I have to have these problems?' Sometimes it's just a big pity party. It's affecting the way I do my job and, obviously, my personal

---

242   The Blue Silence   Tim Chapman

life." She looked down at the floor. "I'm sorry, Sean. This is awkward."

He bent down, trying to catch her eye, but she avoided his gaze. "I'm willing to try, if you want. I enjoyed our dates."

"That's sweet of you. No. This is something I have to work on by myself. Well, with my therapist. I can't be in a relationship with another person if I can't think of them as something other than a mirror." She stood up to leave. "Oh. I almost forgot. You were right about Logan. He admitted that he planned to burn the Poe manuscript in front of us. In fact, he's the one who forged it. He had the real one in a safe in his library. He couldn't afford it but thought he could get away with keeping it if he could convincingly claim that his friend had sold him a fake. That's why he needed you to verify it was a forgery. Then he could burn it so his friend couldn't examine it and see that it wasn't the same one he sold him."

"That's a pretty complicated scheme. Plus, he'd never be able to tell anyone he owned an original Poe poem. What was he going to do, take it out once a month in private and stare at it?"

"I guess. Collectors can get a little crazy. He's broke now, though. He gave the manuscript back and is selling off the rest of his collection. He even moved out of that expensive condo, though I hear he's keeping the butler."

"I guess 'broke' is a relative term."

Nina moved toward the door, and McKinney followed her. He reached to take her hand, thinking to kiss her goodbye, but she pulled away and scurried down the steps. He started to close the door but heard Angelina and Hendrix coming back in.

"Wow! That lady was in some hurry. What did you say to scare her off?"

McKinney smiled a little sadly. "Honey, I think she scared herself."

❧

McKinney sat on the hood of his car in the parking lot of the Methodist Church and watched as the Live For Today meeting participants filed out. He was a little nervous but felt that, after the events of the last couple of months, there wasn't much that could shake him. It was a warm evening and humid, but there was a lake breeze, and the air smelled good to him. Finally, he saw Beth lock the door and come down the steps. She was dressed a little conservatively, he thought, having traded her paisley skirt for black slacks. Her blouse, though, was fuchsia. He waved and went to meet her at the bottom of the steps.

"Sean, hi. You missed the meeting. We just finished."

"Yeah. I saw everyone leaving."

"Well, I'm sorry you didn't make it." She sat on the bottom step and slipped off her shoes. "I'd like to get my hands on the person who invented high heels. Whoever it was must have hated women." She pulled a pair of sandals from the big canvas bag slung over her shoulder. "We've got another meeting in two weeks, same night, same time. I hope you can come to that one."

McKinney extended his hand and helped her to her feet. "I didn't really come here for the meeting. I was kind of hoping you'd like to go with me to get a bite to eat." She looked skeptical, so he added, "Or a cup of coffee."

"I really don't think I should date a group member. It seems like that might present some kind of ethical conflict."

"Not a problem. I hereby officially quit the group."

Beth grinned at him and looped her arm through his. "Good answer," she said.

Tim Chapman is a former forensic scientist for the Chicago police department who currently teaches writing and tai chi chuan. He holds a Master's degree in Creative Writing from Northwestern University. His short fiction has been published in The Southeast Review, the Chicago Reader, Alfred Hitchcock's Mystery Magazine, Chicago Tribune's Printers Row Journal, and the anthology, *The Rich and the Dead*. His first novel, *A Trace of Gold* (originally published as *Bright and Yellow, Hard and Cold*), was a finalist in Shelf Unbound's 2013 Best Indie Book competition. His short stories have been collected under the title, *Kiddieland and other misfortunes*. In his spare time he paints pretty pictures and makes an annoying noise with his saxophone that he claims is music. He lives in Chicago with his lovely and patient wife, Ellen, and Mia, the squirrel-chasingest dog in town.